First Edition

ISBN 0-9647694-2-5

Library of Congress Catalog Card Number 98-65707

Published by Nanticoke Books

For permission to reproduce selections from this book
write to Permissions, Nanticoke Books, Box 333, Vienna, MD 21869

Also by the author: *Conversations In A Country Store*
You Can't Never Get To Puckum

Men's evil manners live in brass;
Their virtues we write in water.

Wm. Shakespeare

Contents

Illustrations

Acknowledgments

I begin these acknowledgments with anxiety, knowing that I am certain to forget someone among the many who have contributed their time, their work, their advice, and their encouragement to this undertaking.

I am first of all indebted to the writers before me who turned their pens to the task of telling the Patty Cannon story, whether their interest was fiction or fact. Most are gone now because the legend has been an enduring one. They are credited throughout the book where their work is sampled and discussed, but I am especially grateful to Robert H. Davis, Ted Giles, William Hartley, Robert B. Hazzard, Anthony Higgins, Theresa Humphrey, F. Arthur Laskowski, George Valentine Massey II, Ellenor Merriken, Robert W. Messenger, Bill Radcliffe, J. H. K. Shannahan, Jr., Dr. Jerry Shields, Sam Smith, and the dean of them all, George Alfred Townsend (Gath).

My gratitude is also tendered to everyone who graciously tolerated my visits, telephone calls, and probing questions. Most of them are named in the text where their contributions are shared, but I want to thank some of them here also: George Figgs, Marilyn Griffies, Jeff Griffies, Mrs. William Handy, Ervin Handy, Jack Knowles, Thomas Marine, Elizabeth Marine, Randy Marine, Mrs. John Messick, Ed Okonowicz, Mildred Parkinson, June Truitt, Bob Wetherall, and Mike Wheedleton.

A special hereafter, if not a sainthood, should be reserved for most of those patient and knowledgeable folks who staff our libraries and archives. My testimonials and recommendations have been forwarded for the directors and personnel of the Delaware Hall of Records in Dover, Delaware; the Historical Society of Delaware Library in Wilmington, Delaware; the Dorchester County Public Library and the Dorchester County Court House, both in Cambridge, Maryland; the Dover Public Library in Dover, Delaware; the Enoch Pratt Free Library in Baltimore, Maryland; The Maryland Hall of Records in Annapolis, Maryland; and the Talbot County Free Library in Easton, Maryland.

During the 1950's, Henry Pervis Cannon II engaged Delaware genealogist George Valentine Massey II to write a history of the Cannon family. The book, which was intended to commemorate the 75th anniversary of H. P. Cannon & Son, Inc., was never published. I am deeply indebted to Mrs. Charlotte Cannon for graciously loaning me the original manuscript and granting me permission to share whatever I felt would be of value to this collection.

Mrs. Cannon, coincidentally, is a descendent of Richard Lee, the progenitor of the distinguished Lee Family of Virginia, whose son, Captain John Lee, patented Rehoboth, a 2,350 acre estate along the Northwest Branch of the Nanticoke River in 1673, very near to where James Cannon would settle soon afterwards.

Excerpts from *Freedom at Risk: The Kidnapping of Free Blacks in America, 1780-1865*, by Carol Wilson, Copyright © 1994 by University Press of Kentucky, are reprinted by permission of University Press of Kentucky.

Excerpts from *Herring Hill* by Ellenor Merriken, Copyright © 1969 by Ellenor Merriken, are reprinted with the permission of Lyal Merriken and Jane Andrew.

Excerpts from *The Star Democrat*, Easton, Maryland, are reprinted with the permission of Publisher and Vice President Larry E. Effingham.

I am much obliged to Jack Knowles for permission to copy and reproduce the photograph of the Handy family in front of

Patty Cannon's house and the undated view of Woodland Ferry. Jack maintains a museum at his home in Woodland where he exhibits historical artifacts from the area and from the Nanticoke River. Jack is an especially valuable source of information about the history of shad fishing on the Nanticoke.

The map on page 244 is adapted from *Maryland/Delaware State Road Atlas*, © 1997 by ADC of Alexandria, Virginia.

It is important to have friends who are willing to take time from their busy schedules to read drafts, point to errors, and be bluntly honest with their reactions. For those favors I want to thank Rick Bowers, Helen Chappell, Dr. Alvin Coleman, Jan Elmy, and Ken Saylor.

Linda Quinter, whose profession is teaching the language in which I write, has also reviewed the manuscript and made recommendations for which I am most grateful. You have saved me from a lot of embarrassment, Linda.

Dr. Jerry Shields, who in all probability is the most informed individual in the world today on the subject of Patty Cannon and her associates, has been an invaluable resource and sounding board. He has generously shared his views and much material, even though he is preparing to write a book of his own on the subject. Dr. Shields also read the typescript and offered valuable suggestions.

The errors and oversights which remain on the following pages are entirely my own.

Foreword

It has been said that she had a hand-
some, fascinating face, but if we can believe her biographers, no
greater monster ever lived.

According to newspaper reports and private diaries, Patty
Cannon died in the Sussex County Jail in Georgetown, Delaware,
on May 11, 1829, while under indictment for four murders. One
hundred and sixty-nine years later, few particulars about her life
are known, and nearly every reported circumstance, including
the account of her death, is controversial.

She has been called "the most celebrated woman criminal in
the history of Maryland and Delaware," "a degenerate creature,"
"a woman void of all human emotions and sympathies," "the
queen of kidnappers and murderers," "the wickedest woman ever

to walk on American soil."

Patty is usually described as having been robust and handsome, with dark hair and eyes and a Gypsy-like appearance. She is reputed to have been fond of music and dance and apparently was a witty and engaging conversationalist. A woman of great strength, Patty is credited with having been capable of lifting as much weight as any man on Delmarva. In her final years, one writer claimed, she visited with prominent Dorchester and Caroline County families, telling fortunes and entertaining her hosts with amusing tales.

But at the time when abolitionists were expanding efforts to liberate slaves by secreting them north via the Underground Railroad, Patty Cannon, her husband Jesse, Joseph and Ebenezer Johnson, and a gang composed of as many as thirty outlaws were engaged in kidnapping blacks, both freemen and slaves, from Pennsylvania, Maryland, Delaware, and Virginia and selling them to slave dealers and plantation owners from the Carolinas through Georgia, Alabama, Mississippi, and Louisiana.

The identity of the individual who initiated the Cannon-Johnson traffic in human life is not recorded, but in that enterprise the principals gained a reputation surpassed by no one else. General robbery also appears to have been a common sideline for the gang—perhaps even river piracy—and murder was a casual act when deemed necessary or when emotions exploded.

During Patty's time the Delmarva Peninsula had many large plantations. Homes were scattered, and their residents were mostly self-reliant. Contact with neighbors was infrequent; transportation was slow; and the tavern played an important role by providing food, drink, lodging, and often entertainment to weary travelers.

Joseph Johnson's Tavern, usually described as the center of operations for Patty Cannon's gang, was located at the intersection of two narrow, unpaved roads on the state line between Maryland and Delaware, several miles west of Seaford. Today, the quiet, tidy community surrounding the heavily remodeled structure is named Reliance; then it was known as Johnson's Corners or Johnson's Cross Roads. It was a relatively remote, sparsely settled area with large tracts of timber.

Less than an hour distant, however, lay a highway by which a horseman or coach could travel to Dover, Delaware's Capitol, or north to Philadelphia, New Jersey, or New York. Several ferries and wharves, one operated by industrious, law-abiding members of the Cannon family, were situated on the Nanticoke River only a few miles from the tavern and Patty's house, which apparently also served as a hostel. This Chesapeake tributary, navigable for seagoing ships, was a convenient artery for reaching northern ports or for moving human contraband south.

In 1808 Congress made the further importation of slaves illegal, and the British Parliament, in 1811, also ended slave trade to its colonies; but because of the annexation of Louisiana in 1803 and the expansion of the plantation system in southern states, the demand for labor increased. Slavers continued for a while to land their smuggled cargo on American shores, as many as 250,000 additional Africans, but the trade decreased as risks intensified. The price for a strong, healthy, male bondsman sometimes rose to as much as a thousand dollars and more, a fortune in the early nineteenth century.

While the importation of Africans became a criminal offense, slave dealing within the borders of the nation remained a legal and lucrative enterprise almost everywhere except Delaware. Laws in the First State forbade exportation of human property for sale. In the neighboring Chesapeake region, however, as profits from the plantation system there began to decline, a brisk trade in Negro lives was inaugurated between Maryland, Virginia, the District of Columbia, and the Deep South.

Then, as the number of available slaves dwindled, the population of free blacks within our boundaries became an ever-widening attraction for kidnappers. Easily accessible from the gang's headquarters, the Maryland counties of Dorchester, Caroline, and Talbot alone, in 1820, were home to nearly six thousand African Americans who had been born outside the bonds of slavery or had labored for or had purchased their liberty.

But even in states where laws prohibited slavery, freedom and independence for these individuals was tenuous at best. They had little education, few rights, and the white majority, through economic and political control, dictated where they would live, work, and even travel.

While the movement against slavery had begun in the North a century before Lincoln issued the Emancipation Proclamation, there was little affection for free blacks on most of the Delmarva Peninsula, and few whites demonstrated any concern for their welfare. Kidnappers raided their cabins and fields or lay in wait to ambush them on country lanes. Some poor blacks were enticed with the offer of jobs, shelter, or assistance. Then, often beaten senseless, chained, and shipped hundreds of miles from home, they found little opportunity for recourse.

With its strong Quaker influence, Delaware had passed a law in 1793 which imposed a penalty on kidnappers of thirty-nine lashes to the bare back, well laid on. After an additional hour in the pillory, with the offender's ears nailed to it, the soft portions of the ears were cut off. This last forfeiture was generally suspended by the governor.

Except for the efforts of Delaware's Attorney General and the courts of that state, the Cannon-Johnson gang experienced little challenge on the peninsula. Even then it took years, chance, and the personal crusade of a Philadelphia mayor to bring an end to the operation.

Patty Cannon's primary biographers have been novelists, and perhaps that is the only direction the literature could have taken. Because of the remote vicinity she frequented and the nature of her business, she lived a secret life and left a mostly-hidden and well-swept trail. In my search to gather the elements that constitute her legend, I have come across a few fragments that apparently have not been widely published, and surely additional documents and tales will surface in time. Some, I know with certainty, are awaiting discovery in drawers and on shelves of state archives; others lie forgotten in private places. Although information will continue to appear in bits and pieces and sometimes, hopefully, in large slices, the controversy and the questions about this "woman of mystery," as author Ted Giles once referred to her, are not likely to end.

In this book I have attempted to collect the oral tradition along with selections from the most influential literature addressing the subject of this notorious woman and her associates. It is, I believe, the most complete review of Patty Cannon's life and legend that has been published to date. In my initial draft of the foreword, I wrote that the book should be accepted as a labor of love intended for reading pleasure rather than as a scholarly study. A friend was quick to point out that there is little about the subject that is pleasurable to read.

In a few places where outdated forms or errors might prove a little too confusing, I have taken the liberty of making minor editorial modifications, which I hope will contribute to ease of understanding without violating the spirit of the original. You will note that until the 1930's, and sometimes later, the word Negro was seldom written as a proper noun.

I begin Patty's story with the controversial 1841 biography and continue it through contemporary documents, letters, newspaper and magazine articles, novels, pamphlets, interviews, and even by surfing the Internet. You will discover many contradictions in the various chronicles and oral traditions presented here, and they will raise many questions. The truth is largely shrouded and inextricable.

NARRATIVE AND CONFESSIONS

.OF

LUCRETIA P. CANNON,

THE FEMALE MURDERER.

See Narrative, Page 13.

Just Published the thrilling and interesting Narrative and Confession of Lucretia P. Cannon, the Female Murderer, who was a short time since, with two of her Accomplices were tried, condemned, and sentenced to be hung at Georgetown, Delaware, for the commission of several of the most Atrocious, Barbarous and Inhuman murders ever committed by one of the Female Sex, which Sex has always been esteemed as having a higher regard for virtue, and a far greater aversion to acts of barbarity, even in the most abandoned of the Sex, than is generally found in men of the same class. And we may truly say that we have never seen recorded a greater instance of moral depravity, so utterly regardless of every feeling which should inhabit the human breast, as the one it becomes our painful lot to lay before our readers in the accounts of Lucretia P. Cannon, the subject of this truly interesting narrative.

It will be found by the Confessions of this ill-fated woman that she has committed eleven murders with her own hands, besides being accessory to more than a dozen others, the accounts of which will be found in the Narrative. Also, the confession of one of her accomplices, who was afterwards executed for Murder, at Cambridge, Maryland.

☞ As many of the circumstances related in this Narrative are doubtless still fresh in the minds of many of our readers who have been eye-witnesses of the facts, it is therefore needless to make any comment regarding

See Narrative, Page 16.

the truth of this statement, as the facts are too well substantiated to admit of a doubt; and will be found to be well worth the perusal of all, both old and young. And we trust that no parent having daughters who are young and inexperienced, will fail of purchasing one of these Narratives, that they may take example from the fate of this unfortunate female, and early learn to refrain from all pursuits or pleasures that tend in the least to swerve them from the path of virtue.

Price of the Narrative, 12½ Cents.

To be had of the person who will soon call for this paper.

The Narrative
And Confessions

Twelve years after the death of Patty Cannon, a twenty-three-page booklet was "Entered According to Act of Congress, in the year of our Lord, 1841, by Clinton Jackson and Erastus E. Barclay, in the Clerk's Office, for the Southern District of New York." No author's name was given, but it seems safe to conclude that Jackson and Barclay were responsible for its contents.

The *Narrative and Confessions of LUCRETIA P. CANNON Who was Tried, Convicted, and Sentenced to be Hung at Georgetown, Delaware, with Two of Her Accomplices* is the first biography of Patty Cannon and has been widely copied by nearly everyone who has written about her life since then.

Apparently this document received little attention on Delmarva until P. Warren Green, Delaware's Attorney General at the time, discovered a copy of it in a New York bookshop in 1934, and a Wilmington, Delaware, newspaper published it in part in a June 19, 1934, article by Norman M. MacLeod titled "SLAYER OF AT LEAST TWENTY-THREE PERSONS, LUCRETIA P. CANNON, DAUGHTER OF MURDERER, CHEATED GALLOWS BY ONE DAY WITH POISON."

A second scenario is that a copy of the pamphlet was discovered in Canada and brought to Delaware sometime in the 1930's. Whatever the source of this rediscovered and now rare volume, it was republished in its entirety in *The Sussex Countian* in 1939, when readers, I have been told, lined up to get copies of each day's segment. It was reprinted again in booklet form by *The Sussex Countian* in September, 1959, with the title *Narrative of LUCRETIA "PATTY" CANNON*.

Yet another reprint, *An Illustrated Version of the Life and Death of the "Wretched" Patty Cannon*, was produced in 1976 and profusely illustrated with conceptual drawings by Daniel G. Costen, Jr.

By today's literary standards the 1841 manuscript, once referred to as "a penny-dreadful" by Delaware writer John Munroe, is tediously wordy and at times almost humorously dramatic. Although it is tempting to edit the copy, especially for punctuation and spelling, the manuscript is presented here in its original form:

NARRATIVE AND CONFESSIONS
OF LUCRETIA P. CANNON

It has probably never fallen to the lot of man to record a list of more cruel, heart-rending, atrocious, cold-blooded, and horrible crimes and murders, than have been perpetuated by the subjects of this narrative, and that too in the midst of a highly civilized and Christian community; and deeds too, which for the depravity of every human feeling, seems scarcely to have found a parallel in the annals of crime.

And it seems doubly shocking, and atrocious, when we find them committed by one of the female sex, which sex, have always been esteemed, as having a higher regard for virtue and a far greater aversion to acts of barbarity, even in the most abandoned of the sex, than is generally found in men of the same class. And we can truly say, that we have never seen recorded, a greater instance of moral depravity, so perfectly regardless of every virtuous feeling, which should inhabit the human breast, as the one it becomes our painful lot to lay before our readers, in the accounts and confessions of Lucretia Cannon, the subject of this thrilling and interesting narrative. And we will now proceed to state the facts as they have actually transpired, and our readers may rely upon the accounts as being correct, as they have been gathered from the most authentic sources.

L. P. Hanly, the father of the subject of this narrative, was the son of a wealthy nobleman—residing in Yorkshire County, in the northern part of England, although he had in the early part of his life received a very liberal education, yet in consequence of being disappointed (by his father's refusing to comply with his request) in marrying the object of his first love, he fell a prey to that soul destroying monster Intemperance, and in a fit of partial derangement brought on by grief and intemperance, he married secretly, a woman who by her intrigue and artfulness, had succeeded in drawing his affections towards her, and who was also very remarkable for the influence which she exercised over the minds of men, as will be seen by referring to circumstances which occurred subsequently, for by her great tact and artfulness she succeeded in marrying her daughters (four in number) to persons of respectability, although they were every one of them prostitutes of the most common character, on this and many other similar accounts she was considered by weak and superstitious persons a witch.

Soon after, his marriage becoming known to his father, whose indignation and anger became so great that he had determined to cut him off without a shilling, and forbade his ever after entering beneath his roof.

Matters had now come to such a pass that he determined to leave his native country, and his wife concurring in the plan, soon scraped up her effects (for she was possessed of a small estate of her own) and turned them into money, they then embarked on board one of his majesty's ships bound for Montreal, where he settled down, and for several years gained a comfortable livelihood by his industry, but as his family increased and their means of living began to grow rather scanty, his evil of intemperance also daily gaining upon him, he forsook all honest courses of getting a living, and joined a gang of smugglers, removing from Montreal to the village of St. Johns situated on the St. Johns River, about thirty miles from Montreal, and here carried on a regular course of smuggling between Montreal and Plattsburg, New York, and Burlington, Vermont, sometimes going as far as Quebec to obtain articles which they could not readily obtain in Montreal, and as his house was situated at a convenient distance from these places, they made it a receptacle for their goods until such time as they should find a convenient opportunity to run them in and dispose of them.

While things were going on in this style, it so happened that an old acquaintance, whose name was Alexander Payne, moved from Montreal and settled in the same neighbourhood [sic] in which Hanly resided, and as they had formerly been on intimate terms the acquaintance was soon renewed, though not with much satisfaction— on the part of Hanly, as he knew Payne to be a man of very

sober and honest habits, and not likely to be easily persuaded to forsake the path of virtue; and it was on this
ground and the fear of detection and exposure that Hanly
dreaded again becoming on any intimate terms with his
old acquaintance, for Payne was as yet entirely ignorant
of the business Hanly was following, for he (Hanly) had
always managed (through the influence of his wife) to
keep up the appearance of honesty and respectability
during his stay in Montreal.

As Payne happened frequently at the house of Hanly,
he soon began to suspect that all was not right. However,
he said nothing on the subject, until one evening he happened to be passing by Hanly's house rather late, and seeing, as he thought an uncommon stir going on at that late
hour he determined on going in, in order to satisfy his
doubts as to what he had before suspected, and there he
found Hanly and two or three more of his gang secreting
goods which he knew had been either smuggled or stolen.
He therefore at once threatened to expose them immediately. Hanly then tried every means of pursuasion [sic] in
his power to induce Payne to join him in his unlawful
pursuits. But all in vain, as Payne said that his duty to his
God and his country, would be the instant exposure of
their mis-doings. Hanly finding that he could not induce
Payne to join him at any rate, he then had recourse to
stratagem.

He begged of Payne to allow him but three days to
settle up his affairs, and leave the country, swearing in
the most solemn manner and calling upon his God to
witness, that if he would grant him his request, that he
would immediately leave off his dishonest course of
living and forever after become an honest man. All this
he said in such an earnest manner, and Payne seeing that
it would also be the utter ruin of his (Hanly's) whole
family, as well as himself, at length yielded to his re-
quests, after the most solemn assurances that Hanly

would do as he had sworn.

But we shall now see how well he regarded his oaths and promises, for no sooner than Payne had left the house, he called in his companions and held a consultation as to what should be done, meanwhile the bottle was circulating freely, so as to steel their hearts and fit them for any fiendish purpose that should suggest itself to their maddened brains, and before they separated they determined (as their only chance of escape and evading the law) to murder Payne; they then separated for the night, resolving to meet the next day, and lay the plan for their diabolical and fiendish purpose which was as follows.

It was agreed that they should meet near Payne's house about dark or soon after, and endeavor by some means to entice him away from his house, towards the river, when they were to fall upon him and kill him with weapons they should provide for the purpose, then they were to tie a large weight around his neck and throw his body into the river. Accordingly they repaired to their place of rendezvous at the appointed time, each one armed for the diabolical purpose with some deadly weapon, after waiting for some time without being able to see or hear anything of Payne, (for he happened to be away from home and did not return until late), they repaired to a low public house near by, to consider what should now be done, as they were frustrated in their previous design, they here drank deeply and urged on to desperation by the maddening and intoxicating draughts they had taken, resolved upon the death of their victim at all hazards.

After disguising themselves as much as possible, they went back again to Payne's house and finding they had returned, stationed themselves one on each side of the house, to give the alarm if they were likely to be discovered. Hanly then entered the house and groping his way through the dark until he came to the room where Payne and his wife slept, Payne hearing the door of the room open, raised himself a little in the bed, and inquired who was there, when Hanly raised an axe he had picked up outside the door and struck Payne upon the head, nearly burying it to the socket, splitting his head in a most shocking manner. He then threw down the axe and drew a large butcher's knife and rushed upon him stabbing him in the heart, and cutting his throat from ear to ear, and otherwise mangling the body in a most horrible manner, during this time Payne's wife was screaming as loud as possible for help, but Hanly paid no attention to her cries, intent only upon the death of his victim. His companions outside fled upon first hearing her cries but persons immediately gathering around, Hanly was taken just as he was coming out of the house, he was carried directly before a magistrate, tried, convicted, and sentenced to be hung. Had he himself fled after striking the first blow with the axe, he too might possibly have escaped, but he was probably too much intoxicated. Thus some means is always left whereby the guilty are sooner or later brought to punishment. It was while on the gallows just before he was swung off, that he made his confession in very near the words above stated. His companions were afterwards taken and sentenced to prison for life for being accessory to the murder.

After the execution of Hanly his family as may be supposed were thrown into the utmost confusion; and it was at this time that Mrs. Hanly saw the necessity of bringing all her artfulness into action, as she had now a large family dependent upon her for support, and her means of living had now become very limited; however, she managed so as to make her house a house of entertainment for persons traveling for pleasure, or those who were spending the summer months in that cool and delightful region, away from the more unwholesome air of a crowded and pent up city. And in this manner, as may be supposed, she formed many new acquaintances, and by keeping up appearances pretty high, and teaching her daughters well the arts of deception she soon succeeded in marrying them all to persons of considerable respectability. She had also an only son who was now nearing the age of manhood, and who by his long associating himself with a set of low, drinking, gambling, and licentious persons, was little better even at this age than a perfect sot, but of him we will speak in another page.

The youngest daughter whose name was Lucretia, and which is the subject of this narrative, was, at the age of sixteen, married to a man whose name was Alonzo Cannon, a respectable wheelwright from the lower part of Delaware, who happening to be traveling through that section of country, stopped for a day or two at St. John's where he was taken sick, and as he had put up at the house of Mrs. Hanly, and she finding her guest to be a man of very good personal attractions and possessed also of considerable money, determined at once, if possible to bring about a marriage between him and her daughter, consequently he was treated with the utmost care and attention during his illness, and Lucretia being his constant and daily attendant, also being an uncommonly agreeable person and by no means bad looking, although rather large. She was extravagantly fond of music, and dancing, a great talker, very witty and fascinating in her conversation, and concealing her real character so well that he soon fell in love with her, and her mother also exerting her influence over him he was induced to marry her immediately on his recovery.

He then returned to Delaware taking his wife with him and settled down on the Nanticoke River near the Maryland line about ten or twelve miles from Lawrel [sic], where he established a ferry now known by the name of Cannon's Ferry, also working occasionally at his trade whenever opportunity presented.

He had not been married long as may be supposed before he found out the real character of his wife, which so preyed upon his constitution, that his health soon began a rapid decay, and at the end of three years he died, as many supposed from grief, but it has since been ascertained by her own confession that he died from the effects of a slow poison, which she had administered to him, thinking no doubt that if she was rid of him, she would then be able to carry out any plan she might devise, for the gratification of her selfish propensities—for she was very sensual in her pleasures, and totally incapable of appreciating that high toned moral feeling, and the true dignity, self respect, and refinement which should govern the female sex. She was almost indifferent to any principal of justice, as well as to human sufferings; she was bold, revengeful, courageous, cunning, and determined in the objects of her pursuits, she was also very deceitful, shrewd and artful in laying her plans, which enabled her to exercise an extensive influence over the lower order of minds.

After the death of her husband she became one of the most abandoned and notorious of women, giving loose to every species of licentiousness and extravagance, and there was no crime too great, no deed too cruel, for her to engage in to accomplish any object of her design, often engaging personally in acts of the most outrageous butchery and robbery.

After living in this manner for some time she moved from her place of habitation down near Johnson's cross roads, on the line between Maryland and Delaware, five miles from her old place of habitation, and here set up a low tavern as she knew she would there have a much greater chance of carrying on her unlawful and wicked practices. Here she made use of a great variety of artifices, to induce slave dealers and others, whom she thought likely to have any quantity of money with them, to put up with her; and she was considered by some, a very hospitable woman seldom charging her visitors anything. She so managed matters as to make her house a kind of headquarters for slave dealers, who generally had plenty of money, and soon got around her a gang of ruffians who were perfect obedient to her will and ready to do the most bloody act when she commanded and planned it. Of this gang she was always the master spirit and the devisor of ways and means—whenever travellers [sic], slave dealers and others called upon her, she marked her man and at once laid her plans and train of means then gave the watchword, and often becoming the leader herself in some of the most horrible murders.

On one occasion a gentleman from Richmond (Virginia) was going to New York, and passing by her house stopped to feed his horse, and called for dinner, she, finding he had a large quantity of money by him placed her unsuspecting guest at table so that his back was near an open window through which he was shot, by one of her accomplices, they then robbed him of everything of value that he had about him, and then secreted the body in the cellar until night when they dug a hole in a side hill near the house and buried him.

At another time two slave dealers called for their dinners, she, finding that they also had money with them, engaged them in conversation and whiled away the afternoon by exciting and gratifying their feelings by her wit and fascinating conversation. Three several times they called for their horses and carriage which were at length tardily brought, but another glass of wine was passed around and they enticed to stay a little longer. Thus she kept them till dark, when they started for Lawrel, which was fifteen miles distant (via.) Cannon's Ferry, no sooner had they departed than she dressing herself in men's attire with three of her gang mounted on some of their fleetest horses, started in pursuit, determined on killing and robbing them. And by taking another route crossed the river above Cannons Ferry, laying obstructions in their road as they passed up a sandy hill, and here they laid in wait for them. Stationing themselves in a convenient place to fire upon them as they came up the hill, accordingly as soon as they approached near the top of the hill, she and her gang rushed out and fired upon them, mortally wounding one so that he died in a few hours, and so frightening the travellers horses that they ran away from both robbers and driver. But the other one though wounded managed to drive safely through to Lawrel that night, his companion died almost immediately on arriving at the inn.

One of the names of this gang was Griffin, who was afterwards executed for murder, at Cambridge (Maryland,) and when brought upon the scaffold declared that although positively not guilty of the murder for which he was about to be executed, still acknowledged that he deserved to die because he had committed many murders, and before he was swung off he begged for a little time, as he said he wished to make a full confession of the murders he had committed and prayed to God to have mercy on his soul, as he said he could not bear the thoughts of appearing before his eternal judge without confessing to the world the awful crimes of which he was guilty, he then proceeded as follows:

I was born, said he, in Cumberland County, Maine, where I lived with my father until I became seventeen years of age, when an uncontrollable desire for travel seized me. I then left my father's house and strolled about from place to place, associating myself with idle and dissipated company and by means soon became one of the most idle and dissolute wretches in existence, in this manner I roved about and finally went to Philadelphia, here I fell in with a young man whose name was Hunt, a low gambling thieving sort of fellow. We agreed to join companionship and share equally in whatever we should make, we then commenced by keeping a sharp look out, and whenever we discovered a man intoxicated after night, or one we thought possible to make so, we enticed them into some dark alley or other secret place and robbed them of whatever money, watches and sometimes clothing, they happened to have with them. At length we began to grow bolder and frequently waylaid persons whom we thought had money, knocking them down, robbing them and leaving them insensible; at one of these times we waylaid a traveller, rushed upon him endeavoring to knock him down, but the blow missing its aim, he made a desperate resistance nearly overpowering us, when drawing a large knife which I always carried about me, I stabbed him in the back when he fell explaining I am murdered, we then robbed him and took to our heels, I seeing the murder advertised publicly the following morning, thought best to leave the city for fear of detection. I then went to Baltimore, dressing myself in good style endeavoring to play the gentleman. I here became enamored of a very pretty young lady whose name was Elizabeth Morton, whose father was a respectable merchant of that city. She received my addresses very cordially for some time but at length began to suspect I was not exactly what I pretended to be, and began to grow daily more cold and reserved in my presence, I then tried to persuade her to elope with me, but this at once she refused, declaring that she would never marry against the will of her parents, finding that I could not induce her to accede to any of my plans, I then determined on her ruin. I persuaded her to accompany me in a short ride for pleasure and conducted her to a house of ill repute, called for a room desiring that we might not be disturbed. I then locked and bolted the door, which she perceiving inquired why I did this, I then told her what my intentions were, promising her at the same time that if she would consent to marry me before returning to her father's house that I would desist, this she flatly refused saying at the same time that she would sooner die then ever permit herself to be led to the altar by me after taking such a dishonourable [sic] course with her, she then attempted to escape but finding I prevented her, she began to cry out for help, which so enraged me that I caught up a towel hanging in the room and tried to force into her mouth, she resisting with all her might, I then twisted it around her neck, choking her until she was insensible, I then accomplished my hellish purpose, and knowing that if she should recover she would immediately expose me, I therefore resolved on her death which I consummated by tying a pocket-handkerchief around her throat so tight as to prevent the possibility of her breathing, I then left her and made my escape from the house unperceived, and fled from the city intending to go to New Orleans or some other southern city, but happening to fall in with one of Lucretia Cannon's gang, I was induced to join them which I did, and was one of the four that committed the murder (before mentioned) of the slave dealer, and that he had been accessory to several other murders, and that Lucretia Cannon was dressed in men's clothes and was their leader and most active operator.

She now moved from her old stand and enlarged her business by adding to it that of negro buying carrying on a regular business in slave dealing, about this time two more joined the gang whose names were Johnson and Bowen, they now fitted out a slaver which used to go to Philadelphia and decoy blacks on board and when full to sail to a convenient point and send them to Lucretia Cannon's headquarters, there to be shipped on board another slaver which plied up and down the Chesapeake, to be transported South. Their plan of operation was this:

They employed a very intelligent negro whose name was Ransom to prowl about the city, giving him plenty of money, mingling with the blacks, treating them freely, and by various pretenses entice the unsuspecting blacks on board their ship when the hatches were closed upon them and they chained, thus half a dozen negroes would sometimes be secured in the course of a single night. They had also an old wench in their employ who kept an infamous house in a low street down near the navy yard, who also used to prowl about the city and use all the inducements in her power to entice young negroes of both sexes to come to her house harboring them free of charge, thus her house was always thronged with a set of lewd and dissolute negroes; it was here that Ransom always went and as he always treated them freely, he soon became a great favourite [sic] there and as he had always some pretense on hand he seldom ever went on board without one of more of these unfortunate wretches. Towards morning the slaver would move down the bay and return the next night to go through the same process until she was loaded.

If they discovered during the day anyone among their unfortunate captives, that was too old, decrepid [sic], or infirm, which would not be worth transporting, they would throw them overboard and drown them, the rest were taken to Lucretia Cannon's as before mentioned; if any of these female negroes had children that were troublesome or likely to expose her by crying, she had a rattan with a large bullet fastened at the end of it which she would strike into their heads and thus dispatch them. She had a secret cave or dungeon dug in her cellar where she always buried these innocent victims to her savage barbarity.

On one occasion, one of the negro women had a little child about five years old sometimes subject to fits, and in these fits the child used to scream in a terrible manner. It happening to have one of these fits while in Lucretia Cannon's house, she became so enraged upon hearing its cries, that she flew at the child, tearing the clothes from off the poor victim of her wrath, beating it at the same time in a dreadful manner; and, as if this was not enough to satisfy her more than brutal disposition, the child continuing its cries, she caught it up and held its face to a hot fire, and thus scorched the child to death in her own hands burning its face to a cinder, she then threw it in the cave in the cellar.

At one time, a traveller put up for the night, intending to start early on the following morning, as he had a long days' drive to reach home before dark, which he wished to do, if possible, as he had been absent from his family for some time, but she determined this should never happen; and while he was at supper, she came behind him, and plunged a large dagger to his heart, killing him instantly. At this time she had liked to have been discovered by some travellers entering the house at the time, but she nothing daunted, caught him up, (being a man of small stature,) and threw him on the table among the dishes, covering him up with the table cloth, and catching the whole together, thrust them into a large chest standing in the room, where she left him until they had departed, then calling in a couple of her accomplices, they then robbed him and took his body in a small boat out into the middle of the river and threw it overboard with a large stone attached to it to prevent it from rising.

At another time, a slave dealer called at her house with two valuable slaves, intending to take them to Norfolk, (Virginia,) but a heavy shower of rain coming on, he was induced to stay all night. She put him in a room separate from the main part of the house to sleep, and during the night, she entered the room by a secret way with one of her gang, armed with a large knotty club, prepared for the purpose, without being discovered by him, and fell upon the unsuspecting sleeper, beating his head until his brains strewed the floor, they then robbed him of what money he had with him, as well as a fine valuable gold watch, they then concealed the slaves in the cellar for upwards of a week, barely giving them food enough to sustain life, she then sent them on board a slaver which happened to be on the coast bound for the south, and sold them. The body of the murdered man they buried in the garden back of the house in a secret place beneath some old rubbish.

At another time, she murdered a negro boy fifteen years of age, whom she feared would expose her, the boy had been in the house for nearly a year, in the capacity of waiter or servant, and her misdoings had always been kept a secret from him, as they were always performed while he was either absent or asleep, until the savage and brutal act of her burning the child, this he heard immediately after it was committed, from one of the negroes that witnessed the horrid deed; he then declared if this was true he would immediately run and give information to some people living nearby, he then started off with this intention, but she discovered him running at some distance from the house suspected something wrong, and immediately sent a man to fetch him back, which he succeeded in doing before the boy had time to give any information, although he ran as if for his life, and declared when taken, that if ever he should get an opportunity he would inform against them. As soon as he was brought into the house, she asked him why he was running away, and upon his answering her the same as he had answered the man, she flew at him catching up a large fire shovel beating him within an inch of his life; she then took him down into the cave in the cellar and locked him up among the dead bodies and skeletons of the children she had before murdered, leaving him in that loathsome place for upwards of two whole days and nights without a single drop of water to cool his thirst, and nothing but the cold damp earth to lie upon, during this time he had nearly perished. She then came down to see if he was still alive and finding him to be so, brought him down some cold victuals and a little water, which he devoured instantly. She then asked him if he would now inform against her if she would take him away from the dungeon, the boy declared that he would, she then caught up a stone lying on the ground, beat him to death, and left him lying in the cave.

It was about this time that she received the news of the death of her mother, and also the death of her only brother, whose name was James, who was hung but a short time before at Kingston, (Upper Canada,) for horse stealing. He had continued his riotous and dissipated course of living for sometime after the marriage of Lucretia, and finally joined a gang of horse thievs [sic] and counterfeiters which infested the country round about the lakes. This gang had a regular line of communication established from Detroit through to Toronto and Kingston and across to the States, clear through to New York and Philadelphia. It is supposed that at one time before the gang was broken up there was upwards of a hundred men engaged in it, although the exact number has never been ascertained—the way they managed was this—a horse was stolen by one of the gang, and run by night to the next station and exchanged or left, and the next night run to another station, the men always returning immediately to prevent suspicion, in this way they managed until they got out of the way of pursuit. They had regular stations where they kept the horses thus stolen until they had collected a sufficient number, when they were taken in small droves to New York, Philadelphia, or otherwise disposed of. The route which James was stationed on was between Kingston and Toronto near Coburg, where he had been engaged in this manner for some time. One time he had been to Kingston with a horse thus stolen, and there received a considerable sum of money for his services to the company, and on his way home he broke into the stable of a British officer, and stole a very valuable horse, but the noise he made awakened an old domestic who got up and perceiving the door of the stable open went and found the horse missing and, giving the alarm to the officer, several men were sent out in pursuit. He was overtaken before he had got ten miles from the place where the horse was stolen, they brought him back to Kingston where he was tried before a magistrate and thrown into prison, until the sitting of the King's Court where he was condemned and sentenced to be hung. He was executed at Kingston sometime late in the year eighteen hundred and twenty-eight.

After hearing this news she became if possible still more cruel and barbarous than before, she now seemed to take no delight whatever in anything but acts of the most bloodthirsty and inhuman nature, nothing now satisfied her murderous disposition but the death of some innocent and to her, unoffending victim, but her career of guilt was nearly run, she had carried it in such a high-handed and impious manner that it was impossible to continue in this way much longer without being overtaken by justice, and it was not long after this that she was by the following circumstances exposed and her gang broken up and nearly all of them brought to justice, for the high-handed and outrageous crimes they had long been committing and had thus far escaped detection.

She had but a few days before she was taken, murdered a traveller who was known to have put up at her house, and had never been seen or heard of after the time he entered her door, and as he was known to have a large quantity of money in his possession at the time, suspicion therefore was strong in the neighborhood that he had been robbed and murdered by her and her gang, as they had now become very notorious in the neighbourhood for their wickedness. However, nothing certain was ascertained about the matter for upwards of a week, when

suspicion became so strong that some neighbours determined on searching the premises secretly, in order, if
possible, to find out something more satisfactory concerning the matter, as well as to satisfy themselves as to
what was going on about the house, for they had suspected
for some time previous, that there was something of this
sort carried on there as there was almost constantly some
of her gang there, and they never appeared to have any
other business on hand, but loitered about exciting the
suspicions of the neighbourhood.

So, accordingly, they went one afternoon and visited
the house, making some pretense for the visit, one of
them saying that he was about to build himself a new
house and begged of her permission to examine her house
and take a drawing of the plan on which it was built,
saying that he wished to build after the same manner, she
not suspecting anything allowed them the privilege,
though not permitting them to enter the cellar, they then
made such examinations as they were able, discovering
however nothing above, to confirm them in their suspicions which were now directed entirely to the cellar and
in her absence from the room for a moment, they questioned an old wench as to what was kept in the cellar, she
replied that she dare not tell for fear she would be killed,
they then promised to liberate and protect her if she
would disclose to them what she knew about the matter,
she replied that there was something awful in the cellar,
but for the life of her she dare not tell what it was, her
mistress coming in again at that instant, prevented any
further discourse with her. They then left the house
concluding that they had now gathered information
enough to convince them that it would now be their duty
to inform the proper authorities and have the house
searched. Accordingly early the next morning a warrant
was placed in the hands of the sheriff, who started with a
party of about a dozen men armed for any emergency that

might happen. Upon arriving at the house and arresting her, she resisted desperately; but seeing the party that surrounded the house was strong and well armed, and that resistance would have been instantly fatal, she and her gang surrendered. They were taken to Georgetown to be tried where one of the company, a young man who had been enticed into the service, turned state's evidence and disclosed most of the facts before mentioned, and to confirm his statement took officers into the garden telling them where by digging they could find numerous skeletons, and in this way several were dug up. He also stated that a great many more were buried there. At the time she was arrested she had twenty-one negroes confined in her house awaiting their transportation south, these were all of them liberated and permitted to return to their former place of abode.

After this examination they were put into prison to await the sitting of the criminal Court, when they were tried, convicted, condemned, and she with two of her accomplices was sentenced to be hung, they were then remanded back to prison to await the day of execution. Three of her gang who it appeared had not been long in the business and who as yet had committed no murders, being only accessory, were sentenced to four years imprisonment at hard labor and three years solitary confinement. While in prison about three weeks before the day on which she was to be executed, she obtained some poison and poisoned herself to avoid the disgrace of exposure and a public execution, which she knew to be inevitable, she died a most terrible and awful death. After the effects of the poison which she had taken, began to take effect, she raved like a maniac, tearing the clothes from off her body, and tore the hair from her head by handfuls, attempting to lay hold and bite everything within her reach, cursing God and the hour that gave her birth. After these fits of insanity had a little subsided and reason had in a measure again restored itself, then the pangs of a guilty conscience, and remorse with all its guilty horrors and bitter anguish, would sear her soul, and she would cry out in the bitterness of her torments, that she already felt the torments of hell, reproaching herself in the most bitter terms for the awful crimes she had committed. Then she would rave again like a madman, cursing and swearing in an awful manner, attempting to destroy everything within her reach, and so strong was she in these fits of raving, that it was with difficulty that three men were able to keep her on a bed. She appeared to be in great agony and pain during the whole time until she died. About an hour before her death she became calm and appeared to be perfectly sensible of the awful situation she was in and expressed a desire to be visited by a priest in order that she might make a confession of the dreadful crimes she had committed. Accordingly one was sent for and she made her confessions nearly as follows. She said that she had killed eleven persons with her own hands and had also been accessory to the murder of more than a dozen others, and that she herself killed the traveller, last mentioned, and that she had been guilty of the shocking crime of murdering one of her own offspring, by strangling it when three days old, and that she also poisoned her husband, and that she and one of her gang had just laid their plans for murdering in their beds two of her neighbors who were considered wealthy, and that they should have committed the murders if they had not been arrested. She was then seized with another fit of despair and fell to raving in a terrible manner, crying out that she then felt the bitterest torments of hell, thus she went on until she sank back on her pillow exhausted, and her immortal spirit winged its way to appear before the tribunal judge there to answer for the dreadful deeds committed in the body. Her death was truly heart-rendering and awful, and should act as a warning voice to all who read the account to be prepared to meet their eternal judge, and render such an account of their past lives as shall be acceptable in his sight. The other two accomplices were executed on the day set, and while on the gallows made a short confession corroborating as far as each was concerned with the above statement.

Concluding Remarks

In confirmation of the authenticity of the facts contained in the foregoing Narrative, the Publishers esteem it not unimportant, to state, that but a very short period has elapsed since the death of this unfortunate and ill fated woman, and one, whom, in consequence of the strong and prevailing propensities ever manifested by her to commit crimes of the most heinous as well as unprovoked nature, was considered by a celebrated and highly respected Phrenologist as a proper subject (after death) for Phrenological examination, and who sought and obtained possession of her skull for that purpose a few months since, at Georgetown (state of Delaware) and which still remains in possession of a gentleman (Mr. O. S. Fowler) of Philadelphia. And the Publishers in delineating and presenting to public view the atrocious crimes of this vile and wicked woman, are in a very great degree prompted by an ardent desire to preserve the honest fame of those who enjoy a good reputation, and to secure the peace of mind of those who are yet unconscious of offense; as it is well known that a cunning artful mind, actuated by ill nature if not checked in youth may pass on by indulgence to acts of fraud and violence and in some instances to cold-blooded murder! as it appears that when even the tenderness of the female sex (of which the foregoing pages furnish an example) is converted into the barbarity of the traitor, that she, who should have made her faithful arm a pillow for the head of her husband conspired to raise it against his domestic peace, his life! that the bosom that should have been filled with fidelity and affection treacherously contrived (in addition to other crimes) a plan of fatal destruction! Hence as has been observed, it is the sincere hope of the Publishers in sending this narrative abroad, that it may not only have the happy and desired effect of rescuing some misguided youth from similar offenses, but to save others of more ripened years from a fate similar to that of the wretched Lucretia P. Cannon.

Although poorly crafted by today's literary standards, this document prevails as an excellent example of the sensational writing which was brought to near perfection in the popular Gothic novels of the period and in later "dime" and "pulp" fiction, and which continues today, at least in spirit, to solicit readers through the tabloids.

In spite of assurances that "Our readers may rely upon the accounts as being correct, as they have been gathered from the most authentic sources," no informant is suggested. Certainly it is doubtful that the author or authors visited Johnson's Crossroads or conducted interviews with residents of that region. Even though many of the details of this story have been repeated in nearly every major reference to Patty since their publication, and continue to periodically appear in historical sketches and news features, scholars consider most of it to be pure fiction.

They also conclude that the names "Lucretia" and "Alonzo" are the result of fictional license. A very plausible theory is that the narrative's scribe—because Patty is often said to have poisoned her husband and herself—chose these names to create an association with Lucretia Borgia, whom legend once marked as a poisoner and who has also been the subject of much literary speculation. Patty has sometimes been referred to as the "Forest Borgia." The name Alonso is also prominent in the Borgia clan. All subsequent uses of the names can be traced to this document.

Although she was commonly called Patty, her given name appears to have been Martha, and *Jesse* Cannon was her husband

In a pamphlet which Dr. Jerry Shields published in 1990, he suggested that the author of the *Narrative and Confessions* may not only have had an interest in selling books—he may have been an abolitionist inclined to put the worst possible face on incidents where whites were abusing blacks. Patty Cannon's atrocious conduct, as reported there, could easily have been designed as a tool to sway undecided minds in what was then the much-debated issue of slavery. If true, it would hardly be the only historical example of employing such tactics.

Let's take a look now at what we can discover of contemporary evidence and then follow the trail of Patty's other biographers.

The Sparse Paper Trail

Patty and Jesse were probably married sometime around 1790 and soon afterward became engaged in criminal activity. For the next thirty-five years, however, we possess only a small handful of documents to inform us of their activities. It is the primary reason that novelists have taken such license with their biographies.

The paper trail I have discovered includes the following:

1813

Patty Cannon: An Order to Arrest

There is an isolated document in the Delaware Archives dated March 16, 1813, which commands that Patty Cannon be arrested on a charge of "trespass and assault." While it appears that the decree originated in the office of the Attorney General of Delaware, I was unable to read the signature under the order ("Russel" seems to be a part of it). Neither have I been able to discover a specific reason for the issuance of the order nor evidence that Patty was ever taken into custody as a result.

> The State of Delaware To the Sheriff of Sussex County Greeting: We Command you upon sight hereof to bring before us Justices of the Court of Oyer & Terminer & General Jaal [sic] delivery now holden [sic] at George Town in and for the said County the Body of Patty Cannon for a trespass & assault to find Surities [sic] for her personal appearance at this present Session to answer the same and all such other matters as on the behalf of the State aforesaid shall be objects against her and if she cannot be taken during this present Session that then so soon as she shall be taken you bring or cause her to be brought before us to find sufficient Surities for her personal appearance at the next Court of Oyer & Terminer and General Jail delivery to be holden for the said County to answer afs. [aforesaid] and further to be dealt with according to Justice of our said Court at George Town afs. this Sixteenth of March in the year of our Lord One thousand eight hundred & thirteen.

While I have discovered no specific information regarding this order for Patty's arrest, we know that her son-in-law, Harry Brereton,[1] was convicted of murder and executed during the same year, 1813, along with an accomplice named John Griffith.[2]

Brereton, who is sometimes also identified as a brother-in-law of Delaware's chancellor, has been described as a daredevil

[1] Brereton is sometimes referred to as Harry Bruinton.
[2] John Griffith is referred to as Joseph in some literature, and his surname is usually erroneously given as Griffin.

and a blacksmith by trade. He was convicted of kidnapping in 1811 and escaped from jail.

In a letter dated May 22, 1837, which is on file in the Delaware Archives, John M. Clayton sets down his version of some of the details surrounding the killing of a man named Ridgell, which occurred either in 1811 or 1812. Ridgell and another trader, according to Clayton, had stopped at Patty Cannon's and were detained by her with "kind treatment" and "apple toddy" until nightfall, when they finally left for the town of Laurel. John Clayton tells his story:

> Bruinton, the first husband of Patty Cannon's daughter, was a great kidnapper. His wife was a real beauty. In his day he and old Patty and the two Griffins were eminently successful both in kidnapping and murdering. Old Patty was a woman of great strength and ferocity. She could & often did knock down a stout negro man, tie him, put him in a cart and carry him over to Johnson's. Persons from the South who visited the line to buy negroes were often missing and after visiting Patty Cannon's were never heard of again. At length these murderers were detected. Two traders with money about them to buy blacks were on their way from Patty's to Laurel. The murderers consisting of Bruinton, Patty Cannon and the two Griffins [who had gone ahead of the traders by a shortcut through the forest] felled a tree across the road and being all around lay concealed near it. It was night. Patty Cannon was dressed as a man and had a musket. When the traders came to the tree their horse stopped and all four fired at them. One was killed but, while mortally wounded, the resistance the two made (for they were armed with pistols, one of which discharged into the bush whence the murderers had fired) drove the murderers from their prey. Gov. Haslett offered a reward for Bruinton & he & the three others were all arrested. One of the Griffins turned state's evidence. His brother & Bruinton

were convicted and hung for the murder. Patty Cannon, that fiend in human shape, escaped on account of her sex, a nolle prosequi[3] being entered on the prosecution against her. After the execution of Bruinton-Griffin, the witness went into Maryland where he murdered two men, and, having made Maryland too hot for him, came back to Delaware where he was arrested & delivered by the Governor to an agent on demand of him from the Governor of Maryland. He was taken to Easton, tried, convicted of murder and executed. Before he was hung he made a confession which I saw published, venting the horrible atrocities & murders he & the rest had committed in Delaware. Patty Cannon still passed unpunished though often indicted or presented for kidnapping. She easily evaded justice by going over for a time to Johnson's house, Johnson after the death of Bruinton having married her daughter.

John Clayton was a conspicuous figure in Delaware and national politics and seems to have developed a personal interest in prosecuting the Cannon-Johnson gang, some have suggested because of his ambitions in the civil arena. Born in Dagsboro, Delaware, to a prominent Quaker family, Clayton graduated from Yale and opened a law office in Dover in 1819. By 1824 he was elected to the Delaware House of Representatives and became Secretary of State for Delaware in 1826. In 1829 he was sent to the United States Senate. Reelected in 1835, he resigned the following year. Then, after having been returned to the Senate in 1845, he was appointed Secretary of State by President Taylor in 1849. Once more a Senator in 1853, he died on November 9, 1856. Considered by his contemporaries among the best debaters and orators of his time, he is best remembered at the national level for negotiating the Clayton-Bulwer Treaty, a mutual agreement with Great Britain to refrain from dominating Central American territory.

The Griffith who was hanged in Maryland was Jesse. Clayton

---

[3] An unwillingness to prosecute

writes that he was executed in Easton, which is in Talbot County. The *Narrative and Confessions* claimed—and on this point they are correct—that he died in Cambridge, the seat for Dorchester. Nothing in the literature suggests a date.

Apparently none of Patty's biographers had discovered Griffith's alleged confession, which most believed would shed significant light on her involvement in criminal activities.

I began a careful search through Easton newspapers on microfilm starting with the year 1813. The best guess, I thought—and others agreed—would be that Griffith was executed about 1815.

When I left the library one evening after exhausting all available material through 1819, I considered dropping the search. Then, two days later, while pursuing a different question in a different library, I came across some abstracts from Maryland newspapers. Jesse Griffith's name appeared in an index. The extract read "EGT [Easton Gazette] Jesse Griffith to be executed 28th inst. for murder of Hinson Tull." The year was 1820.

Back at the microfilm reader in the Talbot County Public Library, I spun an *Easton Gazette and Eastern Shore Intelligencer* strip quickly through the first six months of 1820. In the July 22 issue, under a headline, "DEATH WARRANT," I found the following notice:

> The warrant for the execution of Jesse Griffith, for the murder of Hinson Tull, was received in Cambridge on Saturday last, and Friday the 28th inst. is the day appointed for his execution.

Directly beneath the notice of Jesse Griffith's death warrant is the announcement of another execution, which had already taken place and which contained a confession made "from the gallows" by a murderer. Reflecting back on Clayton's letter, I wondered immediately if someone might have inadvertently (or deliberately) combined the two news items.

Those executed were Morris N. B. Hull and a man named Hutton. It was Hull who made the speech, and it was reported by a witness standing near the gallows.

Both men, according to the reporter, "exhibited the utmost fortitude and calmness, particularly Hull," who went so far as to adjust the rope about his neck "with particular care." The results demonstrated, however, that it is best to leave such matters to a professional: Hull suffered great agony in the process of expiring, while Hutton, whose rope had been set by the hangman, died almost instantly.

As an interesting sidelight, the account ends with this comment: "Soon after the criminals were swung off, a person of genteel appearance was detected on the ground in picking a pocket. He was arrested and committed to prison."

The headline proclaiming Jesse Griffith's execution appeared on August, 19, 1820, almost a month after the announced date:

EXECUTION OF JESSE GRIFFITH

Mr. Editor.—There are two classes of men whose biography are peculiarly interesting to the public, they are those of the best and those of the worst character. The subject of the following sketch has been considered as belonging to the latter class. If you think this no infringement on the rights of your Gazette, you may give it to the public through that medium.

CIVIS

Dorchester County, Aug. 1820.

The poor unfortunate Jesse Griffith was a native of Sussex County, in the State of Delaware. He appears to have been of humble parentage, and had no education, either literary or religious. His father died when he was but a child, and his mother, indulgent to criminality, brought him up in idleness, & allowed him the practice of those things which idleness generally leads to. When he became a man, he seems not to have entered upon any constant employment for a living, yet he could do as good a day's work as most men, and followed different occupations at different times, and in different places, until he, with his brother John formed an alliance with that notorious negro trader and kidnapper of Lewis Town. (H. B.) [Harry Brereton] They went on in the traffic of human flesh until the beginning of the year 1813, when an unsuccessful attempt in a desperate enterprise, brought John and H. B. to the gallows at George Town, in their native county, and Jesse escaped only by turning state's evidence in the case. They had engaged to sell a negro to a foreign trader, and agreed to meet him at a certain hour of the night, at a stated place, between Cannon's Ferry and the town of Laurel, in order to deliver the negro and receive the money.—Before the time of meeting, the conspirators went to the place, threw something in the road to stop the horse, and waited with loaded muskets, with an intention to shoot and kill the trader as he should ride up in his carriage, and then rob him of his money. They succeeded so far as to wound him mortally, but a man who happened to be in the carriage with him, and who was not hurt, drove on to Laurel.

This affair was a broad, black stain on the already spotted character of poor Jesse, a stain which he could never wipe off but with his own blood. The public mind was very much exasperated against him, and almost every direction he took was hedged up, every neighborhood was alarmed at his approach, and trembling seized the man who chanced to met him without proper implements of defence [sic]. He lived generally in the most retired places on the Nanticoke, above Vienna, sometimes in Maryland and sometimes in Delaware. His habitation was generally a temporary hut, where he lived with little family except his wife, and wrought at small jobs of work wherever he could get employ. Awful and lamentable stories were continually afloat about him, and sometimes companies of men would collect and go in quest of him in the night, drive him from his solitary retreat, and demolish his humble dwelling place.—If common report is to be depended on, every persons smoke-house and hen-roost, &c. in the neighborhood, were in danger, as well as the life of any man who was daring enough to oppose him. These bad accounts of him were not always groundless, nor did they always stop within the bounds of truth. He seemed at any rate to possess the noble quality of bearing almost insuperable difficulties with fortitude and courage.

He and his wife disagreeing, they parted, what became of her the writer of these lines knows not, but he took up with Betsy Askridge, and lived after the manner to which he had been accustomed.—Betsy's mother living with them, and perhaps a female or two beside. These were about his family when the fatal affair took place which ultimately terminated in his ignominious exposure on the gallows.

He had erected his cabin on an Island of a half acre of land, lying between the Nanticoke river and a large swamp or cripple, in Dorchester county. A disagreement took place between him and one McOlister about the wood which they were cutting in the swamp; Griffith struck McOlister, and threatened to make beef of his oxen— McOlister swore the peace against him, as it is called. The constable refused to take him, saying an attempt of that kind would be attended with serious consequences, and that he was the best off who had the least to do with him. There was, however, one Kirkley who proffered his services as constable, if he could be deputised [sic] as such, which the magistrate took the liberty of doing, and Kirkley went off with a warrant to take this terror to the neighborhood. After one or two unsuccessful attempts to take him, he summoned a posse of men from the Walnut Landing to take him by surprise in his own house by night. They all had loaded guns except the unfortunate Hinson Tull, and he had a sword. Griffith was sick with the measles, and was lying on his bed when they came. Tull went in first and was shot down. Griffith immediately surrendered and was carried to jail. This took place in the month of December 1818.

Before Court he escaped by some means from jail, taking a negro or two out of jail with him, which some say he sold to a Georgia man.

In the Spring of the present year, 1820, he was brought by the Sheriff of Dorchester from the jail of Sussex, and put in jail here, where he lay in irons until the calling of the special court, which condemned him to die.

He did not only plead not guilty at the bar, but, persisted in his denial of the murder for which he was condemned, to the very last.

He received his awful sentence on the 27th of June; the judge pronounced it with a profusion of tears, and Griffith was conducted back to prison to await the accomplishment of the same. He was repeatedly visited by the Rev. Mr. Weller and other preachers, who labored to bring him to a sense of his lost estate by nature, and of the necessity of a speedy preparation for another world, [several words blurred] best information we have, he was a good deal engaged for his soul's salvation. He professed to have obtained mercy of God, and the pardon of his sins, but persisted in his innocence as to the murder for which he was condemned.

The manner in which he accounts for the death of Hinson Tull, is as follows, which we will simply state without comment, nearly in his own words. "When Kirkley & his men came to take me," says he, "Tull pushed open the door; I asked who was there, he said 'no body shall hurt you, but Kirkley & his men have come to take you.' I ordered him out, he was about to say something, when James LeCompte, who had gone round the house and pulled off a plank or two, put his gun through and shot him down." To the question what could induce J. LeCompte to shoot him, his answer was, "Jim LeCompte was drunk, and when he is drunk he is crazy & no doubt he thought it was me trying to escape."

The death warrant was received in Cambridge on the 16th July & Friday the 18th was to be the fatal day, but on account of a long letter, which one of the associate judges wrote to the Governor in his favor, his Excellency gave him a respite until the 16th of August, that he might have time to be better informed on the subject.

On the fatal day the said 16th of August, about 11 o'clock he was brought out of the jail dressed in his shroud, and seated in the cart which was followed by several ministers to the place of execution. He was then asked by the Sheriff if he had any thing to say, after observing in a faint voice, that he had then to die, and professing his strong confidence in God that he would save his soul, he said, "but as to the crime for which I am to die, God knows I am innocent of it—I never hurt a hair of his head, nor do I tell who it was that did, through malice or ill will, but it was James LeCompte who killed the man, and I have now to die for his fault." He then warned the young people against drunkenness, and bad company, &c. &c. A few verses of that awful Hymn beginning with these lines,

"And must I be to judgment brought,
To answer in that day, &c. &c."

was then sung by the ministers who attended him, and the throne of grace addressed in his behalf by the Rev. Daniel Baine. Shortly after being asked by the Sheriff if he was ready, and answering ALL READY, he was launched into eternity.

This eyewitness report of Griffith's execution certainly does not match the one given in The *Narrative and Confessions*, where, as in John Clayton's letter, he is called "Griffin."

One has to wonder whether the author or authors of the 1841 pamphlet had access to Clayton's 1837 letter, or did they know Clayton personally. Could they have been referring to him when they claimed "the most authentic sources?"

And where, we might reasonably ask, is Patty Cannon in this "confession" of Jesse Griffith? Only Brereton, by his initials, "the notorious negro trader and kidnapper of Lewis Town," and Jesse's brother, John Griffith, are mentioned as having been present at the ambush on the road to Laurel. Was there another document published in which Griffith implicated Patty Cannon? I doubt it.

1816

Jesse Cannon: Convicted of Kidnapping

According to the Governors' Register, on May 10, 1816 the Governor of Delaware: . . . issued a pardon unto Jesse Cannon for that part of the Judgment of the Court of Quarter Sessions of the Peace, (held at George Town for Sussex County,) rendered on the 23rd day of April, 1816, which adjudges him the said Jese [sic] Cannon "to Stand in the Pillory for the Space of one hour with both of his ears nailed and after the expiration of the hour to have the soft part of both his ears cut off," Being so much of the Judgment of the Supreme Court rendered upon the Conviction of J. Cannon for kidnapping a certain free negro Boy named William Rob.

To my knowledge this morsel of information is not supported by surviving court records, so we are not fully informed of the details of Jesse's conviction. We are aware that Delaware law invoked a penalty of thirty-nine lashes to the back in addition to pillorying and loss of the ears and can assume the former punishment was administered.

1821-22

Joe Johnson: Convicted and Whipped

On July 23, 1821, the *Easton Gazette* distributed the following story to readers in Talbot County, Maryland:

On the 14th inst. three writs were issued in Sussex County in this state (Delaware) against James Jones, Jesse Cannon, Joseph Johnson, and ? Goslin, to replevy[4] Thomas Carlisle, negro, another to replevy Nochre Griffith, negro, and a third to replevy Isaac Griffith, negro. The sheriff had also in his hands two writs to arrest Joseph Johnson, on two bills of indictment found against him several years past, for kidnapping other free negroes.

On Monday morning about 10 o'clock Miles Tindall and Purnell Johnson, two deputy sheriffs, with two or three constables, and several other inhabitants of that County went to the house of Jesse Cannon, situate in North West Fork Hundred, within a few hundred yards of the Maryland line, to execute their writs. There they found Johnson and Cannon.

At first Johnson threatened to shoot any person who should attempt to enter the house, or to arrest him. After a little parley, Johnson, finding that the officers were determined at all risks to have him, surrendered.

The house was opened, and after securing Johnson, they searched for the three negroes mentioned in the writs of replevy.

They found the negroes and ten others, all confined in the house and some of them in irons, waiting the arrival of a vessel for transporting them to some of the Southern states.

Johnson and the negroes were all taken to Georgetown (Delaware). Johnson was immediately committed to pris-

---

[4] recover possession of

on and secured in irons. He had a long time eluded the officers, and more than once when they, unarmed, had met him, he had kept them off with fire arms. He generally went prepared for action. On this occasion he was taken by surprise. Two guns were found in his room, but they were both unloaded. Johnson is a strong active athletic man, a very determined fellow, and said to be long versed in this type of traffic.

Account of the names, ages, residence and situation of the negroes:

1. Samuel Carlisle, aged about fifty-five, lived near Milford, Kent County and was the slave of Nancy Griffith, who sold him on the 10th of July 1821, to James Jones, and Mosiah Marvel, and by them to Joseph Johnson.

2. & 3. Nochre and Isaac Griffith, the first aged about nine, and the other about four, also lived with the aforesaid Mrs. Griffith, were her slaves, and sold by her with Samuel, to Jones and Marvel, and by them to Joseph Johnson.

4. Lowel Thorpe, aged twenty-three years, is the slave of Mr. Stockton Armstead, near Plymouth, Washington County, North Carolina, was kidnapped by Obed Smith, in Baltimore, July 3, 1821, from the schooner, Roanoke of Tombstone and brought from thence to the house of Jesse Cannon, in this County, by a vessel, commanded by Capt. W. Bell on July 9, 1821.

5. & 6. Jacob and Spencer Francis, the first aged twenty and the other nineteen years, are brothers, free born, were kidnapped on Thursday June 14, 1821, in Baltimore, by Capt. Bell and brought from thence, in Bell's vessel to the house of the aforesaid J. Cannon, are the sons of Elizabeth Francis, a mulatto, who lives near Pancotrague [sic], Accomac County, Virginia, on the land of Peter Hack.

7. Jacob Eveson, aged seventeen years, lived in Pennsborough, Penna., is the son of Cassey Eveson near Penns-

borough, is free born, and was kidnapped at Wilmington, Delaware, on June 16th by Lewis Duvall and brought from thence by John Russell to the house of the aforesaid J. Cannon, and there sold by him to Joseph Johnson.

8. George Williams, aged 19 years, is the son of Brooks Williams, in Baltimore, was free born, and kidnapped in Baltimore, by Jesse Gunn, brother-in-law to Joseph Johnson, on July 6, 1821, and thence brought to the house of the aforesaid J. Cannon, and by him sold to Jesse Counard.

9. John Todd, aged 11 years, is the son of Betsy Todd, who resides in Philadelphia, with Captain Hudson, in Clover Alley, S. Third Street, was free born, and kidnapped in Wilmington (Delaware) by Lewis Duvall about the 15th of June, 1821, and from thence brought to the house of aforesaid J. Cannon by John Russell, and sold by him to Joseph Johnson.

10. James Morris, aged 16, is the son of Jacob Morris, a mulatto, lived in Philadelphia, with his mother, Anne Morris, free born, came to Wilmington (Delaware) about April 1, 1821, and lived with Mr. Eli Sharp, was kidnapped, in that place by Lewis Duvall, about June 1, 1821, and thence brought to the house of the aforesaid J. Cannon by Jesse Gunn, and sold by him to Joseph Johnson.

11. George Morgan, aged 15, is the son of John Morgan of Baltimore, lived in Baltimore, with his sister, Rachel Jones, was free born, and kidnapped there on Saturday June 16, 1821, by Eben Johnson, and from thence brought to the house of the aforesaid J. Cannon, and sold by him to Joseph Johnson.

12. John Dominick, aged about ten years, is the son of Susan Dominick, lived in Baltimore with Sally Brown, a mulatto, was kidnapped in Baltimore by Eben Johnson on June 16, 1821, and from thence brought to the house of the aforesaid Cannon, and sold by Eben to Joseph Johnson.

13. Henry Ingram, aged about 13 years, was the slave of Margaret Ingram of this County, was sold by her to John Gunn, and by him to James Jones, and by him to Joseph Johnson about June 1, 1821, is the son of Jacob and Hannah Wesley of Georgetown, Delaware.

Those persons are now in Georgetown where their friends may make application for them, for which purpose it will be necessary that they should produce proper vouchers of their being authorized to receive them.—Del Gaz.

The personal information presented in this article provides us with some idea of the range and diversity of the gang's activity at that time.

A question is raised by a reference to the house of Jesse Cannon as being "within a few hundred yards of the Maryland line." As we examine other writings we will repeatedly be told that Patty's house was situated squarely on the state line between Maryland and Delaware. Does the reporter here make an incorrect statement, or was there a residence involved which has not been mentioned in other literature?

On the same day as the above mentioned writs were issued against Joseph Johnson—July 14, 1821—a deed was recorded in Cambridge, Maryland, for the transfer from James Willson (or Wilson) to Joseph Johnson of one hundred and sixteen square perches[5] of "Willson's Plain Dealing." The property was identified as being "adjacent to Willson's Cross Roads, near Northwest Fork Bridge and Cratcher's [sic] Ferry."[6]

It was on this property that Johnson would construct his tavern, and Willson's Cross Roads would come to be known as Johnson's Cross Roads. Where was Joe living at the time of his arrest? He had not yet had time to build his tavern. Did he just

---

[5] a little less than one acre

[6] "Near" is a relative perception. It was six and one half miles as the crow flies from Johnson's Cross Roads to Crotcher's (Cratcher's) Ferry, and crows did not build the winding country roads of that or any other day.

The Sparse Paper Trail   46

happen to be at Jesse's house, or was it also his residence?

The names of a number of kidnappers and dealers are recorded here. Did they collectively compose an organized gang, or was it a loose association in which every man conducted his own raids, made his own purchases, then sold or resold the unfortunate individuals to Joe Johnson and Jesse Cannon?

Next, our attention is drawn to a series of six documents which continue the story of Johnson's arrest and detail his conviction and punishment. These court records, which were first discovered and reported by J. H. K. Shannahan, Jr., include the unexplained and unresolved indictments of Patty, Jesse, and their two children.

November 12, 1821

Indictment. Kidnapping. True Bill. The State of Delaware versus:
Joseph Johnson
John Stevenson
Jesse Cannon
Jesse Cannon, Jr.
Martha Cannon
Mary Johnson

The defendant, Joseph Johnson, pleaded "Not Guilty."
"Guilty," says the Attorney General.

Historians and genealogists are certain that "Martha Cannon" in the indictment was Patty; Jesse Cannon was Patty's husband; Jesse, Jr., their son; and Mary[7] Johnson, their daughter and the wife of Joseph Johnson. For the Cannons, then, contrary to some of the accounts you will read, kidnapping was apparently a family business.

---

[7] She has also been called "Margaret" and was referred to as "Margaretta" in *The Entailed Hat.*

Keep the date of November 12, 1821, in mind when you consider claims that Jesse died shortly after his marriage to Patty, either of shock and disillusionment over the discovery of her true nature or by poison administered by her hand.

I assume this indictment was one of the bills carried by the sheriff from "several years past." There is nothing to explain why Johnson alone was singled out for prosecution.

April 25, 1822

Continued upon affidavit of defendant and now to wit: this 25th day of April, 1822, Joseph Johnson was brought to the bar of the Court and a Jury drawn, verdict of the jury "Guilty,"

April 30th, 1822

Notice by council for defendant to show cause why the said verdict should not be set aside because there was reasonable grounds for the jury to entertain doubt of the guilt of the defendant.

May 1, 1822

Upon agreement, rule was discharged.

May 3, 1822

Now to wit: the third day of May, 1822 the defendant was brought into court by the Sheriff of Sussex County, Delaware, being convicted of having feloniously kidnapped, taken and carried away from this State into the State of Maryland, a free negro man named Thomas Spence.

The sentence of the court is that Joseph Johnson shall be publicly whipped on his bare back with 39 lashes, well laid on, and shall stand one hour in the pillory with both ears nailed thereto, and at the expiration of the one hour shall have the soft part of each ear cut off and shall pay the cost of this prosecution, and the above judgment to be executed on Tuesday, the fourth day of June next ensuing, between the hours of 10:00 A.M. and 4:00 P.M.

This sentence was reported by the Delaware Gazette in a brief article and also in the Easton Gazette on May 25, 1822.

June 12, 1822

On Tuesday, the fourth day of June, between the hours of 10:00 o'clock A.M. and 4:00 o'clock in the afternoon, the punishment upon Joseph Johnson was inflicted a-greeable to the order of the Court, except the cutting off of the soft part of the ears, which was remitted by the Governor.

(Signed) William Ellegood, Sheriff

In his 1837 letter John Clayton comments on Johnson's arrest and trial:

Joe Johnson's house (now Michael Millman's) lies on the edge of three counties and two states. It is in Dorchester County Maryland and within a stone's cast of Caroline County in Maryland and Sussex County in Delaware. It has been the old stand and residence of the most celebrated kidnappers and murderers this country has produced. Johnson himself made a fortune at the business and easily escaped justice by removing from one county or state to another when pursued by an officer with a posse, for none but an officer with a posse could take him. He was a powerful man 6 feet high & the best built man I ever saw. He was arrested at last in 1822[8] by

---

[8] The arrest was made in 1821.

the Sheriff of Sussex with a posse at the house of the notorious Patty Cannon which is in Sussex County Delaware. He was the second husband of Patty Cannon's
daughter. Her first husband was the kidnapper & murderer Harry Bruinton alias Brereton. Patty Cannon's
house was but a short distance from the house of Joseph
Johnson. Johnson had gone to her house where his wife
was at the time. They had 15 or 20 negroes in chains hid
about the premises at the time and were surprised by the
Sheriff & his posse at midnight. In 1822 at the April term
in Sussex I assisted the Attorney General and James
Booth to prosecute Johnson. I was employed by the Quakers to do so. He was defended by Vandyke, T. Clayton,
Wells and Cooper. He feed [paid] counsel well & his trial
lasted seven days. He was convicted, received the penalty
of our old law which was more severe than the present—
except the cutting off the ears which was remitted.

There are numerous discrepancies between the news reports
filed in 1821 and Clayton's letter, just as there are with the ambush of the slave trader and Griffith's execution and "confession." Clayton is writing years after the events occurred. Has
time distorted his memory, or was he misinformed? Can we
trust any of his statements?

I find it interesting that Clayton refers to "the house of the
notorious Patty Cannon" and focuses on her, but Patty is not
even mentioned in the news accounts at the time. In them it was
"the house of Jesse Cannon."

Later in his letter, Clayton continues with this comment on
Joe Johnson:

After Johnson's conviction in 1822 he went South
and is said lately to have been a Judge of Probate in a
South Western State under a feigned name. Powell of
Seaford told me he saw him about a year ago [1836] on the
levee at N. Orleans & knew him, but he did not expose him

as Johnson said he passed under another name & was a Judge of Probate in the territory of Arkansas & begged Powell not to mention anything of him.

If Joseph Johnson did travel south after his whipping, there is evidence that he did not remain there. Personal observations and at least one document bear witness to time spent on Delmarva between 1822 and 1829.

But it does appear that Johnson made himself scarce after his 1821-22 encounter with justice, and that raises a very large question in my mind: If the tavern property at the crossroads was purchased by Johnson at the time of his arrest, and if he was largely absent from Delmarva and more secretive than before, how is it that the tavern became and remains the center for most of the legend?

And did Joseph Johnson really become a probate judge in Arkansas? Jerry Shields says he has found nothing to discount that.

1824

A Petition for Freedom

A petition for freedom—Negro Hannah McColly versus Joseph Johnson and James Garum[9]—was scheduled to be heard by the Sussex County Court of Common Pleas in Georgetown, Delaware in 1824.

On April 12 of that year, a commission was issued to John Stockley to take depositions from witnesses and present them to the court on April 21. Elisha D. Cullen, attorney for the plaintiff, prepared a set of interrogatories which included references to Jesse and Patty Cannon. This document is an example of some rather tedious legal wording of its day and is almost devoid of punctuation. A copy in the Delaware State Archives reads as

---

[9] This name is very difficult to read on the documents, sometimes appearing to be "Orem," "Gram," "Grim," or "Grum."

follows:

1. Do you know the parties plantiff [sic] and Defendant or any and which of them and how long have you known them respectively.

2. Do you or do you not know that the Petitioner and when was held as a slave by a certain Elzey Spicer did and whither said Spicer and about what time sold her to a certain Horace Boyce of Sussex County Delaware.

3. Do you know or have you ever been informed by said Boyce or by William B. Spicer that said Boyce sold said Hannah to said William B. Spicer or that said William B. Spicer ever and at what time bought said Hannah of said Boyce or any other person.

4. Do you know whether said William B. Spicer sold and at what time said Hannah as a slave or in what other manner to a certain Joseph Johnson or any other person with intent to export said Hannah from this to some other and what State [several words illegible].

5. Do you know whether said Johnson ever claimed said Hannah as his slave or in any other manner and if you do you or do you not know of whom said Johnson Bought her or to whom he sold her and whether to a citizen of this State or some other State did he or did not inform you thereof.

6. Do you know or have you ever been informed whether a certain James Garum of the State of Maryland ever owned or claimed said Hannah as his Slave and can you say whether she said Hannah was ever confined at the house of said Garum and whether of not she ever escaped therefrom and to what place, set forth and declare.

7. Can you say whether or not the said Horace Boyce William B. Spicer Joseph Johnson and James Garum or any and which of them support the character of Negro traders or persons who buy and sell Negroes with intent to export them out of this into another State contrary to the

laws of this State and did you ever hear any & which of them say so or to that effect.

8. Did you or did you not see the said Hannah and if yea at what time and place in the possession of said Joseph Johnson or his agents on the way to the house of Jesse Cannon Patty Cannon or Joseph Johnson. Do you no [sic] whether said Hannah was sold and if yea by whom to any person and whom residing out of the State of Delaware.

9. Do you know of any other matter or thing which will benefit the petitioner or have you heard of any other matter or thing that you believe which will benefit the plantiff petition at the trial of their cause if yea set forth the same fully and at large.

I have found no record of answers to the interrogatories and nothing to suggest the outcome of the investigation, and we are left uninformed as to when the mentioned incidents occurred. Two years had passed since Johnson's trial, whipping, and alleged relocation south.

One can only speculate whether this document, when it names Jesse Cannon, is referring to Patty's husband or to her son. If it alludes to the senior Jesse, as it appears to do, then Jesse may still have been living in 1824.

The Noose Tightens

In 1990, repeating earlier claims by historian Littleton Bowen, Dr. Jerry Shields wrote that Joe Johnson left the area in 1826 and that the other members of Patty's family had departed even earlier, that Patty "was not up to carrying on the family business alone. Now living in Maryland . . . , she apparently sank into semi-retirement.

"Accounts of her between 1826 and 1829 record her as visiting in prominent Dorchester and Caroline County homes, where she entertained her hosts and hostesses with gossip and amusing stories and told their fortunes to supplement her diminished income." Friends apparently blamed her reputation in crime on Joe Johnson and other male associates.

I have been unable to discover any documented contemporary

accounts of Patty's personal activities during this period; however, in 1963, the Delaware State Archives came into possession of a series of six letters which provide us with information about the movements of her primary associates during a part of the decade and clearly show that the gang's criminal activity extended at the very least from Philadelphia, Pennsylvania, through Maryland, Delaware, and as far as the state of Mississippi.

The first letter which is addressed to Joseph Watson, Mayor of Philadelphia, is dated February 14, 1826, and is signed by James Rogers, Attorney General of Delaware:

> I have noticed in the *U. S. Gazette* of this morning a letter which had been received by you in reference to several kidnapped Negroes. The two Johnsons particularly I have had much information on for several years. Joseph is certainly the most celebrated Negro stealer in the country. Efficient means should be used to bring both these persons—particularly Joseph—to the bar of Justice.
>
> If prompt measures are used, and with proper information to the execution of them, they may be corrected. Their place of residence is not in Delaware, but within a few feet of the line dividing this state from Maryland, near Nanticoke Run, and distant from Laurel in the County of Sussex of this state about nine miles or perhaps some little more. But little reliance can be placed for their arrest by persons in their immediate neighborhood.
>
> If the publick [sic] authority in your state should intend to make an attempt to punish these persons I will cheerfully afforde [sic] any advice or information in my power to give to facilitate such object.

From Thos. Garrett, Jr., Wilmington, Delaware, To Joseph Watson, February 20, 1826:

> I find by one of our papers that thou hast received a communication from the State of Mississippi respecting

several coloured persons said to be kidnapped, one of which is stated to have lived in this place. There is a female of the name of Charity Fisher that left this place the 6th day of last month expecting to return in a few days, that has not since been heard of by her friends. Every circumstance but the first name would induce me to believe it was the same.

I will furnish thee with what information I have on the subject, and should anything transpire to make it necessary to have more information on the subject, I will cheerfully attend to it at any time.

The mother's name is at this time Elizabeth Hirons, and lives here. She says Charity was born near Downingtown, Penna., that she was removed when young with or by her mother to the neighborhood of Smyrna (Delaware). After living there a few years she was sent to James Fourney near Downingtown where she staid [sic] till about 21 years of age. She then went to Wilmington and staid till the time above stated when she left here.

It may not be amiss to state that she had while here left behind her a male child about nine months old named Matthew, that she never was married. She is supposed at this time to be about 24 years old, lusty make and light complexion for a descendent of Africa. Looks a little on one side when sewing or doing any work of that kind, thinks she has a small blemish on her left eye.

Her mother says she had a daughter living in Cherry Alley, Phila., with friends of the name of William and Mary James. Her name is Debby Fisher. I think it is probable she can give some more information on the subject. If anything more transpires on the subject I shall be glad to hear from thee as the mother is anxious to hear the fate of her daughter.

From Tos. S. Layton in George Town, Delaware, to James Rogers, February 23, 1826:

Your esteemed favor of the 18th just was received by Tuesday's mail, and hasten to enclose you the copies requested in mail, not meeting with a private conveyance.

I have seen the letter spoken of by you to the Mayor of Philadelphia and have also made some inquiry here. Concerning the Mulatto John Smith and Collins. As to Collins I cannot learn anything about. We have in our place a Mulatto by the name of Spencer Francis who is strongly suspected of being the John Smith. It is a well known fact that in the course of the last summer he was repeatedly at Robert Brereton's, in company with Joe Johnson and was leaping to and from Philadelphia, often in the Summer and Fall.

Further, a black man belonging to Mrs. T. J. C. Wright of Cannon's Ferry, who made his escape last summer, has been taken and says that Spencer passed under the name of John Smith in Philadelphia. Wright's Negro was also engaged in decoying blacks.

From James Rogers in New Castle, Delaware, to Joseph Watson, March 5th, 1826:

In each of your letters to me I have marked a mistake you have fallen into, as to the names of one of the Johnsons. You called Ebenezer F. Johnson "Abraham Johnson." I mention this that a similar mistake may not happen in the indictments, which may be processed.

The [illegible word] and must be made of the Execution of Maryland as their indictment is in that state and perhaps are there at that time. If either or both of them should take up a situation within this state I shall direct their arrest.

To accomplish the arrest of these men will require more than ordinary performance from the public authority of your state.

From Joseph Watson in Philadelphia to Spencer Franz with a copy to James Rogers, March 20, 1826:

From the information contained in the written letter from James Rogers, Esq., and by him forwarded to me I return you my thanks. I put it into the hands of the bearer Samuel Garrigues one of the high constables of this city, an excellent officer and fully possessing my confidence.

He will probably be in your place and if so will wish to confer with you fully on his mission to your state. I give him this letter as well for the information it contains as that it may act as a support to your confidence in favor of Garrigues. Any service that you can render will particularly oblige.

From Joseph Watson in Philadelphia to James Rogers, February 24, 1827:

In a letter which I have this moment received from J. W. Hamilton of Rocky Spring, Mississippi, the gentleman in whose possession the Negroes are that were kidnapped by Johnson:—he gives the following description of Mary Fisher, who discloses that she was kidnapped from near Elkton [Maryland].

I avail myself of the permission you gave me to trouble you on this occasion. I think I have conclusive proof of the cases of the four boys which I shall [send] immediately to Mr. Henderson.

I should like if it could be so managed to obtain depositions as [to] the general infamous character of these kidnappers, or the official word of their convictions. Do you know the mulatto John Smith, or Tom Collins, mentioned in Mr. Henderson's letter?

The letters offer additional endorsement of the notoriety of Joseph Johnson and clearly indicate that Delaware authorities had long been aware of his activities, but on the subject of Patty Cannon, the missives are tantalizingly silent.

We can only wonder why none of the correspondence involves authorities in Maryland where the Johnson brothers resided. What can be inferred by the statement: "But little reliance can be placed for their arrest by persons in their immediate neighborhood?" Is the Attorney General of Delaware saying that no dependence can be placed on Maryland authorities to accomplish the arrest, or is he suggesting that the Johnsons have such a strong base of support in their community as to preclude a successful raid? I am reminded of the newspaper account of Jesse Griffith's hanging, where the story is told of a constable once refusing to arrest Griffith, obviously out of fear for the officer's personal safety.

It is a stroke of good fortune that the letters have survived. They offer us solid contemporary information and whet our appetites for more.

Professor Carol Wilson has done much to satisfy that appetite in *Freedom at Risk: The Kidnapping of Free Blacks in America, 1780-1865*, a University Press of Kentucky book. In an excerpt published by *Washington College Magazine* in its 1994 summer issue, Wilson, a professor of history at Washington, fills in many details of the story behind the Watson Letters. Here is a portion:

> The extent of the Patty Cannon Gang's activities was fully revealed in 1826 in a kidnapping case that involved some two dozen victims from Pennsylvania to Mississippi. These abductions brought notoriety to the gang when Joseph Watson, the Mayor of Philadelphia, made them his personal crusade. Evidence of the kidnappings first surfaced when Joe Johnson's brother Ebenezer stopped at the home of John Hamilton, a planter in Rocky Spring, Mississippi, and offered three boys and two women for sale. One of the boys told Hamilton that he and the others

were not slaves but had been stolen from Philadelphia. Hamilton sent for a justice of the peace, who questioned Ebenezer Johnson. Johnson produced a bill of sale for the blacks, but agreed to let them remain at Hamilton's until this proof was verified. Johnson then left, supposedly to obtain further evidence of his ownership. Meanwhile, the alleged slaves told their stories to Hamilton.

Samuel Scomp, at about age fifteen, the oldest boy, was an indentured servant from Princeton, New Jersey, who had run away from his master. He went to Philadelphia, where a mulatto calling himself John Smith offered Scomp work unloading a ship. On board, Scomp encountered Joe Johnson, who tied Scomp's hands, put irons on his legs, and threatened to kill him with a knife if he made any noise.

A second boy, Enos Tilman, about nine years old, told Hamilton that he had been an apprentice in Philadelphia when he was lured aboard the ship and chained by Smith. Another Philadelphian, Alexander Manlove, related a similar story. Mary Fisher, a free black woman from Delaware, explained that she had been gathering wood near the state border in Elkton, Maryland, when she was attacked by two men who took her to Joe Johnson's house. She said that a kidnapped boy called Joe had died on the journey to Mississippi. Another boy previously with them, Cornelius, had apparently been sold in Alabama. One woman among the group was a slave who had been legally purchased.

In his letter to Philadelphia Mayor Joseph Watson, John Hamilton's lawyer, John Henderson (later U. S. senator from Mississippi), suggested that if the statements of these unfortunate blacks proved accurate, they should be published so that "the coloured people of your city and other places may be guarded against similar outrages." He added that he had no doubt as to Johnson's guilt. Henderson's belief was certainly correct, but he probably never imagined that he had helped uncover one of the largest mass kidnappings in American history.

Apparently Watson followed Henderson's advice and publicized the incident, as the mayor received several letters in the next few months concerning the activities of the Cannon-Johnson gang. Delaware's Attorney General, James Rogers, described his earlier attempts to bring the Johnson brothers to justice, and offered any information or assistance Watson requested. A Wilmington abolitionist, Thomas Garrett, provided information about one of the victims, known as Mary Fisher. He stated that he had read about the blacks' plight and believed the woman to be Charity Fisher, a Wilmington resident who had recently disappeared. Garrett added that he would continue to follow the case and asked Watson to keep him apprised of any new developments. Jesse Green, of Concord, Delaware, wrote that Ebenezer Johnson had just returned from a slave-selling trip to Alabama and had resumed kidnapping blacks in the area. James Bryan of Cambridge, Delaware,[1] also offered information of the Johnsons and stated his belief that half of the suspected fugitive slaves on the peninsula were actually kidnapping victims taken by Johnson's "emissaries,"[2] who worked the field from Philadelphia to Accomak [sic], Virginia. They numbered some thirty men, "as desperate as Johnson." Bryan also placed some of the blame on the Delaware legislature, which he claimed was more concerned with recovering runaways than with liberating kidnapped free blacks.

As a result of the publicity given to the incident, the

---

[1] There is no town named Cambridge in Delaware. Cambridge is the seat for Dorchester County, Maryland, where Johnson's Tavern was located and where Bryan family lineage boasts a James Bryan in each generation during the period under study.

[2] In a review of contemporary newspapers from Maryland and Delaware, I find no edition which does not contain advertisements offering rewards for "runaway slaves."

gang's black confederate, John Smith, was located. A resident of Georgetown, Delaware, Thomas Layton, wrote to James Rogers informing him that Smith had been seen in the area and was using the alias Spencer Francis. In response, a Philadelphia constable was sent to investigate.

In Mississippi, John Hamilton had examined the documents relevant to the case, concluding that the slaves offered for sale by Ebenezer Johnson had in fact been kidnapped. Hamilton contacted Mississippi authorities. The state's attorney general, Richard Stockton, wrote to Mayor Watson at Hamilton's request and notified him that everything was being done to effect the return of the victims to their homes and the prosecution of the kidnappers. Although Mississippi was a slave state, Stockton assured Watson, "There is no community that holds in greater abhorrence that infamous traffic carried on by Negro stealers." He added that no other state made it easier for those held illegally in slavery to gain their liberty.

In June a deposition was taken in the Philadelphia mayor's office from Samuel Scomp, who had been returned to the city with some of the other blacks after spending several months at Hamilton's plantation. Scomp's statement confirmed and elaborated upon the account he had given to John Henderson in Mississippi. After John Smith had lured him on board a ship docked in Philadelphia, Scomp was secured in the hold with two other boys, Enos Tilman and Alexander Manlove. They said that they had been abducted the night before, also enticed aboard by Smith. Two more boys were brought to the ship later that day, Cornelius Sinclair and the ironically named Joe Johnson.

That night the ship sailed. In a week, it landed near the kidnapper Johnson's house along the Delaware-Maryland border, where the captives were confined in an attic. They were later moved to the Cannon house and chained there for about a week. There, two women, Mary Fisher, a free woman from Delaware, and Maria Neal, a slave, joined them. The whole group was then transported by boat to the Deep South; Scomp was unsure exactly where they landed. The victims were forced to walk through Alabama, where they were offered for sale.

Cornelius Sinclair was the first to be sold, bringing four hundred dollars in Tuscaloosa. The rest were forced to walk on to Mississippi, where they finally stopped at Rocky Spring, site of John Hamilton's plantation. Scomp estimated that they had traveled about thirty miles each day on foot and had received a severe whipping if they complained. When Scomp tried to escape, he was beaten "with a hand saw and with hickories" by Ebenezer Johnson. The deposition noted that an examination of Scomp's back confirmed the beatings.

About seven miles outside Rocky Spring, the boy called Joe Johnson died from the beatings and from frostbite of the feet. At Hamilton's, all but the slave Maria Neal were taken in and cared for. After several months, the planter obtained passage for them to New Orleans, from where they sailed to Philadelphia. Mary Fisher, who did not want to travel by sea, remained at Hamilton's.

Philadelphia Mayor, Joseph Watson, kept the Pennsylvania Abolition Society informed of his ongoing investigation. In July, William Rawle, PAS president, received word from Watson that Ebenezer Johnson had been arrested for possessing the body of the boy who had died on the journey. Watson reported the return of most of the victims and added that Cornelius Sinclair was expected to arrive shortly. The Grand Jury of Philadelphia County issued indictments against Ebenezer and Joe Johnson, John Smith, and Thomas Collins, another gang member. Warrants for their arrest were forwarded to Delaware, Maryland, Virginia, Alabama, and Mississippi. Watson also told the PAS that he had forwarded documents that supported the victims' statements.

But the case did not end there, for the activities of the Johnson brothers exceeded the scope of the initial reports. In December 1826, evidence of another kidnapping by the gang surfaced. David Holmes, governor of Mississippi, and Joseph E. Davis, lawyer and state legislator of Natchez, notified Watson of the story of Peter Hook, a slave in Mississippi. In a deposition recorded by lawyer Duncan S. Walker, Hook revealed that he had been kidnapped in Philadelphia in June 1825, one night when a black man named John invited him to a ship near the Arch Street wharf for a drink. On board, Joe Johnson took him below, tied him up, and chained him to a pump. Two others, William Miller and Milton Trusty, were brought down the same night and chained with Hook. Clement Cox and William Chase, two more kidnapping victims, arrived the next night. After several days, the ship sailed, and eventually all the victims were taken to Joe Johnson's house, where they were shackled in the attic. Several more victims arrived over the next few days—John Jacobs, a cart driver, James Bayard, a sweep, Benjamin Baxter, "little John," and Henry. All were boys except Henry, who was a young man.

Two girls, Lydia Smith and Sarah (Sally) Nicholson, were chained in a different part of the attic. According to Hook, the entire group remained at Johnson's house for about six months and were then taken to Rockingham, North Carolina, and were sold. Hook reported that they were severely beaten when they asserted their free status. Two other black men, Staten and Constant, who said they had been abducted from Philadelphia, joined the group near Rockingham. Miller and Sutler, slave traders, purchased the blacks from Johnson and sold them at various points. Hook was sold to a man named Perryman in

Holmesville, Mississippi, along with three of the other boys.

In January 1827, Mayor Watson thanked David Holmes and J. E. Davis for the information they had added to the state's case against the Cannon-Johnson gang. He told them of the gang's other kidnappings and explained that he hoped "to develop the mazes of this infernal plot, by means of which a great number of free born children during several years past, have been seduced away and kidnapped, principally, and almost wholly as I believe, by a gang of desperadoes, whose haunts and head quarters are known to have been on the dividing line between the states of Delaware and Maryland, low down on the peninsula, between the Delaware and Chesapeake Bays."

. . . Watson had found white witnesses who could identify three of the boys, although he recognized the difficulty of getting whites to testify to the identity of the blacks, especially after so much time had elapsed. The city council of Philadelphia authorized the mayor to issue a five-hundred-dollar reward for information leading to the arrest and prosecution of anyone involved in the kidnappings of 1825. The council also approved five hundred dollars to the mayor for expenses incurred in the investigation. This proclamation was issued to newspapers the following day. Watson advised Duncan S. Walker, the Mississippi lawyer working to secure the freedom and safe return of the victims, "to leave no stone unturned" in his efforts to help the blacks. The Philadelphia mayor clearly followed the same policy himself.

Walker brought freedom suits for five of the blacks. His brother, Robert J. Walker, also an attorney, investigated the circumstances of the six whose whereabouts were unknown. Duncan Walker sympathized with Watson. "I can appreciate the difficulty you anticipate, of identifying black children, by the evidence of white persons," he wrote. "But however onerous it may be on all hands, we must do our duty." It seemed surprising that Walker, a southerner, would expend so much effort to assist people of color. Yet he was sincere: he refused any fees for his services, despite Watson's offer of compensation, and he assured the mayor, "Our soil affords no stone for building Penitentiaries, but our forests supply gallows for the kidnapper; while our laws protect slave property, they will restore the free." Walker also sent the statement of another of the victims, Lydia Smith of Delaware. An indentured servant, she had been among numerous masters for many of her twenty-three years. Her last master, Bill Spicer,[3] had been jailed for attempting to sell her as a slave. When he was released, he sold Smith to Ebenezer Johnson for $110. Chained for about five months in the home of Johnson's sister, Smith there encountered Ephraim Lawrence, John Jacobs, and little John. They were eventually taken to Rockingham, North Carolina.

Watson then asked James Rogers, attorney general of Delaware, if he could "obtain depositions as to the general infamous character of these kidnappers." The Philadelphia grand jury would be sitting in March, and Watson believed that the Johnsons would be indicted for kidnapping. He planned to ask Pennsylvania Governor John Schultze to demand the Johnson's extradition from Mississippi and to make arrangements for the children's return. Watson had no doubt that they had all been kidnapped. In fact, he believed that most of the kidnappings that had occurred over the past ten years in the mid-Atlantic region were the work of the Johnson brothers, whom he characterized as "very desperate ruffians, and utterly infamous."

The Cannon-Johnson family managed to avoid ap-

---

[3] This appears to be the same William Spicer mentioned in the interrogatories prepared in 1824 as a result of Hannah McColly's petition for freedom.

prehension, however. As a Delawarian, Jesse Green, reported in March 1827, the Johnson brothers had returned to Patty Cannon's home in Delaware and planned to resume their kidnapping operation, with blacks "to assist and decoy." Stating that "the poor Free Negroes feel much alarm at their return," Green added that while he would continue to provide authorities with any information he could, he was too old to offer any other help. He also wanted his name kept secret for fear of the gang's revenge.

The same month, a Natchez, Mississippi newspaper editorial spoke out against the kidnappings. "Policy, as well as humanity, requires that our citizens take every measure in their power to assist in restoring these unfortunate beings to their homes, and their families." Despite the tone of most of the editorial, however, it claimed that "for the most part free Negroes are the worst description of people that could ever be willingly brought among us." The extensive laws passed by Mississippi and other southern states reveal an intensive attempt to prevent free blacks from entering their borders and to control the existing black population. Perhaps the efforts of southern citizens to return the victims of the Cannon-Johnson gang to their homes were an indication not of sympathy for fellow human beings in trouble, not of obedience to anti-kidnapping laws, but of the desire to expunge a group of people they viewed with distaste and fear.

Professor Wilson continues with other examples of efforts to free the Johnson's victims and stresses the dilemmas often encountered by society and by laws themselves:

However, difficulties were encountered . . . in obtaining "strictly legal proof—that is to say, the evidence of white persons in open court." This was a common problem. Even though there were witnesses to the crime, many kidnapping cases were lost in court because of the inadmissibility of black testimony in cases involving whites. Even when white witnesses were available, they were frequently reluctant to testify. Fear of retribution and racism prevented many whites from testifying in cases of kidnapping, which usually involved a black plaintiff and white defendant.

Ironically, when members of the Cannon-Johnson kidnapping ring were finally brought to justice, it was not for the crime of kidnapping. In fact, few of the gang were ever convicted of that offense.

The Watson letters and the exemplary academic detective work of Professor Wilson present us with a clear and focused picture of the range and brutality of the Cannon-Johnson kidnapping operation and suggest that perhaps *all* was not quiet domesticity in and around the Cannon household after Joe Johnson's conviction and whipping in 1822.

Patty Cannon's Arrest and Death

On April 1, 1829, the world of Patty Cannon came crashing down. The story of her arrest spread rapidly by word of mouth from Johnson's Crossroads to Seaford, to Georgetown, and beyond. Citizens clustered, it has been said, in astonished disbelief, frequently in anger over the grisly discoveries that led to her confinement. Some claimed their long-standing suspicions were finally vindicated.

The contemporary news media, which often consisted of little more than town criers and a few scattered weeklies, were slow to respond. It was not until April 17 that Samuel Harker, a former crafter of rush-bottom chairs and then editor of Wilmington's *Delaware Gazette,* headlined the following story:

A Horrible Development

The murders in Sussex—We stated briefly in our paper of Friday last [April 10]. Some circumstances respecting a most diabolical course of conduct which, for some years past, has been carried on in Sussex County, in this state, the evidences of which have just been brought to light, and promised in our next number to give further particulars.

From our correspondent's account we gather the following particulars: About ten days previous to this writing, a tenant, who lives on the farm where Patty Cannon and her son-in-law, the celebrated Joseph Johnson, negro trader, lived for many years in Northwest Fork Hundred, near the Maryland Line, was ploughing in a field in a place generally covered with water, and where a heap of brush had been laying for years, when his horse sunk in a grave, and on digging he found a blue painted chest, about three feet long, and in it were found the bones of a man.

The news flew like wild fire and people from many miles around visited the place; among whom it was universally agreed that a negro trader from Georgia, named Bell or Miller, or perhaps both, had been murdered by Johnson and his gang about ten or twelve years before, and that the bones now discovered were those of one of them; as the man or men had been missed about that time, and the horse on which one of them rode was found at Patty Cannon's, who laid claim to the animal until a person from Maryland, who had lent the horse, came forward and claimed his property; and she alleged at the time that Bell or Miller had sailed a short time previous, with a cargo of negroes for the South.

Since that time he had not been heard of, and it is said that a few days before he was missed, he was heard to say he had with him fifteen thousand dollars with which he proposed to purchase negroes. The supposition now is that the knowledge of his having this money in his possession formed the inducement to take his life, and that to conceal the body it had been deposited in the place where the bones have been found.

The excitement produced by the discovery, as may naturally be supposed, was very great in the neighborhood, and on the second instant, one of Johnson's gang, named Cyrus James, who has resided in Maryland, was caught in this state, and brought before a justice of the peace in Seaford, and on examination stated that Joseph Johnson, Ebenezer F. Johnson, and Patty Cannon, had shot the man while at supper in her house, and that he saw them all engaged in carrying him in the chest and burying him; and stated moreover that many others had been killed, and that he could show where they had been buried. The officers and citizens accordingly accompanied him to the places which he pointed out, and made the necessary search.

In one place, a garden, they dug and found the bones of a young child, the mother of which, he stated, was a negro woman belonging to Patty Cannon, Which, being a mulatto, she had killed for the reason she supposed its father to be one of her own family. Another place a few feet distant was then pointed out, when, upon digging a few feet two oak boxes were found, each of which contained human bones.

Those in one of them had been of a person about seven years of age, which James said he saw Patty Cannon knock in the head with a billet of wood, and the other contained those of one whom he said they considered bad property; by which, it is supposed they meant that he was free. As there was at the time much stir about the children and there was no convenient opportunity to send them away, they were murdered to prevent discovery. On exam-

ining the skull of the largest child, it was discovered to be
broken as described by James.

The fellow James was raised by Patty Cannon, having
been bound to her at the age of seven years, and is said to
have done much mischief in his time for her and Johnson.

Another witness named Butler has already been secured, and it is thought that some others will be brought
forward who are acquainted with the bloody deeds of
Patty and Joe. This woman is now between sixty and
seventy years of age, and looks more like a man than a
woman; but old as she is, she is believed to be as heedless
and heartless as the most abandoned wretch that lives.

Patty Cannon has been lodged in the jail at Georgetown; James and Butler were also placed there at the same
time; and it is highly probably that ere this the trial has
taken place, and the result of it will soon be known.

James stated that he had not shown all the places
where murdered bodies had been buried, and at the time of
writing, our correspondent informs us, the people were
still digging.

Joe Johnson, who is said to be residing at this time in
Alabama, is stated to have been seen in this state in December or January last; and the probability is that his
business here was to do something at his old business of
kidnapping. He was convicted of this crime some years
since at Georgetown and suffered the punishment of the
lash and the pillory on account of it. He is a man of some
celebrity, having, for many years, carried on the traffic of
stealing and selling negroes in which he was aided and
instructed by the old hag, Patty Cannon, whose daughter
he married, after she had lost a former husband on the
gallows.

He [Johnson] continued to reside near his tutoress
until within a few years, when a reward of $500 was of-
fered by Mr. Watson, Mayor of Philadelphia, when hav-

ing obtained information of the fact before any others in his neighborhood, he suddenly decamped, and has since been very cautious in suffering himself to be seen in that part of the country.

The former husband of Joe's wife was hung for the murder of a negro trader, the plan for which is said to have been arranged at her mother's home.

From the circumstances which have already taken place, it would appear probable that such developments may be expected to take place as will present the wretched actors . . . as successful rivals in depravity of the infamous Burke[1], whose bloody deeds and recent execution in Scotland have occupied so large a portion of the public prints.

The neighborhood in which these terrible events occurred, the borders of Delaware and Maryland, have long been famous for negro stealing and negro trading—and Patty Cannon and Joe Johnson are familiar names to us.

In 1965, without stating a source, Ted Giles wrote, "When Patty was arrested in 1829 . . . the town crier calling the hours bellowed, 'Three o'clock and Patty Cannon taken.'"

A week later the *Delaware Gazette* amended its story, reporting that the anticipated trial had not occurred, and on April 25, 1829, Hezekiah Niles, a Pennsylvanian who migrated to Baltimore, Maryland, by way of Wilmington, Delaware, elevated Patty Cannon to national attention. *Niles Weekly Register* has been called *Time, Newsweek*, and the *Sunday New York Times* all rolled into one. At least in its day it was a highly regarded source of information. Later, on May 23, Niles published this brief report:

Murders in Delaware

---

[1] William Burke was an Irish criminal who moved to Scotland and there, for the value of their bodies, murdered by suffocation at least fifteen travelers, selling the corpses to an anatomist. He was hanged on January 28, 1829.

The *Delaware Journal* says "At the Court of Quarterly Sessions recently setting in Sussex County, the grand jury found three indictments against Patty Cannon for murder, and one against each of the brothers, Joe Johnson and Ebenezer Johnson, at The Court of Oyer and Terminer in October—the others reside out of the state—where, is not exactly known, but we take it for granted that the proper steps will be taken to discover and bring them to justice.

Patty Cannon died in jail on the 11th instant.

Such an austere announcement: "Patty Cannon died in jail on the 11th instant." Levi Sullivan, a resident of Broad Creek Hundred in Sussex County, kept a private diary from 1818 to 1844. On its pages we find this notation, nearly as concise as the one in Niles *Register*: "May 11th 1829 Patty Cannon deceased in Georgetown Jail said to have committed murder." And that was about all America would have to say about Patty Cannon until years later.

While records of Patty's arrest seem to have vanished, her indictment survives in the Delaware Archives:

Be it remembered that at Court of General Sessions of the Peace and Goal Delivery of the State of Delaware held at George Town in and for the County of Sussex on the 13th day of April, 1829.

Patty Cannon, late of North West Fork Hundred, widow, not having the fear of God before her eyes and being moved and seduced by the Devil, on the 26th day of April, 1822, with force and arms in and upon a certain infant female child to the aforesaid unknown then and there lately born and alive in the Peace of God and of the State of Delaware then and there being feloniously, unlawfully and of malice aforethought did make an assault, and that the said Patty Cannon with both her hands about the neck of the said infant and—did choke and strangle, of which said choking and strangling the said female child to the jury aforesaid unknown so being alive, then and there instantly died. Patty Cannon did kill and murder against the peace and dignity of the state. . . [and] did cast and throw the infant child on the ground and cover over with earth.

Joseph Johnson, Ebenezer Johnson, and James Melson were named with Patty for the murder of a male child on April 26, 1822. Patty and Joe Johnson were cited for the murder of an unknown male who was struck and beaten with a stick on the right side of the head, the blow or blows inflicting, the indictment states, a "mortal bruise." Patty and Joe are also accused of the murder of a Negro boy "with a certain large piece of wood of the value of one cent, lawful money of the State of Delaware." The latter crime was said to have taken place on June 1, 1824.

Attorney General James Rogers must have taken pleasure in finally signing murder indictments against the principals of the gang, a jubilance diminished by the fact that Joe and Ebenezer remained at large. In the end neither the Johnsons nor James Melson were ever brought to trial on the charges.

H. C. Conrad, whose three volume history of Delaware has been highly acclaimed, discovered what appears to be an unsigned letter in 1927, which is now housed in the Delaware Archives and which provides an additional contemporary account:

Much excitement now prevails in this county in consequence of the discovery of the bodies of several persons, interred upon the premises of the celebrated Patty Cannon, who lives upon the line of the state and whose house has been for a long time the resort of all the kidnapping and negro traders in this part of the Peninsula.

About a week since, a person who was ploughing in the orchard adjoining the house of this woman, observed the ground to sink in a particular spot, which induced him to suppose that money might be found there. Upon going home he communicated the fact to several others, who in the hope of some valuable prize went to examine it. They dug up the earth until they came to a chest, which upon opening to their astonishment contained the bones of a man with some remains of clothing.

This chest has been identified as one formerly in the possession of Mrs. Cannon and the deceased is supposed to have been a Southern trader, who about ten years ago suddenly disappeared from the neighborhood.

In consequence of this discovery the people in the vicinity were in dread to make further search, and a few days since, in the enclosure they dug up the bodies of three other persons, one of them a child with the skull fractured. The bones of the child and of one other were found in the same pit, the child uppermost.

Mrs. Cannon has since been arrested and is now confined to Jail to await a further investigation by the Grand Jury. A man by the name of Cyrus James, who was raised by Mrs. Cannon and who has been inmate of her family ever since, is likewise imprisoned. He was present at the disinterring of the bodies and directed the persons engaged in it where to find them.

It is said that he stated before the Justice who committed Mrs. Cannon that he saw the mortal wound inflicted upon the child that was found and that Mrs. Cannon on another occasion carried out a black child, not yet dead, in her apron, but that it never returned.

How the truth is, or who was the actual perpetrator of those horrible deeds, it may be difficult to ascertain, but there is no doubt that these persons have been murdered and the suspicion at present rests upon this degraded woman.

On this document is a note in another hand which reads:

The ploughing and discovery of bones happened about the first of April, 1829.

Mrs. Cannon lived in Maryland, just adjoining to the State Line. She had formerly lived in Delaware, on the land where the bones were found. It was sold by the Sheriff, and now belongs to Isaac Cannon and Jacob Cannon. Their tenant lives on the land, and he made the first discovery. Mrs. Cannon, it is said, came voluntarily into the state and there was arrested as also did James.

In a comment dated June 6, 1927, Mr. Conrad indicated that he was unaware of the source of the letter but that Henry M. Ridgely authored the note contained thereon.

There is disagreement concerning the race of Cyrus James, apparently the state's only witness against Patty Cannon in the 1829 indictments. Most writers have referred to him as a Negro. Almost singularly, George Alfred Townsend made James' counterpart a white character in his novel, *The Entailed Hat.*

What do we have for contemporary evidence? In reports from the period, James is not referred to as either black or white, but notice that blacks in these documents and stories are consistently alluded to by their race; whites are not.

James is said to have been "raised by Mrs. Cannon" and "has been inmate of her family ever since." At another point he is said to have been "bound to her at the age of seven years." To be bound is not necessarily an indication of slavery; white individuals known as indentured servants were commonly bound to masters, usually for a specific time in payment of a debt or for instruction in a trade.

Very important to the consideration of James' race is the knowledge that blacks were not legally permitted to stand as witnesses against white defendants, and this has influenced some historians to conclude that Townsend was correct.

One is swayed to join these scholars, but there always seems to be another bit of evidence to keep the question alive. Later we shall read the memoirs of Robert Hazzard, a man who witnessed

Patty's procession on its way to the Georgetown Jail, who knew neighbors of hers, and whose father once assisted a man who escaped from her attic. Hazzard identifies James as a Negro.

There is also disagreement concerning the details of Patty Cannon's arrest. While the bodies of the victims were discovered in Delaware on the premises of her old homestead, Patty was then living in Johnson's Tavern, just across the state line in Maryland; but it appears evident from contemporary information that she never went through extradition proceedings.

We have been told above that she came across the state line voluntarily, and that appears to be the official position taken by Delaware authorities. There are, however, other claims, which include the conspiracy versions in which a Maryland deputy is alleged to have distracted her through conversation while casually crossing the border, or else pushed her across into the arms of a Sussex County officer.

Carroll Dulaney, in a 1935 story in the *Baltimore Sun*, gives credit to Thomas Holliday Hicks for Patty Cannon's arrest, as have others. Dulaney claims that Hicks, whom he calls a Dorchester constable, turned Patty over to Delaware authorities. George Alfred Townsend, in *The Entailed Hat*, also involves Hicks in Patty's arrest. It is an interesting theory, especially since Hicks became governor of Maryland and earned many distinctions. He is credited with averting his state's secession from the Union—Maryland was a slave-holding state—by refusing to call the General Assembly in 1861.

My examination of family records informs me that Thomas Holiday Hicks was born in Dorchester County in 1798, that, in spite of a limited education brought about by family financial woes, he was elected constable of East New Market shortly after reaching majority and remained in that post until 1824, when citizens of Dorchester chose him to fill the office of county sheriff. Upon retiring from the latter position in 1827, the family sketch claims, Hicks moved to a farm on the Choptank River. In 1829, the year of Patty's arrest, he was elected to the Maryland House of Delegates. And so, while it reads well to have

had this statesman and friend of Lincoln responsible for appre-
hending the infamous Patty Cannon, it might better be considered a romantic notion.

Another Dorchester deputy sometimes given credit for the
arrest is Jacob Wilson. Wilson lived in the district where Johnson's Tavern was located and there is a better chance that he was
involved in the arrest, but we are not likely to ever know with
certainty what happened that day.

The account of a pitched battle between Patty's gang and a
posse of lawmen, which some versions of her capture include,
are, with certainty, no more than fictional efforts to sensation-
alize the incident.

Yet another controversy is the matter of a trial. Several writers claim she was tried by a Sussex County jury, declared guilty,
and sentenced to death, and that she thwarted the hangman by
ingesting a dose of arsenic before the appointed hour.

Such a conclusion might have legitimately been surmised
from Samuel Harker's statement in the *Delaware Gazette* of
April 17: ". . . it is highly probably that ere this the trial has taken place"; but if these journalists had read subsequent editions,
they would have found an apology for that misinformation in
the *Gazette's* April 17 release:

> We inadvertently stated that her trial might be expec-
> ted to take place about the time of the publication. It was
> the court of Common Pleas which was then in session,
> and by the Constitution of our State the trial for capital
> offenses is confined to the Supreme Court, whose regular
> session does not take place in that County until August
> next. Several bills of indictment were found against the
> old woman, but she has saved the Court the trouble of
> trying, and perhaps the Sheriff that of performing even a
> more unpleasant duty, as she died in jail on the 11th
> instant.

The *Gazette's* editor traveled to Sussex County on a fact-finding trip and returned with a tale involving one of Patty's Negro allies. This decoy, Harker was told, persuaded a slave in Worcester County, Maryland, along with his free wife and seven children, to follow him to Camden, Delaware, for a meeting with Quakers, who were to provide safe passage to New Jersey. Instead of leading the family to Camden, however, the Judas delivered them to Johnson's Crossroads. They were never seen again by relatives and friends.

As further support for the contention that Patty was never tried, we also have the *Delaware Journal* statement: "At the Court of Quarterly Sessions recently setting in Sussex County, the grand jury found three indictments against Patty Cannon for murder, and one against each of the brothers, Joe Johnson and Ebenezer Johnson, at The Court of Oyer and Terminer in October." This, some claim, is a clear indication that the trial was set for October.

In a footnote in *The Entailed Hat*, its author indicated that: "She was to have been tried in October. . . ."

Ted Giles, author of *Patty Cannon—Woman of Mystery*, asked Judge Charles S. Richards, retired Associate Judge of the Supreme Court of Delaware and also a former Judge of the Superior Court, and Judge James B. Carey, Richard's successor in those two posts, for their opinions. Judge Richards, in his thirty-four years of service on the bench, had been in a position to obtain testimony from contemporaries about the events. The judges agreed that no trial had ever been conducted, and Giles asserts that they should be considered authorities in support of that conclusion.

And the cause of Patty Cannon's death—still more disagreement. You can choose between self-administered poison, natural causes, or assassination. Or, you may prefer the premise of Ashworth Burslem, former assistant city editor and drama critic of Wilmington's *Journal-Every Evening*. Burslem's belief was that influential citizens from the Cambridge, Maryland area—people who had benefited from Patty's business ventures—bribed the Georgetown jailers to permit Patty to escape and then assisted her flight to Canada.

The last two hypotheses seem to be the most remote, and poison, though it remains the most widely accepted claim, raises several questions. First of all, where did she get it? Some proponents of the poison theory claim it was hidden in the hem of her skirt; others say in a locket. One believes it was delivered to her in prison. We can only wonder if a person of Patty's alleged temperament would have been so quick to take her own life, and would the fact she died of self-inflicted poison not have been newsworthy? We do have John Clayton's letter from 1837 which includes the statement "She was arrested & put in goal in Sussex, but upon her trial this demon took arsenic and died by her own hand." Did Clayton know more about the details of her death than was shared with reporters, or was he simply repeating a common rumor? Why would authorities want to hide the fact that Patty committed suicide? She was apparently in her 60's, already beyond the average life expectancy for her time; a death from natural causes would not have been extraordinary.

You would expect that the demise of a prisoner, especially one with such a notorious reputation, would be a well-documented event. So also, we argue, should a lot of other details about Patty Cannon be a matter of indisputable record, but they are not. The times were very different then. The sense of history was not so acute, nor were policies concerning records so specific as they are today.

Since we have no evidence that anyone attempted to claim Patty's body, nor that there was even a living family member who might have had an interest in doing so, it seems reasonable to believe that she was interred on the premises of the Sussex County Jail as tradition claims. Judges Richards and Carey concurred with this theory and confirmed the custom of jailyard burials for unclaimed bodies. Several prisoners were laid to rest over the years behind the court house and jail, near the whipping post.

Sometime after the turn of the century, most likely between 1902 and 1905, the remains of those prisoners were moved to unmarked graves in Potters Field, next to the Sussex County Correctional Institution outside Georgetown. Some say three individuals were transferred, all women. It was the responsibility of the Levy Court to keep such records, but, if they ever existed, they have been lost.

I have also encountered rumors which suggest that the remains of Patty Cannon were taken to Galestown, Maryland, a few miles below the site of Cannon's Ferry, but I can find no evidence to support such a thesis. After investigating the possibility, Ted Giles concluded that if she had been brought to Galestown, someone would have remembered the incident.

But Jerry Shields is not ready to completely dismiss the possibility. If her body had been interred in the vicinity of this small, rural, Maryland community, Shields believes it would have been in the Twiford family cemetery, which he describes as being just on the western side of the state line on the north bank of the Nanticoke. After conducting a terse investigation of the area, Shields concludes for now that the Twiford burials have been plowed over and cultivated for many years. And why would Patty Cannon have been brought to the Twiford tombs? Betty Twiford and Patty are said to have been sisters.

More will be said later about the earthly remains of Patty Cannon.

The Entailed Hat

For more than a century now, those who inquire as to the best source for information about Patty Cannon, her gang, and her nefarious exploits are often directed to the novel *The Entailed Hat* by "Gath." This peculiar pen name was apparently suggested by a verse from Samuel: "Tell it not to Gath," a term which includes the initials of the author, George Alfred Townsend.

Townsend was born in Georgetown, Delaware, on January 30, 1841, almost twelve years after Patty Cannon died in that town's jail and the same year in which the *Narrative and Confessions of Lucretia Canon* was published. His father was a carpenter and itinerant Methodist preacher who later in life practiced medicine. The writer lived in nearly a dozen towns on Delmarva and traveled the peninsula extensively in his early years. He visited Reliance, saw the tavern and its attic before the building was remodeled, had personal contact with individuals who had known Patty Cannon, her family, and the gang of cutthroats, and so was able to get, among other details, accurate physical descriptions of the participants. As far as can be determined, the names of her mob used in the story are those of actual individuals.

The "hat" in the title has no connection to Patty Cannon but claims its origin in a curious will written by one of the author's ancestors in which he bequeathed to a son: "My best hat, to him and his assignees forever."

Townsend became a reporter for the *Inquirer* in Philadelphia and then for the *Herald* and *World* in New York. His coverage of the last battles of the Civil War and the assassination of Lincoln brought him national recognition. After reporting the Austro-Prussian War, he settled in Washington where he became a syndicated columnist and began to sign his articles "Gath."

Gathland Park, near Burkittsville, Maryland, contains one of the five homes Townsend built there, as well as a huge stone arch he erected as a tribute to writers and artists, both Union and Confederate, who reported the Civil War. It is the only monument dedicated to war correspondents in the world.

Turning, in 1882, to the allure of historical fiction, Townsend devoted two years to writing *The Entailed Hat*, his first novel.

In 1990 Jerry Shields reported that he had been told that Harper & Brothers had quickly withdrawn the first edition because of objections from some prominent families in Maryland and Delaware, and then, after modifications were made, republished it later in 1884 in the form we know. If such an edition existed, it would be a valuable collectors' item today. I contacted several rare book dealers and experts and asked if they had ever heard of such an issue. None had, and all considered the possibility to be remote.

When I questioned Shields on the source of the rumor, he said he had been told about someone in possession of such a volume, but " I borrowed the book, checked it thoroughly against the edition I had, and found there was no difference."

Shields, having since come into possession of a large amount of Townsend material, has published the book, *Gath's Literary Work and Folk*.

"What I have learned," Shields says, "is that Townsend made cuts himself and obviously avoided calling certain key names of prominent families, but gave enough evidence so that if you were really interested you could find out who they were. The initial rumor that I heard," he concluded, "turned out to be unsubstantiated."

Townsend died in 1904, but his popularity is evident in the fact that *The Entailed Hat* went to several printings when first released in 1884 and was then revived in 1912 and again in the 1920's. Tidewater Publishers gave it yet another lease on life in 1955.

A large portion of the novel is dedicated to the activities of the Cannon-Johnson gang with a romance woven into the fabric of evil.

Here are some excerpts to give you the flavor of Townsend's skills as a writer and Patty Cannon's nefarious deeds:

"Do you know Joe Johnson, Dave?"

"Yes, Marster Phoebus, you bet I does. He's at Salisbury, he's at Vienna, he's up yer to Crotcher's Ferry, he's all ober de country, but he don't go to Delawaw any more in de daylight. He was whipped dar, an' banished from de state on pain o' de gallows. But he lives jess on dis side o' de Delawaw line, so dey can't git him in Delawaw. He calls his place Johnson's Crossroads: ole Patty Cannon lives dar, too. She's afraid to stay in Delawaw now."

"Why, what is the occupation of those terrible people at present?" asked Mrs. Custis.

No answer was made for a minute, and then Dave said, in a low, frightened voice, as he stole a glance at both of his companions out of his fiery, scarred eyes:

"Kidnappin', I 'spect."

"It's everything that makes Pangymonum," Jimmy Phoebus explained; "that old woman, Patty Cannon, has spent the whole of a wicked life, by smoke!—or ever sence she came to Delaware from Cannady, as the bride of pore Alonzo Cannon—a-makin' robbers an' bloodhounds out of the young men she could git hold of. Some of 'em she sets to robbin' the mails, some to makin' an' passin' of counterfeit money, but most of 'em she sets at stealin' free niggers outen the State of Delaware; and, when it's safe, they steal slaves too. She fust made a tool of Ebenezer Johnson, the pirate of Broad Creek, an' he died in his tracks a-fightin' fur her. Then she took hold of his sons, Joe Johnson an' young Ebenezer, an' made 'em both out-laws and kidnappers, an' Joe she married to her daughter, when Bruington, her first son-in-law, had been hanged. When Samson Hat, who is the whitest nigger I ever found, knocked Joe Johnson down in Princess Anne, the night before last, he struck the worst man in our peninsula."

"They [residents of Delmarva] hated free niggers as if they was all Tories an' didn't love Amerikey. So, seein' the free niggers hadn't no friends, these Johnsons an' Patty Cannon begun to steal 'em, by smoke! There was only a million niggers in the whole country; Louisiana was a-roarin' for 'em; every nigger was wuth twenty horses or thirty yokes of oxen, or two good farms around yer, an' these kidnappers made money like smoke, bought the lawyers, went into polytics, an' got sech a highhand that they tried a murderin' of the nigger traders from Georgey an' down thar, comin' yer full of gold to buy free people. That give 'em a back-set, an' they hung some of Patty's band—some at Georgetown, some at Cambridge."

"At last the Delawareans marched on Johnson's Crossroads an' cleaned his Pangymonum thar out, an' guarded him, an' sixteen pore niggers in chains he'd kidnapped, to Georgetown jail. Young John M. Clayton was paid by the Phildelfy Quakers to git him convicted. Johnson was strong in the county—we're in it now, Sussex—an' if Clayton hadn't skeered the jury almost to death, it would have disagreed. He held 'em over bilin' hell, an' dipped 'em thar till the courtroom was like a Methodis' revival meetin', with half that jury cryin', 'Save me, save me, Lord!' while some of 'em had Joe Johnson's money in their pockets. Joe was licked at the post, banished from the state, an' so skeered that he laid low awhile, goin' off somewhar—to Missoury, or Floridey, or Allybamy. But Patty Cannon never flinched; she trained the young boys around yer to be her sleuth-hounds an' go stealin' for her; an', till she dies, it's safer to be a chicken than a free nigger.

"Now, I never been by this place before," Jimmy Phoebus muttered, "but, by smoke! yon house looks to me like Betty Twiford's wharf, an', to save my life, I can't help thinkin' yon white spots down this side of the river air Sharptown. If that's the case, which state am I in?"

He rose to his feet, bailed the scow, which was nearly full of water, and began to paddle along the shore, and, seeing something white, he landed and parted the bushes, and found it to be a stone of a bluish marble, bearing on one side the letter M, and on the other the letter P, and a royal crown was also carved upon it.

"Yer's one o' Lord Baltimore's boundary stones," Phoebus exclaimed. "Now see the rascality o' them kidnappers! Yon house, I know, is Betty Twiford's, because it's a'most on the state-line, but, I'm ashamed to say, it's a leetle in Maryland. And that lane, coming down to the wharf, is my way to Joe Johnson's Pangymonum at his cross-roads."

A sound, as of some one singing, seemed to come from

the woods near by, and Phoebus, listening, concluded that it was farther along the water, so he paddled softly forward till a small cove or pool led up into the swamp, and its shores nowhere offered a dry landing; yet there were recent foot-marks deeply trodden in the bog, and disclosed up the slope into the woods, and from their direction seemed to come the mysterious chanting.

"My head's bloody and I'm wet as a musk-rat, so I reckon I ain't afraid of gittin' a little muddy," and with this the navigator stepped from the scow in swamp nearly to his middle, and pulled himself up the slope by main strength.

"I believe my soul this yer is a island," Jimmy remarked; "a island surrounded with mud, that's wuss to git to than a water island."

The tall trees increased in size as he went on and entered a noble grove of pines, through whose roar, like an organ accompanied by a human voice, the singing was heard nearer and nearer, and, following the track of previous feet, which had almost made a path, Phoebus came to a space where an axe had laid the smaller bushes low around a large loblolly pine that spread its branches like a roof only a few feet from the ground; and there, fastened by a chain to the trunk, which allowed her to go around and around the tree, and tread a nearly bare place in the pine droppings or "shats," sat a black woman, singing a long, weary, throat-sore wail.

. . . The chain, strong and rusty, had been very recently welded to her feet by a blacksmith; the fresh rivet attested that, and there were also pieces of charcoal in the pine strewings, as if fire had been brought there for smith's uses. Jimmy Phoebus took hold of the chain and examined it link by link till it depended from a powerful staple driven to the heart of the pine-tree; though rusty, it was perfect in every part, and the condition of the staple showed that it was permanently retained in its position, as if to secure various and successive persons, while the staple itself had been driven above the reach of the hands, as by a man standing on some platform or on another's shoulders.

"There's jess two people can unfasten this chain," exclaimed Jimmy, blowing hard and kneading his palms, after two such exertions, "one of em's a blacksmith and t'other's a woodchopper. Gal, how did you git yer?"

. . . "My husband brought me here," she said, between her long sobs. "He sold me. . . ."

"I reckon you don't belong fur down this way. You don't talk like it."

"No sir; I belong to Philadelphia. I was a free woman and a widow; my husband left me a little money and a little house and this child; another man come and courted me, a han'some mulatto man, almost as white as you. He told me he had a farm in Delaware, and wanted me to be his wife; he promised me so much and was so anxious about it, that I listened to him. . . ."

"You say he sold you?"

. . . "We moved our things on a vessel to Delaware, and come up a creek to a little town in the marshes, and there we started for my husband's farm. He said we had come to it in the night. I couldn't tell, but I saw a house in the woods, and was so tired I went to sleep with my baby there, and in the night I found men in the room, and one of them, a white man, was tying my feet. . . .

"I thought then of the kidnappers of Delaware, for I had heard about them, and I jumped out of bed and fought for my life. They knocked me down and the rope around my feet tripped me up; but I fought with my teeth after my hands was tied, too, and I bit the white man's knees, and then he picked up a fire-shovel, or something of iron, and knocked my teeth out. My last hope was almost gone when I saw my husband coming in, and I cried to him, 'Save me! Save me, darling!' He had a rope in his hand,

and, before I could understand it, he had slipped it over my neck and choked me. . . .

"The white man tried to sell me to a farmer, and then I told what I had heard them say. He believed me, and told them the mayor of Philadelphia had a reward out for them, for kidnappin' free people, already. Then they talked together—a little scared they was—and tied me again, and brought me on a cart through the woods to the river and fetched me here, and chained me, and told me if I ever said I was free, to another man, they meant to sell my baby and to drown me in the river."

"I never 'spected to come yer," Jimmy Phoebus observed, "but I've hearn tell of this place considabul. The big, barn-roofed house is Joe Johnson's Tavern for the entertainment of Georgey nigger-traders that comes to git his stolen goods. It's at the crossroads, three miles from Cannon's Ferry, whar the passengers from below crosses the Nanticoke fur Easton an' the north, an' the stages from Cambridge by the King's road meets 'em yonder at the tavern. The tavern stands in Dorchester County, with a tongue of Caroline reaching down in front of it, an' Delaware state hardly twenty yards from the porch. Thar ain't a courthouse within twenty miles, nor a town in ten, except Crotcher's Ferry, whar every Sunday mornin' the people goin' to church kin pick up a basketful of ears, eyes, noses, fingers, an' hair bit off a-fightin' on Saturday afternoon. They call the country around Crotcher's, Wire Neck, caze no neck is left thar that kin be twisted off; the country in lower Car'line they calls 'Puckem,' caze the crops is so puckered up. They say Joe's a great man among his neighbors, an' kin go to the Legislater. The t'other house out in the fields is Patty Cannon's own, whar she did all her dev'lishness fur twenty years, till Joe got rich enough to build his palace."

. . . the only face which arrested his attention was a woman's, standing in the door of the enclosed space at the end of the porch, at right angles to the central door of the tavern, and just besides it. The whole building was without paint, and weather-stained, but the room on the porch was manifestly newer, as if it had been an afterthought, and its two windows revealed some of the crude appendages of a liquor bar, as a fire somewhere within flashed up and lighted it.

By this fire the woman's face was also revealed, and she was so much interested in the fight that she turned all parts of her countenance into the firelight, slapping her hands together, laughing like a man, dropping her oaths at the right places, and crying:

"I'll bet my money on little Owen Daw! Cy James ain't no good, by God! Yer's whiskey a-plenty for Owen Daw if he gouges him. Give it to him, Owen Daw! Shame on ye, Cy James!"

There was occasional servility and deference to this woman from members of the crowd, however they were absorbed in the fight. She was what is called a "chunky" woman, short and thick, with a rosy skin, low but pleasing forehead, coal-black hair, a rolling way of swaying and moving herself, a pair of large black eyes, at once daring, furtive, and familiar, and a large neck and large breast, uniting the bull-dog and the dam, cruelty and full womanhood.

Behind this woman, whom Phoebus thought to be Patty Cannon herself, the moonlight from the rear came through the door in the older and main building, shining quite through the house . . .

"Jimmy," said Samson, "if it's ever known in Prencess Anne—as I 'spect it never will be, fur we're in bad hands, neighbor—dar'll be a laugh instid of a cry, fur old boxin' Samson, dat was kidnapped an' fetched to jail by a woman!"

"You licked by a woman, Samson?"

"Yes, Jimmy, a woman all by herself frowed me down, tied my hands an' feet, an' brought me to dis garret. I hain't seen nobody but her an' dese yer people, sence I was tuk."

"Hah!" exclaimed the dejected mulatto, "that's a favorite feat of Patty Cannon. She is the only woman ever seen at a threshing-floor who can stand in a half-bushel measure and lift five bushels of grain at once upon her shoulders, weighing three hundred pounds."

"I ain't half dat," Samson smiled, quietly, "an' she handled me, shore enough. You remember, Jimmy, when I leff you by ole Spring Hill Church, to go an' git a woman on a little wagon to show me de way to Laurel?"

"Why, it was only yisterday, Samson!"

"Dat was de woman, Jimmy. She was a chunky, heavy-sot woman, right purty to look at, an' maybe fifty year ole. She was de nicest woman mos' ever I see. She made me git off my mule an' ride in de wagon by her, an' take a drink of her own applejack—she said she 'stilled it on her farm. She said she knowed Judge Custis, an' asked me questions about Prencess Anne, an' wanted me to work fur her some way. We was goin' froo a pore, pine country, a heap wuss dan Hardship, what Marster Milburn come outen, an' hadn't seen nobody on de road till we come to a run she said was named de Tussocky Branch, whar she got out of de wagon to water her hoss. At dat place she come up to me an' says. 'Samson, I'll wrastle you!' 'Go long,' says I, 'I kin't wrastle no woman like you.' 'You got to,' she says, swearin' like a man, an' takin' holt of me jess like a man wrastles. I felt ashamed, an' didn't know what to do, an', befor' I could wink, Jimmy, dat woman had give me de trip an' shoved me wid a blow like de kick of an ox, and was a-top of my back wid a knee like iron pinnin' of me down."

"The awful huzzy of Pangymonum!"

"De fust idee I had was dat she was a man dressed up like a woman. I started like lightnin' to jump up, an' my legs caught each oder; she had carried the cord to tie me under her gown, an' clued it aroun' me in a minute. As I run at her an' fell hard, she drew de runnin' knot tight an' danced aroun' me like a fat witch, windin' me all up in de rope. De sweat started from my head; I yelled an' fought an' fell again, an', as I laid with my tongue out like a calf in de butcher's cart, she whispered to me, 'Maybe you're de las' nigger ole Patty Cannon'll ever tie!"

"Tindel, your torch!" Van Dorn exclaimed, and, after a moment's delay—the old house and shady yard meantime illuminated by lightning, and sounds of thunder rolling in the sky—a blazing pine-knot, all prepared, was pro- cured, and Van Dorn, holding it in his left hand, and with nothing but his rude whip in his right, bounded in the door shouting:

"Patty Cannon has come!"

At that dreaded name there were a few suppressed shrieks, and the great windows at the gable side fell inwards with a crash as the kidnappers came pouring over. Van Dorn's quick eye took in the situation as he waved his torch, and it lighted ceiling and pilaster, the close-fastened doors on the left and the great stairway- well beyond, filled with black forms in the attitude of defense.

"Patty Cannon has come!" he shouted again; "follow me!"

An instant only brought him to the base of the stair- case, and the lightning flashing in the gaping windows and fallen floor revealed him to his followers, with his yellow hair waving, and his long, silken mustache like golden flame.

A mighty yell rose from the emboldened gang as they

formed behind him, with bludgeons and iron knuckles, billies and slings, and whatever would disable but fail to kill.

Van Dorn, far ahead, made three murderous slashes of his whip across the human objects above, and, with a toss of that formidable weapon, clubbed it and darted on.

At the moment loud explosions and smoke and cries filled the echoing place, as a volley of firearms burst from the landing, sweeping the line of the windows and raking the hall. The band on the floor below stopped, and some were down, groaning and cursing.

"They're armed; it's treachery," a voice, in panic, cried, and the cowardly assailants ran to places of refuge, some crawling out at the portal, some dropping from the windows, and others getting behind the stairway, out of fire, and seeking desperately to draw the bolts of the smaller door there.

"Patty Cannon has come!" Van Dorn repeated, throwing himself into the body of the defenders, who, terrified at his bravery, began to retreat upward around the angles of the stairs.

One man, however, did not retreat, neither did he strike, but wrapped Van Dorn around the body in a pair of long and powerful arms, and lifted him from the landing by main strength, saying:

"High doings, friend! I'm concerned for thee."

Van Dorn felt at the grip that he was overcome. He tried to reach for his knife, but his arms were enclosed in the unknown stranger's, who, having seized him from behind, sought to push him through the square window on the landing into the grass yard below, where the rain was falling and the lightning making brilliant play among the herbs and ferns.

As the kidnapper prepared himself to fall, with all his joints and muscles relaxed, the boy, Owen Daw, lying bloodthirstily along the limb of the old tulip-tree, aimed his musket, according to Van Dorn's instructions, at the forms contending there, and greedily pulled the trigger.

The Quaker's arms, as they enclosed Van Dorn, presented, upon the cuff of his coat, a large steel or metal button, and the ball from the tree, striking this, glanced, and entered Van Dorn's throat.

McLane went to his portmanteau and unlocked it, and took out rolls of notes and a buckskin bag of gold.

The yellow lustre seemed to flash in Patty Cannon's rich black eyes, like the moon overhead upon a well.

"How beautiful it do shine, Cunnil!" she said. "Nothin' is like it fur a friend. Youth an' beauty has to go together to be strong, but, by God! gold kin go it alone."

As he made one step to penetrate the darkness with his dazzled eyes, Patty Cannon silently thrust against his heart a huge horse-pistol and pulled the trigger: a flash of fire from the sharp flint against the fresh powder in the pan lit up the hall an instant, and the heavy body of the guest fell backward before his chair, and over him leaned the woman a moment, still as death, with the heavy pistol clubbed, ready to strike if he should stir.

He did not move, but only bled at the large lips, ghastly and unprotesting, and the cold blue eyes looked as natural as life.

Patty Cannon took the chair and counted the money.

A table stood in the middle of the main room, on which was an old moldered chest with the earth clinging to it, and beside the chest were bones and shreds of clothing on the riven lid of the chest.

"You swear that the evidence you give shall be the truth, the whole truth, and nothing but the truth, so help you God!" exclaimed a small, chunky, Irish-looking person, presenting a book to be kissed by a scrawny, chinless, goose-necked lad . . .

"Yes, Mr. Clayton."

"Do you know the nature of an oath? What is it?"

"I'll be fried like a slapper on the devil's griddle ef I don't tell right," whined Cy James, zealously.

"No you won't; at least, not first. If you don't tell me the truth I'll have your two ears cut off on the pillory, and no slapper shall enter that hungry stomach of yours for a month. Goy!"

He looked at Cy James as if he had a mind to bite his nose off as a mere beginning.

"Now, Holliday Hicks, you and Billy Hooper and the other constables take away this box, which smells too loud here, as soon as the witness has sworn to it. When did you last see this box, James?"

"About ten year ago, sir, when I had been bound to Patty Cannon four year, I reckon, I see Patty an' Joe Johnson an' Ebenezer, his brother, all totin' this chist to the field an' a-buryin' of it."

"What did you see them put in that chest?"

" A dead man—a nigger-trader. I can't tell whether his name was Bell or Miller; she killed two men nigh that time, an' I was so little that I've got 'em mixed."

". . . She said he come to Joe's tavern with a borreyed hoss from East New Market, where he told the people he was buyin' niggers, an' would take fifteen thousand dollars wuth if he could git 'em. He was followed out, an' Ebenezer Johnson got in ahead of him. They told him the tavern was full, an' he would be better tuk care of at a good woman's little farm close by. They made him think, she said, that a gentleman with much money wasn't allus safe at the tavern. Aunt Patty got him supper. He sit at the table after it a-pickin' of his teeth. She got her pistol an' went out in her garden a-hoein' of her flowers. Once she come up on him at the window to shoot, but he turned quick, an' she says to him: 'Oh, sir, I only want to see if you didn't need somethin' more.' 'No, no,' says he; 'I've made a rale good supper.' 'I loves my flowers,' Aunt Patty says, 'an' likes to hoe 'em at sundown, so they can sleep nice an' soft.' 'Do you?' says he; 'I reckon you're a kind woman.' He turned around agin an' begin to look over his pocket-book. She hoed an' hoed, an' hummed a little tune. All at once she slipped up, an' I heerd her say, 'Boys, I give it to him good, right in the back of the head, an' he fell on to the table, an' the water he had been drinkin' was red as currant wine,'"

"James Moore, I'll swear you next," the magistrate said to the new tenant of the farm, and this man proceeded to testify concerning the finding of the chest as he was ploughing in a wet spot where he had removed some brush.

Cy James, being recalled, gave testimony as to other buried bodies, chiefly of children slaughtered in wantonness or jealousy, or to avoid pursuit.

The dawn had not broken when that fleet traveler, Joseph Johnson, anticipating his enemies by hours, noiselessly tied his horses at the tavern he had erected, and nearly fell into the arms of Owen Daw.

"Joe," said the scapegrace, "thar's queer people hangin' around yer. They say a blue chest has been dug outen the field yonder, an' bones in it. I 'spect they're a-lookin' fur you, Joe.

"Joe!" said a voice, and Patty Cannon threw her arms around him.

"To burning fire with you!" bellowed the filial son. "Take your arms away!"

"Let us make up, Joe! Everyone has run away from us. . ."

Joe Johnson's face became almost livid pale, and, rushing upon Patty Cannon with both hands raised, he struck her to the floor and put his boot upon her.

"If I had the time, I'd have your life," he hissed. "But it would lose the uptucker a job. Tonight I leave you forever. Margaretta, your daughter, wishes never to see you again. Take this crib and the blood you still must shed to keep your old heart warm, and take my curse to choke you on the gallows!"

The morning was well advanced, and the sun made the gaunt and steep old tavern rise like a mammoth from the level lands, and filled its upper front rooms with golden wine of light, as Patty Cannon sat in one of them by a window near the piazza, and talked to Van Dorn, whom she had tenderly washed and re-dressed, and placed him in her own comfortable rocking-chair of rushes, with his feet raised, as all unaffected Americans like, and blanketed, upon a second chair.

Her woes and his relief made Patty social, yet tender, and the instincts of her sex had returned, to be petted and beloved.

"Oh, Captain," she said, fondly, "how clean and sweet you look, like my good man again. Don't be cross to me, Van Dorn! My heart is sad."

"Chito, Patty! chito! Fie! you sad? I like to see you saucy and defiant. Let us not repent! So Joe has left you?"

"With cruel curses. My daughter hates me, he says, and means to be a lady where I can't disgrace her. Oh, honey! to raise a child and have it hate an' despise you goes hard, even if I have been bad. There's nothing left me now but you, Van Dorn; oh, do not die!"

He coughed carefully, as if coughing was a luxury to be very mildly exerted, and wiped a little blood from his tongue and lip.

"I'll try not to die till I comfort you some. The ball is at my windpipe, and, when the blood trickles in, it makes me cough, and I must beware of emotions, the surgeon says, lest it drop into my lung and break a blood-vessel by some very spasmodic cough. So do not be too beautiful or I might perish."

"Captain," called Patty, "I see men and boys all over the fields yonder, running and digging and dragging away the bresh. Is them ole burryin's of mine suspected?"

"Pshaw! darling, 'tis your warm imagination, and Joe's unkindness. I would make you happy with the memory of your daring acts. Que maravilla! In your little pets you stamped a life out, when another woman would only stamp her foot. There was that morning when your fire would not burn, and a little black child bawled with the cold and angered you; if its body is ever dug up where it was laid, the skull cracked with the billet of wood will tell the tale. You once suspected me of truantry from your charms—Quedo, quedo! exacting dame—and the pale offspring of poor Hagar you threw upon the blazing backlog, and grimly watched it burn. The pursued children whose cries you could not still, that yet are stilled till hell shall have a voice, not even you can number. Evangelists, O Patty, dipping their pens in blood of saints to write your crimes, could make the next age infidel, where you will seem impossible, and all of us mythology!"

"Be still!" the woman cried, rising and walking, in her rolling gait, to watch things without that stirred her mind more than her lover's recitation; "What good kin these tales do you, Captain? My God! The roads is full of people, and they are all looking yer. Is it at me, Van Dorn?"

He pointed his white finger at her in an ecstasy, with a mocking smile in his blue eyes, like fading stars at dawn, and then the rosy morning flowed all round his mouth, as the bullet, detached in his emotion, fell towards the lung, and wakening hemorrhage, and to the last of his strength he pointed at her, and then fell back, in crimson linen, smiling yet in death.

As they knelt, with closed eyes, the room slowly filled, and Patty Cannon's arms were seized by two constables, and the warrant read to her. She heard it with humility, making no answer but this:

"Once I had money an' friends a plenty; my money is gone, and so is my friends; there's no fight now in pore ole Patty Cannon."

As Patty Cannon came out of the tavern the cross-roads were full of people, taking their last look at the spot where she had triumphed for nearly twenty years.

The Maryland constable marched Patty Cannon down to the little bridge of planks where ran the ditch nearly on the State line, and tradition still believes the figment that Joe Johnson at that moment was hiding beneath it.

There, driven across the boundary like some border's cow, the queen of the kidnappers was seized by the Delaware constable, and placed in a small country gig-wagon, and, followed by a large mounted posse, the road was taken to the little hamlet of Seaford, five miles distant.

The evidence of Cy James and other cowardly companions in her sins was quickly given, and the procession started through the woods and sands to Georgetown, twelve miles to the eastward, where Patty Cannon was received by all the town, waiting up for her, and the jail immediately closed her in.

For a while Patty Canon, by her affability and sorrow, had easy times in jail, and was allowed to eat with the jailer's family; but, as the examination proceeded before the grand jury, and her menials hastened to throw their responsibility in so many crimes upon her alone, an

outer opinion demanded that she be treated more harsh-
ly, and some of the irons she had manacled upon her
captives were riveted upon her own ankles. Very soon
dropsy began to appear in her legs and feet, and, after it
became evident to her that neither money nor friends
were forthcoming in her defense, she fell into a passive
despair.

Fear was relative in her: she had neither the fear of
men nor of shame, and only death as it involved a
hereafter. Whether that hereafter was a latent conviction
in her mind, or the vivid admonition of guilt and dead
men's eyes peering over her dreams and into the silent,
lonely watches of haunted midnights, who shall tell?

So had this woman, conscious of her deserts, bullied
eternal justice through its long postponements, never
doubting, while ever vexing, the spirit of God, until the
number of her crimes crowded the tablet of her memory,
and out of the hideous gulf of her past life gazed faces
without names and deeds without memoranda; a procession the longer that strangers were in it, and, shrink-
ing from her, yet pressing on, exclaiming her name or
only shrieked "'Tis she!" as if her name was nothing to
her curse.

Sleeping in her chains, there were children's eyes
watching her from far-off corners, as if to say, "Give us
the whole life we would have lived but for you!"

As her swollen limbs festered to the irons, there were
babies' cries floating in the air, that seemed to draw near
her breasts, as if for food, and suddenly convulse there in
screams of pain, and move away with the sounds of suffocation she had heard as they expired.

All night there were callers on her, and whom they
were no one could tell; but the jailer's family saw her lips
moving and her eyes consult the air, as if she was faintly

trying bravado upon certain business-speaking ghosts who had come with bills long overdue and demanded payment, and went out only to come again and again.

Some of these mystic visitors she would jeer at and defy, and stamp her feet, as if they had no rights in equity against her soul, having been on vicious errands when they met their ends, and bankrupts in the court of pity; but suddenly a helpless something would appear, and paralyze her with its little wail, like a babeless mother or a motherless babe, and, with her forehead wet with sweat of agony, she would affect to chuckle, and would whisper, "Nothin' but niggers! nothin' more!"

Day brought her some relief, but also other cares, and of these the chief was the care of money. She had been a spendthrift all her life, and robbed mankind of life and liberty to enjoy the selfish dissipation of spending their blood-money; and what had she bought with it? Nothing, nothing. To spend it for such trifles as children want— candy and common ornaments, a dance and a treat, a gift for some boor or forester or even negro she was mislead- ing, or to establish a silly reputation for generosity: generous at the expense of human happiness, and of robbing people of liberty and life, merely for spending- money!

Now she had none to appease the all-devouring greeds of habit intensified by real necessity: no money to buy dainties or even liquor; no money to spend upon the jailer's family and keep the reputation of kindness alive; no money for decent apparel to appear in court; none to corrupt the law or to hire witnesses and attorneys.

The two demons she had created alternately seized the day and the night: the demon of money plagued her all day, the demon of murder pursued her all night.

Every morning she had insatiate wants; all night she had remorseless visitors; and, close before, the gallows filled the view, with the Devil tying the noose.

That Devil she plainly saw, so busy on the gallows, fitting his ropes and shrouds and long death-caps, and he evaded her, as if he had no commerce with her now.

He was a cool and wistful man, perfectly happy in the prospect of getting her, and not anxious about it, so sure was he of her soon and complete possession.

He was always out in the jail-yard when she looked there, fixing his ropes, sliding the nooses, examining the gallows, like a conscientious carpenter; and in his complacent smile was an awful terror that froze her dumb: he seemed so impersonal, so joyous, so industrious, as if he had waited for her like a long creditor, and compounded the interest on her sins till the infernal sum made him a millionaire in torments.

A Devil it was, real as a man—a slavemaster to whose quiet love of cruelty eternal death was not enough; a man whose unscarred age, old as the rising sun, still came and went in immortal youthfulness and satisfaction, but for the nonce forgetting other debtors in the grip he had on her, as his majestic expiation for his own shortcomings.

He looked like a storekeeper, a man of accounts, a cosmopolitan kidnapper, who knew a good article and had it now. She was so terrified that she wanted to cry to him, and see if he would not remit that business method and become more human, and sauce her back.

But no; the longer she watched, the less he looked towards her, though she knew his smile meant no one else. To hang upon his cord was very little; to go with him after it was stretched, down the burning grates of hell, and see him all so cool and busy in her misery, was the gnawing vulture at her heart.

In vain she tried to throw responsibility for her sins upon a vague, false parentage and fatherhood, and say that she was bred to robbery and vice; a something in her heart responded: "No, you had beauty and health and chaste lovers whom you rejected or tempted, and a mind that was ever clear and knew right from wrong. Conscience never gave you up, though drenched in innocent blood. The often-murdered monitor revived and cried aloud like the striking of a clock, but never was obeyed!"

Thus haunted, deserted, peeped in upon from the hereafter, racked with vain needs, her outlets closed to every escape or subterfuge, revenge itself dead, and disease assisting conscience to banish sleep, the wretched woman crawled to her window one day and saw the helpless effigy of her sex [a black woman on display in the jail's pillory] exposed there for doing an act of humanity; and instantly an instinct she immediately obeyed exacted from her one last familiar, heartless deed, to show the crowd that even she, Patty Cannon the murderess, had "no respect for a nigger."

That doctrine long survived her, though she found it old when she came among them.

She aimed an egg at the breast of her sex, and, with a barefaced grin, she saw it strike and burst. The next moment the crowd had recognized and defied her.

In the exasperation of their shout, and of being no longer praised even for insulting a negro, a convulsion of desperate rage overcame the murderess.

Too helpless to retort in any other way, yet in uncontrollable recklessness, she exclaimed, "They never shall see me hang, then!" and swallowed the arsenic she had concealed in her bosom.

That night she died in awful torments.

John A. Munroe once described *The Entailed Hat* as a "remarkable" book and called it "Delaware's expiation for the sins that accompanied slavery." Some might disagree with the latter statement, but few challenge its literary achievement.

I have recognized that Townsend had access to whatever records existed in his lifetime and also to people who actually knew Patty Cannon and her associates. As a scrupulous and

respected reporter who was fortified with an abundance of experience, we can be certain of his interest in truth and accuracy.
What we cannot know is where in *The Entailed Hat* its creator
crossed the line between fact and invention.

Johnson's Tavern as one artist portrayed it, circa 1880

At the Turn of the Century

Of all the reports and stories written about Patty Cannon, only one, as far as I can determine, boasts an author who actually saw her; he was Robert B. Hazzard of Seaford, Delaware.

Hazzard's memoir, apparently written sometime in the 1890's, first appeared in the Salisbury *Tribune*, later in the Baltimore *Sun*, and finally became a chapter in his book, *The History of Seaford*. Its accuracy was attested to by Mrs. Hageman, wife of the *Tribune's* editor, who had been born and spent her early youth in the immediate vicinity of Patty's homestead.

Hazzard's story, titled "Pat Cannon. Joe Johnson.," is presented here in its entirety:

The History of Seaford
Pat Cannon. Joe Johnson.

I am unwilling to close up my little history without reference to one of the most exciting tragedies, or rather many of them, which took place in that age. It did not occur in Seaford, but so near that I deem it pertinent to these reminiscences. Patty Hanley came to the neighborhood of the crossroads, now called Reliance, about the first of this century. She was said to be a handsome, fascinating woman, and also said to be a gypsy. She was found to be a very strong and masculine woman, could stand in a half bushel measure and shoulder as much grain as the strongest man around. In after years she could take hold of a negro man, however young and strong, trip and throw him up on his face, and tie him before he could recover himself. Such was said to be her plan in securing the many she bought and stole for the southern market. She found a fine young mechanic in that neighborhood or near it, a man of fair moral character and of good family, by the name of Jesse Cannon. She drew her cords of fascination, perhaps pure love, around him. They were married, had two children, and he died leaving her a widow which she remained to be, and carried the sobriquet of Pat Cannon the balance of her life, and became one of, if not the most cruel, profane, avaricious and notorious women of any age or place. Her name struck terror to the hearts of slaves and free people of color from the northern county of Delaware and its parallel county in Maryland to and through Northampton County, Virginia. She formed an alliance in the business of buying and stealing negroes with Joe Johnson, who married one of her daughters[1] and made his residence in the large two storied and attic house which then

---

[1] We know of only one daughter.

and for many years stood at Johnson's Crossroads, now Reliance, where the beautiful home of W. Matthew Smith now stands. She had for her home the small farm and house which is still standing and occupied as a home in the field nearly opposite the Gethsamanee M. P. Church on the north side of the county road.

George Townsend, an author of fiction, some years ago wrote a book of that class called *The Entailed Hat*, the basis of which was largely these two wretched persons. He made his story to start in an old furnace village near Snow Hill and Princess Ann in Somerset, and ply their nefarious traffic between the last named place and Johnson's Crossroads, and up beyond that as far as negroes could be enticed by their wiles or bought or stole. In those far away back times, there lived a man by the name of Twiford, who, it was said, married Betty, a sister of Patty Cannon, and owned the farm, now and for more than sixty years known as the Truitt farm, on the Dorchester side of the Nanticoke river, a mile or more above Sharptown. The author of *The Entailed Hat* made that home a stopping place for the Johnson crew, and Twiford an abettor in his trade. While *The Entailed Hat* was written in fiction, still it was a wonderful portrayal of facts, even to the very names of the persons who figure in it. I remember the persons and scenes he names in his book vividly, even the dilapidated vault and the exposed persons of Twiford and his wife as they lay in their coffins sixty years ago or about.

The facts that I give in this history are only such as I have retained in my memory or gathered from older persons than myself of that period. Johnson sailed a schooner from Cannon's Ferry to Baltimore and stole all the negro men he could hire and induce to go as stevedores in the hold of his vessel; and when he had gotten them there, would quickly put on the hatches, fasten them down, and sail for home and leave them in the care of Pat.

I was about five years old when she was arrested, yet I remember a fact distinctly that my mother gave me, as proof of the fact I have stated. One of the men who Johnson stole and brought off from Baltimore, was leg-ironed and put in the loft or stairs of Pat Cannon's house. The room was over her cook room and had a trap door instead of stairway. It was in February and a bright and pleasant day, she left the house and was out so long that he took the opportunity to get away. He lifted the door, let himself down, and fell upon the floor; got out and to Seaford, ironed as he was, without being overtaken and recaptured. The only probable reason we can think of for this was that he was gone some hours before she missed him. My own father took him to his home, broke off his fetters, healed his frost-bitten feet, and sent him to his home in the city. There was back from her house a pine growth mixed with sedge, and back of that a large body of oak and gum woods; it was said of her that she kept her purchased and stolen negroes chained in warm weather in that thicket. The author of *The Entailed Hat* describes the prison with its cells in the Johnson house, and it was a well authenticated fact that the prison in that attic was there long after the death of Pat and the absconding of Johnson.

I was conversing one day with Asbury Dean, who lived but a few miles below there, and he told me that he and others were there the day she was arrested. That, as it was said, when she bought or stole a woman who had a babe, if it annoyed her or gave any inconvenience, she would kill it. They procured spades, went into the garden where it was said she buried them, and began to dig diagonally across the squares and soon unearthed several child skeletons. Said he, we became so enraged, that if she had been there, we would have lynched her.

The murder for which she was arrested and committed to prison was committed about fourteen years before her arrest. She was believed to be a murderer long before her arrest, but she managed so well to cover her tracks, and other influences were at work to screen her, that she kept on in her desperate career until one of these things which corroborated the old saying, "murder will out," occurred. A man who often called upon her for food and lodgings and to purchase her negroes, called upon her one summer day to feed and dine. He unwisely showed her a bag of gold that raised the devil avarice in her. She, in a very pleasant mood apparently, set his dinner before an open window. When he took his seat at the table and began to eat, she sped to the window on the outside and shot him dead.

She had a negro man living with her for many years who was in such abject fear of her that he would divulge none of her terrible doings, and if he had, he was a chattel, and his testimony was not admissible before a court. Her plan for hiding that crime was, as she could not procure a coffin or box long enough for his body without being detected, to cut him in two and press the body thus severed into a large chest she had, and with this negro to assist her, buried him in her orchard. This negro was the Cy James character in *The Entailed Hat.* About fourteen years after she hired a man with a double team to plough that orchard field; the land was very wet and the horses in passing over that grave broke in, and that led to her arrest and commitment.

Her location gave her some advantage over the law or its officers in that she could slip in a few minutes over to Johnson's, who lived in Maryland. Suspicion had by this time become rife, and the excitement in the county all around intense. She knew this, and on the morning of her arrest went over the state line to the home of Johnson. At that time Joseph Neal was the sheriff's deputy in Sussex, and Jacob Wilson the deputy in Dorchester. As the crime for which they wanted her was committed in Delaware, these two men planned that Wilson should engage her in a walk and conversation, and Neal should take her as soon as she stepped over the line. The ruse was successful. Wilson was a young, single and fine looking man, and so absorbed her thought that before she was aware of it she was in the clutches of the law and the hands of the Delaware officer. She was taken to Seaford, committed by Dr. John Gibbon, then justice of the peace, taken to Georgetown and imprisoned for trial. Her case was hopeless and she procured poison and put an end to her own life, and thus closed one of the most daring, cruel, bloodthirsty and vicious lives that ever characterized any person living in a civil and Christian land. I saw that woman that day on her way to the prison. I was very small, I suppose five or six years old. I was at school, and the large party who accompanied her to the justice I remember well as we were on the playground when they passed.

Johnson sped himself away after her arrest and went to New Orleans, and was seen there by Jacob Wright when he took his cargo of negroes down there in 1836 or '37. Major Allen told me a short time before his death that Johnson gave Wright a fine gold watch. He supposed it was intended as a bribe to keep him mum.

Now my readers will naturally inquire how such terrible crimes could be committed in any civil and Christian country for so long a period without detection. We will give you some facts which may at least partially answer that question. First, the lower part of Sussex was almost wholly pro-slavery in both sentiment and practice. It had Maryland on the south and west of it, a slave state; nearly all the farmers who owned land were slave holders, many of them, a large number. The interest between the buyer and seller and owner was so dovetailed, that many who knew facts about this nefarious traffic kept mum. Secondly, the pro-slavery sentiment was so much larger than the anti-slavery sentiment, that many who were not really in sentiment pro-slavery, kept mum because they had not the courage of their convictions. Another reason was that the neighborhood of Johnson's Crossroads was then sparsely settled. In all that opening where now there is more than a dozen good homes, there was then not more than four or five immediately around; the place seemed to be a God-forsaken country, and you felt, or I did years after as I passed through or by it, a painful sense of that fact. Now, as all my readers may know, it is a pretty little thriving village, occupied, both in the village and country around, with a class of citizens who will compare favorably with any surrounding communities.

While Hazzard wrote his account from memory and more than sixty years after Patty Cannon died, he was closely acquainted with the vicinity of Reliance and personally connected to individuals who knew Patty and Joe. His only interest appears to have been a presentation of the truth to the best of his ability.

Tales of Old Maryland

Obviously borrowing from *The Entailed Hat,* J. H. K. Shannahan, Jr. also utilized court documents and conversations with Delmarva residents in writing a story which was published in the Baltimore *Sun* on March 31, 1907, and in a small book, *Tales of Old Maryland,* copyrighted the same year.

As far as I can determine, Shannahan is the first writer to conduct a search of court records in Georgetown and publish the chronicles of the trial and whipping of Joe Johnson, which were included in the second chapter, "The Sparse Paper Trail."

Most of Shannahan's story of Patty Cannon is a repetition of details you have already read, but he adds one anecdote I would like to share with you:

I have been told that some years ago a young attorney

of Baltimore was visiting near the old tavern and was dared to spend a night in it. The forfeit being posted, the young man went to the house, made himself a bed on the floor and went to sleep. He was awakened towards midnight by the sound of a chain dragging across the floor. Having an easy conscience, he struck a light and instituted a search which revealed the presence of a dog which had broken loose from his kennel and had wandered into the house, dragging his chain after him. Being wide awake, the young man determined to find the mysterious chamber, the location of which so long defied detection, finally locating its entrance from a closet with a false door.

Meantime, several belated travelers, seeing lights in the old house, fled to Seaford, swearing that Patty Cannon had come back.

Patty Cannon
Administers Justice

At least a few residents of Delmarva seem to have been outraged with the villainous characterization of Patty in *The Entailed Hat* and perhaps also by Townsend's general portrayal of the temperament of the community. Some believe that R. W. Messenger, by representing her as repentant in his novel, *Patty Cannon Administers Justice*, was endeavoring to compensate for that.

While Messenger has captured some of the mystique of the times, critics suggest that his book is historically very inaccurate and rather unprofessionally crafted. It is indeed burdensome to read. At one point Messenger joins his censors and refers to the effort as "a story without much real merit."

Messenger was clearly an idealist and concludes his drama with this emotional plea: "God give us men! God give us women! God give us true patriotism, world patriotism as well as merely national, and God give us law reverence, national and international, and a proper abhorrence of law breaking with all the degradation it leads to!" He was a bit impassioned to say the least.

While the novel portrays a fictional Patty who finally "administers justice" to Joe Johnson in the form of a rifle ball to the head, it contains some exciting scenes. But of more interest to us here, it offers footnotes in which Messenger provides what appear to be intended as factual comments. Although some of his information conflicts with documentation you have read or which will be introduced later, these notes are interesting and worthy of examination. In places Messenger's wordy sentences and often spare punctuation present a text which is difficult to read. I have injected a few commas at points to relieve some of the confusion.

[Joe Johnson was] a man guilty of every crime in the calendar. Lacking [Patty Cannon's] generalship, he was nevertheless a "hand to execute" anything which she could plan and could dominate the men under him and change plans to meet changed or unforeseen conditions better than any mere lieutenant. In fact, legend shows plainly that he resented Patty Cannon's leadership and aspired to full leadership himself, but he had enough judgment to realize that her wonderful ability to keep in favor with those charged with law-enforcement, plus her ability to control a few loyal ruffians, plan their law-breaking for them and arrange the division of the plunder, made her an extremely valuable ally. He was probably a little over 35 years old at this time, big and strong, possessing a great reputation as a fighter and a still greater one as a bully; was pointed to on all sides as the undoubted leader of a gang of kidnappers of both free blacks and slaves but had never been convicted in the courts.[1] He had been developed by Patty Cannon in his career of crime and married to her daughter, who disappeared altogether not very long after the marriage, probably, though not certainly, dying a natural death. Legend is not clear on that subject though it does say that her first husband was hanged for murder. Joe Johnson is a very real character and many seemingly authentic sayings and doings of his have been handed down from father to son for one hundred years. To the "pack" he was a hero in his day, because for years he defied the law and "got away with it." In the end he paid the penalty of his crimes, though not in the manner described in this story. And as the scales fell from the eyes of the "pack" he was visualized properly as a dirty miscreant, a scoundrel of the deepest dye, a compound of villainy.

Certainly 45 years old if not more at this time, Patty Cannon must have appeared much younger than that. She had been engaged in a career more or less criminal ever since soon after her marriage more than 25 years earlier, yet through sheer force of personality had escaped paying any penalty for her many crimes. A remarkably handsome woman whose charms only seemed to develop with age, she was noted not only for her bold, brunette type of beauty, but also for her physical development, which, while womanly in every line and curve, made her possessed of a strength and a trained ability to use that strength to the best advantage, which was positively uncanny. She was probably never bested in "side hold" wrestling, (as soon as any part of either participant's body except feet, hands or knees touched the ground, a halt and fresh hold required) her very favorite trick was to throw down and, with the aid of a rope concealed under

---

[1] Joe Johnson was convicted of kidnapping in 1822.

her skirts until needed, tie up the strongest man. She was reputed to have kidnapped black men herself this way. Many feats of strength were assiduously cultivated by her and from a modern athlete's view point she kept "in condition" all of the time, being very temperate in her own use of liquor of all kinds, though encouraging over-indulgence among her gangsters. Her greatest offense against society was the harboring and developing of these gangsters and the planning for them of their kidnapping raids. Her own daughter's first husband was aided in his downward path by her and was hanged for murder almost before his honeymoon was over. Before the daughter's death her mother's influence over her second husband, Joe Johnson, was greater than the wife's, and after her death the mother's influence became unquestioned until he developed in villainy to the point where he became a greater one than she had ever been. On the other hand, she possessed a dual character, or, more properly speaking, a many-sided character, which enabled her to entertain as landlady in splendid style, and she was often in George-town, Denton and Cambridge—(the county seats of the three counties which cornered right in front of the hotel which Johnson built from his gains in his first illegal operations)—in high favor with many of the men form-ing the "political element" in these counties. She was a favorite with part of the legal fraternity in these counties, and to as great an extent as possible kept "in right" with the right people. She was like many others who are en-gaged now in somewhat questionable practices, which will be looked back at 50 years hence as we look back at kidnapping blacks now. A most remarkable woman and probably no piece of fiction will ever do her justice.

The following paragraph (in part) describing Johnson's Tavern is contained in the novel:

. . . up six steps to a wide porch, across the floor of the same and through a door easily entered by the stretcher, which meant a wide door. After making fourteen steps straight ahead, a full one hundred and eighty degrees turn was made to the left, then up a stairway seventeen steps, straight ahead four steps, a square turn to the left again through a narrow door . . . .

and is followed by this footnote:

This building is still standing but it was cut down in size and entirely remodeled in the author's youth, with the result that all of its distinctive features have disappeared. Before being remodeled its arrangement was, as near as the writer can recollect, exactly as described . . . . One very peculiar feature of the old building not mentioned in these pages was a large double chimney, which, built on the outside of the house according to the custom of that time, was really two chimneys more than six feet apart at the ground, each one of which furnished a large open fireplace in each of two rooms. About ten feet from the ground these chimneys were gradually drawn together and, by means of a very creditable piece of brick-laying work, were finally united over the Gothic arch thus formed in making one large chimney with two flues. The stairway from the lower to the second floor was located exactly as described, though it has since been entirely changed. The second floor hallway and rooms are also truly described as they were at that time. They are very different now.

Joe Johnson's horse, Yaller Corn, was about as much of a celebrity as the rider was. Raced all over the peninsula by his master and almost always winning, the animal well-deserved its reputation. One of the most authentic legends of the day, however, has it that in a semi-public race at Bucktown [Maryland] the judges decided Yaller Corn had lost by a nose, but the decision was reversed by Joe Johnson himself in one of the greatest exhibitions of bravado and bullying tactics which that celebrity ever used to intimidate a spineless gathering.

From the novel, speaking of the location of Johnson's Tavern:

... the hotel stood in one corner of Dorchester County in an acute angle of an irregular cross roads and exactly fronting the State line between Maryland and Delaware, while a still more acute angle of Caroline County cornered almost exactly in front of the hotel, the line between Dorchester and Caroline Counties of Maryland being formed by the Federalsburg road which ran in a northwesterly direction from Johnson's Cross Roads, while the Delaware State Line ran a trifle west of north.

Across the line in Delaware, well back from the road leading towards Seaford but only a few hundred feet from the hotel, was Patty Cannon's own home. Hayward had heard that whenever officers of any one of the three counties, two in Maryland and one in Delaware, ever attempted to make an arrest of any of the Johnson-Cannon gang they were always in some other county and generally in another state. The various county seats were all more that twenty miles away, and Cambridge, the county seat of Dorchester, in which county the hotel was really located, was more than twenty-five miles away.

with the following footnote:

This describes the exact location of the building, but the reader may not readily grasp the rather complicated situation of the lines cornering as they do without the aid of a good map showing what a strategic location the hotel proper had. A visit to the spot will give any one a ready understanding of the subject. The hotel building looks entirely different from what it did, but the splendid big maple trees are the ones which were there one hundred years ago and part of the house itself is still the same. The remains of Patty Cannon's old home on the Delaware side of the line were partly utilized for an out building when a new home was built on the property and may still be seen between the home and the barn. There is a store on the same location of the original store mentioned in this story, but there is now a parsonage directly across the road in front of the hotel and a beautiful little church in the edge of what remains of the fine grove of oaks.

Footnotes continue to describe the tavern:

. . . there was a false trapdoor in one of the first floor closets leading to a very small cellar,[2] which has not been mentioned and which might conceivably have been used for some of the most blood curdling of crimes.

. . . it stands to reason that the secret of the dungeon in the attic was known to many outside of the immediate followers of the kidnappers. This secret should have been disclosed years before it finally came out if those who knew it had done their full duty before the law and for humanity's sake. An extreme "rottenness" existed to a greater or less degree over the whole section surrounding Johnson's Cross Roads, otherwise such an abhorrent condition as actually obtained in the nest of villainy itself positively could not have been reached. . . .

---

[2] The argument over the existence of a cellar has been raised repeatedly over the years. There is no cellar in evidence today, and writers have quoted A. Hill Smith, resident from the 1890's to the 1960's, as denying the existence of one. But one Reliance old-timer has told me that Smith once mentioned a small cellar which had been "closed off."

The following description of the secret method of entrance to the attic and of the dungeon existing in that attic, which was so well built and so carefully built that several experienced carpenters and iron workers must have assisted in its construction and shared in the secret of such construction for many years, is just as true as the recollection of forty years ago can bring it back to the writer. Just before the house was remodeled he visited it as a boy, and as what he saw made a lasting impression on him it would be correct almost to the nail. Joe Johnson and Patty Cannon had been only a memory for sixty years at that time, but the evidence of their kidnapping activities was then almost as plain as it ever had been. The door of the dungeon is still being preserved at Reliance.[3]

From the novel:

Steps such as are used in the companionways of most sailing vessels, but very much steeper and taller, led from the floor of one section of the double-closet to the attic floor above. The closet door opened flush against these steps. . . . there was no ceiling to the closet and a few steps upward would put [one] on the attic floor.

Two small square attic windows lighted the [nearest] end of the attic. . . . There seemed to be no light at all in the other end and none at all except what came from [those] two windows.

The other end of the attic was done off solidly with heavy oak planking. . . . Two-inch planks were laid on the floor, more two-inch oak was nailed to the under side of the rafters to form a ceiling for the dungeon, and at the point where the rafters came within a little less than three feet of the floor, double planking of one and a half inch oak was laid, giving a total thickness of three in-

---

[3] I have been unable to locate anyone who has knowledge of the door.

ches, reaching from the rafters to the floor. The back and front ends of the dungeon were similarly planked with hard white oak seasoned until an auger would have had difficulty in penetrating it.

Exactly in the center of the front end was a door which . . . was made of five thicknesses of white oak, made up over each other diagonally, with a good-sized window in it strongly grated with iron bars. . . . On very short notice the companion ladder could be pulled up and the false top dragged into place by one man.

To give you a little more of the flavor of Messenger's prose, here is the scene near the end of the book where Joe Johnson is killed. Keep in mind that the event as described is entirely fictitious:

The attention of all three of them had been drawn to the other schooner and the shouted warning came because Joe Johnson himself, partly recovered from the effects of the heavy blow, reeling, dimly seeing the chance offered him to regain possession of the Pretty Polly, with the courage of a man driven to his last extremity and the venom of the scoundrel that he was, had suddenly emerged from the companionway, steadied himself with his left hand on the edge of the house and drew from a hiding place on his person a pistol, which he leveled and pulled the trigger of, almost in one motion.

Hayward whirled at the warning and started to raise his gun, but of the three Virgie had been the quickest. With an exercise of instinct rather than any reasoning power, she had sprung between Hayward and the leveled pistol just as the trigger was pulled and at a distance of only a few feet the heavy pistol ball went clear through the girl's body a little above her left breast, then penetrated Hayward's clothing and after drawing blood from him also glanced from one of his ribs and fell to the vessel's deck.

The shock turned him partly around. Before he could recover himself and lift his gun to his shoulder there came the crack of a rifle from Windward's quarter. Shrieking out one last curse Joe Johnson threw up his arms and fell backwards, a bullet squarely through his brain, while Patty Cannon dropped the butt of the rifle which had fired the shot to the schooner's deck with the words. "I was the right one to do that job, and now it's done and done properly. That's my idee o' jestice."

Messenger's 1926 edition, which numbered less than a thousand copies, was reprinted by Tidewater Publishers in 1960.

A Century Later

While I am not aware that any specific attention was paid to the centennial of Patty's death, there were a number of interesting accounts and opinions rendered on the lady's life and legend around that time. One article I have seen, which does not carry the banner line of the newspaper it was clipped from, was written by Charles. M. Hackett:

Patty Cannon Legend
Grows More Fantastic As Time Flies

The exploits and infamies of the notorious Patty Cannon, whispered up and down these counties for nearly a century, grow more fantastic as time takes its flight. She has become a dim, legendary figure in folklore of the Peninsula, a sort of human were-wolf whose name has been a constant rattan to frighten small boys the State over. Like all tales transmitted through generations by word of mouth, the legend takes on stature with each successive raconteur; what it loses in historical accuracy it makes up for in vivid representation and enlargement of detail. Perhaps in another century a real saga will have developed, comparable to Neiberlung [sic][1] and the Cid[2], with the villainous Mrs. Cannon either as a black-hearted wretch or a haloed heroine.

Some day a gifted bard will collect all the tales and weave a glorious epic of early tidewater; indeed, Patty has not been shunned by the literary in search of inspiration. George Alfred Townsend's *The Entailed Hat* is built upon the theme and the same material, handled quite freely, has been moulded [sic] into a blood and thunder romance called *Joe Johnson's Last Stand*.[3] Both, while drawing on the legend for their story, are really concerned more with literary presentation than with historical fact, and rightly, for the true saga should not be weighed down with authenticity.

Without specifically crediting the 1841 *Narrative and Confessions*, Hackett borrows freely from it, with one notable deviation. This is how he describes Patty's initial venture into kidnapping:

Then Patty conceived the idea of hi-jacking slaves. A

---

[1] I believe Hackett must be referring to the Nibelungenlied, a circa 1200 German Epic in which Siegfried captured a treasure possessed by a race of dwarfs called Nibelungs. It was also the subject of a libretto, "Der Ring des Nibelungen," written by Wilhelm Richard Wagner 1863.
[2] Rodrigo Diaz de Bivar, circa 1040-1099, known as El Cid (The Lord), was a Spanish military captain and hero of the wars against the Moors.
[3] I can find no book by this title. Perhaps Hackett was referring to Messenger's *Patty Cannon Administers Justice* which has the subtitle *Joe Johnson's Last Kidnapping Exploit.*

gentleman named Tavannes arrived one evening with four Negroes and a villainous one-eyed sailor, called Stump, as assistant. The widow decided to put her plan into execution. She dallied with the kidnapper throughout the evening, plied him with drink, then calmly cut his throat. His lieutenant, seeking escape, was speedily cut down by the brigands under her wing. She then dispatched Joe Johnson to Baltimore with the Negroes, where he negotiated their sale. Richer by the price of the slaves, plus the contents of the two ill-starred adventurers' pocketbooks, she was delighted with the successful execution of the venture. It was repeated with equally satisfactory results for several years, and so potent was her spell that she never wanted for customers. Officers of the law who called upon her were completely disarmed by her grace and beauty, and she plied her trade in perfect safety. The fact that her victims were outlaws provided their associates with no recourse, and she was able to continue her murderous career at will.

After lamenting the fact that William Randolph Hearst was not living at the time to exploit Patty's fame, Hackett closes with this observation:

Whether she will eventually pass into legend as a feminine Robin Hood or as the black-hearted cutthroat she was, is uncertain—such being the vagaries of the phenomenon of folklore. Certainly she was one of the most colorful figures to ever grace or disgrace this peninsula. But as a heroine, she deserves no more adulation than do the gangsters of the present day, for she struck in the dark and her victims never had a chance. It is unfortunate that her undeniable abilities could not have been directed into useful channels, for she was undoubtedly an extraordinarily capable person. Born into the present age, where women are upon an equal footing, her capabilities would doubtlessly have been placed into proper fields; at worst she would be a silken wolf of Wall Street.

The Laskowski Papers

F. Arthur Laskowski was a native of New York who moved to Cambridge, Maryland, and there served as manager of the Department of Employment Security. Fascinated with tales of Old Dorchester, he began in the 1930's to explore and write about its history, and the results have come to be known as *The Laskowski Papers*. Only five copies were produced on a typewriter, and each was bound in two volumes by Cornell Maritime Press. One of these transcripts can be viewed in the Maryland Room at the Dorchester County Library in Cambridge.

Laskowski's anecdotes about Patty Cannon and her times were derived from conversations he had with area residents, but the author indicates that he could not recall specific sources. His account is the product of telling and retelling the stories over several generations, and some commonly known information is reported incorrectly.

This is what Laskowski wrote about Patty Cannon:

About 1802 there came to this neighborhood a young woman, Patty Hanley, who would reveal neither her place of birth nor whence she came. In a short time she married a mechanic, Jesse Cannon, and lived in a small house in a field just across the Maryland border. This humble dwelling of the infamous Patty has since been removed from its original site, converted into a barn and is now in an extreme state of dilapidation.

Besides murdering and robbing travelers, another purpose of the partnership was the stealing and selling of Negroes.

It is said that on one occasion her artistic temperament was ruffled by the crying of a little Negro child, so she threw it into the fire.

When buyers were found for the slaves, they were removed from the attic of the tavern in which they were
kept prisoners, to the river three miles distant. If wind
and tide were favorable, they were taken to Truitt's[4]
Wharf down the Nanticoke and placed on board a sailing
vessel. Were conditions not favorable, they were often
kept in a little house on Lucas Island until ready for
shipment. Another shipping point was Crotcher's Ferry
at Brookview[5].

Patty and her son-in-law continued their unholy
alliance for twenty years when she was arrested and died
in the jail at Georgetown, Delaware before her trial. Joe
Johnson disappeared, going, it is said, to Texas.

It is told that when the law officers of one state appeared she went to that side of the house lying in the other
state. Though this conception is undoubtedly romantic,
she could not have done so as her house was in Delaware.
It might have been that, leaving the house, she crossed the
line into another state.

While in this vicinity, should the visitor be interested,
it is worth one's while to cross the Delaware line at this
point, proceed a distance of perhaps one hundred feet
where the church stands and turn to the right. By driving
down this road for three miles one reaches Woodlawn
[sic], or what was formerly Cannon's Ferry. Here, the
quaint little ferry is still in existence and the cheerful
ferry man will not only gladly convey you unto the other
shore, but will give all the information he knows on the
subject of Patty Cannon.

It seems that in this neighborhood the humblest hew-
er of wood and carrier of water is acquainted with *The
Entailed Hat* and undoubtedly as traffic becomes heavier,
some enterprising gentleman will build a hot-dog stand
in the shape of the entailed hat and call it by this name.

---

[4] At that time the wharf was named Twiford's.
[5] Crotcher's Ferry became Brookview circa 1900.

At Cannon's Ferry is Cannon's Hall, the large dwelling in which lived Isaac and Jacob Cannon, brothers of Jesse.[6] These enterprising gentlemen were large landowners, and woe betide the unfortunate tenant who failed to pay his rent, as the Cannon brothers would sell him out lock, stock and barrel or take all his earthly possessions.

In the kitchen was an enormous fireplace with a large brick platform. In front of this a man was murdered and a short time ago the blood stains could be easily distinguished.

In the little church yard at the ferry are the graves of Isaac and Jacob. Isaac Cannon died May 6, 1843, aged 73 years. Jacob Cannon, born September 6, 1786[7], died April 10, 1843. Here is also buried Elizabeth, wife of Jacob Cannon.

Leaving Cannon's Ferry, if the traveler drives along the road for a little more than two miles, he comes to Lucas Island, and should he desire the pleasure, he may stay all night in the little house in which many an unfortunate person lost his life. Further down the river is Truitt's Wharf where many stolen slaves were shipped to the cotton plantations of the South.

Although Joe Johnson's Tavern still stands with but little exterior change, the interior has been so remodeled and modernized that Patty would not now recognize it. The southeast corner of the building was the barroom and extended out where the south end of the porch now stands. Though it has been told in story that there was a cellar, none ever existed. The attic, however, was used as a prison for the captured Negroes until they were ready to sell. Mr. A. Hill Smith, the present owner, now regrets that his father who owned the property before him, had not left

[6] Jesse was not a brother to Isaac and Jacob. Relationships will be discussed later in the chapter "Cannon's Ferry and the Cannon Family."
[7] Jacob's vault epitaph says he was born on September 10, 1780.

the attic as it was in Patty's day as a feature of historical interest.

The building, a two-story structure, painted a shade of yellow, is on the border line of Dorchester and Caroline counties. Above the second story is the famous attic. The original framework and studding are still in the old house but it is a matter of regret that the building is not in its original state.

However, the atmosphere of Patty Cannon still pervades and busses of school children from as far as New Jersey come to visit the place.

One woman visitor insisted that the river came up near the tavern and was quite indignant when told that it had never been nearer than three miles.

So even though the old tavern is modernized, and though hard, smooth concrete roads pass its door, one can still visualize the line of chained slaves moving through the darkness to the Nanticoke, or see in the mind's eye the blurred figures of Patty and Joe Johnson in the blackness of midnight, burying some unfortunate victim in the field on which we stand.

At the north end of the brick wall of the Christ Church Cemetery on High Street, Cambridge, opposite the court house is a little frame structure that is now the office of Thomas Simmons, attorney at law.[8] Lawyers, like doctors and ministers of God, hear stories that if woven into fiction would hold the reader spellbound. Years previous to Mr. Simmon's tenancy, this little building was the law office of Honorable Josiah Bayly, one of the most clever attorneys in Maryland. He was born in Somerset County, Maryland October 31, 1769 and died in Cambridge August 15, 1846, where he is buried in Christ Church Cemetery. In 1790, he moved to Cambridge and being in quest of a

---

[8] In 1997 Bayly's office is occupied by Jo Ann Shepard, (J. D.) and Vernon Phillips III, (CPA).

situation, entered the home of Congressman Scott as private tutor to the congressman's daughters. In consideration of the education of these girls, Scott promised Mr. Bayly that he should have his board, the use of his law books and succeed him in his practice. The Scott girls were very tractable and pliant and submissive to scholarly discipline, yet they would not eat at the table with Mr. Bayly as they looked upon him as a hireling for wages.

Mr. Bayly practiced law in Cambridge, becoming a leading member of the bar and was later distinguished as the first Attorney General of Maryland.

It is said that on one occasion Mr. Bayly was defending a client accused of horse stealing. He requested permission of the court to speak privately to his client in the hall. Here, Mr. Bayly told him that he was guilty and there was no way for him to escape sentence and advised him to leave the premises as quickly as possible. A short time later Mr. Bayly reappeared before the bench signifying his readiness to proceed with the case. When the court asked where his client was, Mr. Bayly looked around exclaiming, "Why, he was at my side but a second ago."

Whether this story be true or not, this sort of practice undoubtedly qualified him for the kind of advice required by the infamous Patty Cannon.

Honorable Josiah Bayly was Patty's legal advisor and undoubtedly there existed between them a splendid spirit of cooperation.

The architectural history of Dorchester County, *Between the Nanticoke and the Choptank*, which was edited by Christopher Weeks, informs us that Josiah Bayly acquired the property at 211 High Street from Christ Church in 1796 and indicates that the structure was erected in that year. It is reputed to be the earliest surviving office building in Cambridge. The book, which was copyrighted in 1984, claims that the property has remained in the possession of Bayly descendants except for a few years at the beginning of the Twentieth Century.

Does it make sense that Patty, a resident of Delaware until her final three years, would seek the services of a Maryland attorney, especially one whose office lay more than thirty miles distant over bad roads and at least one ferry? Jerry Shields thinks it may.

"After his whipping in 1822," Shields argued his case, "Joe Johnson and Patty were pretty much persona non grata. And in 1826 when Johnson left for the Deep South, he sold Patty the tavern and she moved across the line into Dorchester County." A deed exists to verify this transaction.

Edward Nabb, Sr. is one of several attorneys I asked about Patty's alleged connection to Bayly:

"The only whispering I ever heard," Nabb told me, "was that old Josiah was one of her admirers—secret admirer—and probably her advisor. I've never seen any documentation, but in a small community people always have an ear for such things."

"I imagine," I said, "if there were any records showing that Bayly had represented Patty, someone would have found them by now."

"Don't have that attitude," Nabb admonished me. "I think you'll find something at the court house."

After visiting Josiah Bayly's grave in the Christ Church cemetery—his gravestone standing among those of other family members only a few yards from his former office—I searched the courthouse indexes and found nothing to confirm a Bayly-Cannon relationship.

Clearly documented among Bayly's clients, however, is the glamorous Betsy Patterson of Baltimore, who became Mme. Jerome Bonaparte, sister-in-law of Napoleon Bonaparte. Bayly represented Betsy in her divorce case against Napoleon's brother.

Laskowski also mentions Whitehall, an estate just outside Cambridge, which, along with numerous other old homes on Delmarva, has the reputation of having once been utilized as a temporary warehouse for Patty Cannon's captives.

The lovely white mansion, built around 1750 for one of the Ennalls children, sits on part of the land originally granted to Colonel Thomas Ennalls. Tradition claims that a tunnel led from the basement to the creek at the rear of the house. Until recent times old iron bars covered the cellar windows.

The Queen of Kidnappers

An account by Anthony Higgins in the Baltimore Sun on November 9, 1930, began with this paragraph:

> Patty Cannon was, more directly, the Queen of Kidnappers. Her reign was the Dark Ages of the Eastern Shore, where her memory lingers, garish and bloody, from the mouth of the Susquehanna to the cypress swamps of the Pocomoke. After a hundred years she is still a nightmare to the back-country Negroes of Delaware and Eastern Maryland.

Higgins borrows his information primarily from The *Narrative and Confessions* and *The Entailed Hat* but weaves a spellbinding presentation of Patty's story. What is different about this essay is the author's introduction of evidence from a rare and little-heralded contemporary publication. Back to Higgins:

> These [victims] she sold to slave dealers from the Gulf country. Cash money passed from the pockets of the dealers to the stockings of Mrs. Cannon. Corn whisky gurgled down to clinch the bargain, and off went the Negroes, whimpering or sullen, consigned to a far-away limbo of sweat. Down the Nanticoke they sailed to Chesapeake Bay and the concentration points of Norfolk and Washington: or the slavers coasted straight to Mobile or New Orleans.
>
> Kidnapped Negroes generally remained so, but there

were some exceptions. In a work called 'The American Slave Trade,[9]' one Jesse Torrey described how he rescued a trio of enslaved freemen, kidnapped in Delaware, whom he found in the City of Washington. They had languished in the tavern dungeon until a slave dealer arrived and bought them from Patty Cannon, and took them across the Bay to Annapolis, herding them from there to the capital.

One of them, a man, had been pounced upon while hunting possums in the woods. The other two were a mother and her baby. The pair had been in bed when three members of the Cannon-Johnson gang broke into her cabin. One man held her down while another pulled a noose around her neck to keep her from screaming. The third assailant blindfolded her and she was done for. Her only comforts were that the baby went with her and she had been able to bite off a piece of her blindfolder's cheek during the fray.

Deeply moved, Torrey set to work. He first got an injunction restraining the removal of Negroes from the District. Then he went to Delaware and obtained proof of their free status, whereupon the captives were freed.

Why Moses Sherman
Did Not Return to Chaptank [sic] River

Bearing a Claiborne, Maryland, dateline, a crumbling, yellowed newspaper clipping outlines the fanciful account of a kidnapping by "Paddy" Cannon. The article was copyrighted in 1931 by Robert H. Davis who is identified in it as a "famous news-

---

[9] *American Slave Trade; or, An Account of the manner in which the slave dealers take free people from some of the United States of America, and carry them away, and sell them as slaves in other of the States; and of the horrible cruelties practiced in the carrying on of this most infamous traffic: with reflections on the project for forming a colony of American Blacks in Africa, and certain documents respecting that project.* Jesse Torrey (1787-1834). Published by J. M. Cobbett, London, 1822.

paperman and author" and a writer for the *Evening News*. Mr. Davis does not seem to have been familiar with Patty Cannon when he was told the tale, and Patty's activities are incorrectly placed in an 1840-1860 time frame. We can only guess how many such wonderful yarns have been lost to time for the lack of a recorder.

Along one of the many indescribably beautiful back roads that intersect the county of Dorchester I came across an ancient black man whose tongue was tipped with legendary lore and fragments of forgotten history. Among other things, he told me about "Paddy" Cannon, an Amazonian white woman who ranged in 1840-50 and '60 along the borders of Maryland and Delaware, where she kidnapped slaves and sold them at a fancy price to the Georgian and Alabama planters.

"Ya-s-s-sir," said he, "dat woman in her stockin's, which she ain't never had on, was mo' dan six feet high and specify dat she could hog tie any color'd man what walk de earth. Dat what she says, and dat what she do. Ya-s-s-sir. Is you ev'r hyerd 'bout Paddy Cannon?"

I confessed my ignorance and plied the old darkey for more details, which he offered somewhat incoherently. Eventually he mentioned a "Massa Frank Sherman, whut op'rate de Claibo'ne-'Knapplis ferry on de Ches'peake. He da man whut know 'bout Paddy. You ax Massa Frank."

As I was traveling toward that artery, which was opened originally by George Washington to shorten his trips between Annapolis and Philadelphia, when we were planning to defy Great Britain, I continued and sought out Massa Frank, the present general manager of the ferry line.

"Yes," he said, when I introduced the subject of the terrible Paddy, "she was one of Maryland's most spectacular renegades and among the Negroes attained the proportion of bugaboo. To this day they tell tales of her raiding that seem almost unbelievable. Nevertheless, she was quite as bad as advertised, if not worse. Her origin is clouded in mystery, but she belonged to that group of utterly lawless characters that infested the South when the tide of civilization began to move Westward. Her husband, equally disreputable, seems to have faded out of the record about 1840, leaving his mate, who dressed like a man and had the strength of Hercules with the courage of a lion, to carry on his enterprises, foremost of which was the kidnapping of slaves which were shipped to Southern points via Tick Island, on the Manacote [Nanticoke] River. Paddy specialized in prime stock, the finest Africans brought to America by the black-birders. Whoever she made up her mind to capture sooner or later disappeared leaving no trace of his whereabouts. Owing to the great distances and the lack of communication it was practically impossible to trace her victims. It was her habit, as you have already heard, that the black man never lived that she could not throw and hog tie without help. More than that, she could carry a 200 pound man on her back for five miles without pausing to rest. The number of slaves she captured and resold into the Georgia and Alabama Market over a period of 30 years will never be known."

"Was there no law in the land," I asked.

"Plenty of it," replied Sherman, "but the Cannon woman knew her onions. The house in which she lived was located on the state line between Maryland and Delaware. Part of the residence in the latter state was in Sussex County. The section occupying Maryland was in Dorchester and Caroline County. Geographically this condition made it possible for her to step into five jurisdictions at will to harass the law, to evade summons and confuse any officer attempting her arrest. Not only could she step out of Maryland into Delaware, but vice versa, and in petty cases into three different counties. Paddy

Cannon was a woman of ideas. The exact spot where Paddy lived was at that time known as Johnson's Cross Roads. It is now the town of Reliance. Across the street from the Cannon house, Johnson's Tavern, also one of her haunts, still stands."

"Who was Richard Sherman mentioned by the Dorchester Negro?" I asked.

"My great-grandfather, who died in 1859. He was famous for the excellence of his slaves among whom Moses, a gigantic black from the Ivory Coast of Africa, stood alone for his strength and courage. Paddy had listed him for capture. One day grandfather directed Moses to hitch up a pair of mules and take a load of corn from Watertown to Ennie's Mill, a distance of 20 miles. The neighbors warned him not to send Moses alone 'unless you want him hog-tied and kidnapped.' 'If Paddy can throw Moses,' said grandfather, 'she can have him.' About sundown the mules, still hitched to the wagon—which was without a driver—ambled into Watertown. A party went out and found along the road near the Chaptank River evidence that a terrific struggle had taken place along the highway in a dense wood. The grass was torn up and the underbrush broken and matted. Moses was never seen again, although his captor ranged the region for 20 years after. Grandfather Sherman never quite forgave himself for sending Moses alone into the domain of the giantess. For years after the people of that region indulged in some extraordinary speculation as to what must have happened when the renegade white woman threw down the gauntlet and the black man picked it up.

"The spectacle must have been worth while. Following the kidnapping of Moses, a wave of terror swept through the Negro population. No slave considered himself secure and few could be induced to travel the country roads of Maryland alone. After the Civil War Paddy, her strength shattered and her market destroyed, became a hunted thing. Eventually she was taken by a posse, escorted to the jail in Delaware, to await the action of the grand jury. Much influence was brought to bear in her behalf, but Paddy, knowing better than any one else how much she had to answer for, took poison and died behind the bars before she came to face the judgment of man. It would be interesting if in the annals of Georgia or Alabama there should be living any of the descendants of Moses Sherman, one time of Watertown, Maryland, where he was a slave on the plantation of my great-grandfather, Richard Sherman."

"And I would like to know, Massa Frank, if Moses was at the ferry when Paddy reached the opposite side of the River Styx—and how!"

I have been unable to locate or further identify either the community of Watertown or Ennie's Mill.

Rivers of the Eastern Shore

Hulbert Footner was a consummate storyteller who practiced his craft with an expertise which has endeared him to several generations. His widely read and cherished *Rivers of the Eastern Shore*, originally published by Holt, Rinehart and Winston, Inc. as part of their "Rivers of America" series, has become a classic against which other books about Delmarva are inevitably compared.

While researching and writing *Rivers*, Footner traveled extensively, gathering tales and observing the peninsula's graceful geography and sometimes hard but appealing lifestyles, at a time when the region was still essentially distant from the rest of Maryland and largely undeveloped. I have spoken with several elderly gentlemen who were still chuckling, many years after the fact, about the fun they had sharing tales with him. One offered a strong suggestion that Footner may have had his leg pulled a little by some of the old timers.

Next to *The Entailed Hat*, Footner's yarn is the one most often mentioned when I ask people what they know about Patty Cannon. In Chapter 9, "The Nanticoke River," six delightfully horrifying pages are devoted to the legend of Patty Cannon. Since they are primarily a summary of the 1841 *Narrative and Confessions*, I shall not repeat them here.

Rivers of the Eastern Shore remains in print from Tidewater Publishers.

Patty Cannon on Stage

Ted Giles believed that a melodrama which drew applause from audiences across England and America in the late nineteenth and early twentieth centuries might have been suggested by one of Patty Cannon's crimes. Production of "The Bells" propelled then little-known actor Henry Irving into a career that eventually brought him world-wide fame.

It is Christmas Eve in a remote tavern in Alsace. The innkeeper, Mathias, is looking forward to the impending wedding of his daughter. Alone, Mathias imagines he hears sleigh bells off in the distance; it is a hallucination he suffers frequently.

We learn that on Christmas Eve, fifteen years earlier, a stranger had come by sleigh to the inn. Mathias fed the man and provided him with a room; then, learning that his guest carried a bag of gold, Mathias murdered him and buried the body in a nearby field.

Over the intervening years the crime has weighed heavily on Mathias, but he lives with the hope that once his daughter is married and her dowry (the gold) is paid, he will be free of the agony.

But alas, there is no respite for the innkeeper. After the wedding vows are spoken and the bride and groom embark on their honeymoon, Mathias hears the bells again. He succumbs to a fit of madness and dies.

I shall permit Giles to inform you of the relationship to Patty as he saw it:

Reference has been made previously to publication, in New York in 1841, of the book *Narrative And Confessions Of Lucretia P. Cannon*, which, along with other activities of Patty's life, tells of the murdered slave dealer. This crime took place during a business lull at the tavern, and a witness testified that Patty shot the man through a window while he was eating. She then took from his body, it was said, a bag which contained $15,000.

The crime was sensational for any period or place. The news of Patty's arrest, indictment and death must have gone abroad to be told and retold. We know that newspapers carried repeated accounts.

Two Frenchmen about the middle of the 19th century collaborated on a book *Le Juif Polonais*. One of these authors was Emile Erckmann, born in 1822. The other was Louis G. Chastrain, born in 1826. It is logical to believe they had heard the story of the Patty Cannon murders, had read newspaper and magazine statements, and might readily have had access to the sensational book published in 1841. At any rate their book, *Le Juif Polonais*, contained the story of the man traveling alone, who was murdered and robbed at a remote inn.

Leopold David Lewis adapted *Le Juif Polonais* into the

melodramatic success "The Bells." To trace this play back to Patty Cannon seems as likely a development as many of the other tales that have emerged from the Maryland-Delaware legend. The chronological progression seems to harmonize.

While some may feel that connecting Patty Cannon to "The Bells" is just another exercise of imagination, there is no question about who inspired the play "Patty Cannon," a three-act production written in 1951 by Ashworth Burslem, assistant editor and drama critic of Wilmington's *Journal-Every Evening*.

"Patty Cannon" was produced in the fall of 1951 as a workshop presentation of the Wilmington Drama League, then was taken on the road for two April 1952 performances to a packed auditorium at Laurel High School in Sussex County, Patty's old stomping grounds. Phyllis Wood Anderson, directed by Charles and Esther Jackson, starred in the role of Patty.

The *Journal-Every Evening* applauded the event as "the first play ever written about Patty Cannon."

An interesting sidelight comes to us through a long-ago conversation between Burslem and popular Delaware columnist Bill Frank. When Burslem informed Frank of his belief that Patty had never died in prison but was secretly released and assisted in escaping to Canada, Frank, to use his own words, ". . . thought I had him on the hip."

"But Ash," Frank said, "in your play, your melodrama, you have Patty Cannon committing suicide. How do you reconcile your theory of her escape to Canada with the final act of your drama?"

"He was sharp as a fox," reports Frank.

"Hell," Burslem retorted, "I could have had Patty sneaking off to Canada in the sunset and all that, but what kind of theater would that be?"

The Case
of the Sobbing Owl

Borrowing a few basic "facts" from the 1841 *Narrative and Confessions* and then exercising a vivid imagination, William Hartley brought Patty Cannon to national attention in 1954. A copy of Hartley's magazine article is housed in the collection of the Historical Society of Delaware with a hand-written note on the tear sheets indicating that it appeared in *Cavalier* in April of that year. The journal is no longer published.

The article was illustrated by Howell Dodd, who depicted Patty as a curvaceous young woman wearing tights, high leather boots, and a low-cut blouse.

"By day," wrote Hartley, "Patty Hanley killed her guests with kindness. By night she just plain killed them. Her final score was 24—a record that still stands."

The child had heard the sound before—a curious throbbing call that came from the woods beyond the cabin clearing. It was clear as a flute during the first seconds, but it always broke into a throaty, gurgling note. Sometimes it penetrated the silence of the dark moments before dawn.

"An owl," the child's mother had said. But Lucretia Patricia Hanley knew it was not an owl. No owl made a sound like that. And no owl could make her father rise from bed at midnight, dress, and stride across the clearing to the woods. The child had often watched from the tiny window in the loft, while her brother and sister lay trembling on the common pallet.

"What is it, Patty?" they had asked. And Lucretia Patricia, turning from the window, had repeated her mother's explanation.

"It's that old owl calling her'n. Go to sleep."

The explanation had satisfied Betty and James Hanley; the owl call ceased to frighten them and they rarely wakened when it sounded from the woods. But Lucretia Patricia always slipped from her place at the edge of the pallet to kneel by the window and stare across the moonlit clearing.

Tonight it had sounded twice. At the first call, in the hour after dark, Lucretia Patricia's father had left the cabin. The second call had come in the pre-dawn hours. There had been a strange violence and urgency in the second call; and Lucretia Patricia, kneeling now at the window, trembled as she gazed across the empty clearing.

The moon was still high enough to give a strong, cold light. With the dying of the owl cry, Lucretia saw her mother step into the clearing. When the owl cry was repeated, she walked toward the center of the clearing. A figure detached itself from the shadows of the woods and ran to meet the woman. Suddenly Lucretia's mother spread her arms and screamed, "Ah-i-i-i!"

At the sound the stranger turned and fled, half-crouching, into the black woods.

Lucretia, hugging her shoulders and trembling, watched her mother stagger toward the cabin. She heard the door latch drop into place. Then a soft mumbling sound filled the cabin—the whimpering of a fright-crazed woman.

Lucretia found her way down the loft ladder.

"What is it?" she whispered to her mother. "What did he say?"

"Ahii-sta . . . . ," her mother muttered in the strange tongue Lucretia knew was gypsy talk. The woman reached for the child's wrists, but Lucretia pulled away.

"In English," she said sharply. "Tell me."

"Your father killed a man," the older woman whispered.

"He'll get away!" Lucretia said fiercely.

"No. His friend said he is caught. He will be killed."

"But what happened?"

"Better you should not know. Go to bed. Ah, God! Don't tell your brother and sister."

Lucretia climbed slowly to the loft and lay down beside Betty and James. Staring into the darkness, she puzzled over her mother's unbelievable words. Why had her father killed a man? What had the man done and what was the meaning of the owl's cry?

Above all, where was her father? "He is caught," Lucretia's mother had said. "He will be killed."

During the days that followed, Lucretia pieced together scraps of information until she know the entire story. From her mother the girl learned that her father, Lucius Hanley, was an Englishmen of noble birth who had outraged his family by marrying a gypsy. Forced out of England by the anger of his father, the young nobleman and his wild, black-haired bride had settled in Montreal. Lucretia had been born shortly after their arrival in the New World.

From Montreal, the Hanleys had moved south to St. Johns on the St. Johns River (today the Richelieu) where Hanley erected a cabin. The settlement of St. Johns, midway between Montreal and the border of the young United States, was an excellent location for smugglers; and Hanley had easily been persuaded to join one of the bands of border ruffians.

The smuggling business had been profitable, for the American government, torn by the aftermath of the Revolution and the disorder of the weak confederation of colonies, was in no position to stamp out smuggling. When the owl sobbed in the night, wealth had poured into the breeches of Lucius Hanley. But the owl had sobbed once too often.

"Your father," said Lucretia's mother, "learned that a man named Payne had spied out his secret."

"Your father," the neighbors told the child, "put his hatchet in Alex Payne's head. In bed, he killed him. A knife in the heart to seal it, child!"

And it was true, of course. Lucretia Patricia had to believe it, for her father had been seized as he fled from Payne's house. The neighbors had deputized three men to take Lucius Hanley to Montreal for trail.

"Hang him up, they will!" Lucretia's mother moaned. "We should never have left Yorkshire for this terrible country!"

The waiting was over almost as soon as it was begun. On a cold spring afternoon, they hung Lucius Hanley.

"That night an owl called from the woods, but it was a true owl. Lucretia Patricia knew it for a fair cry, because it ended in a shriek rather than a sob, and it pierced her brain like a needle. Until the day of her death, Lucretia would never be far from the call of the sobbing owl.

When the period of mourning was finished, the gypsy hardiness of Lucretia's mother asserted itself. She was still young and still had the reserves of energy born out of her early years in the gypsy camps of England and France. She decided to enlarge her cabin and turn it into a tavern and inn. The location, midway between Montreal and the upper reaches of Lake Champlain, was excellent, for travelers passed through St. Johns both by river and by land.

The tavern prospered. By the day of Mr. Washington's inauguration, Mrs. Hanley's tavern was respected throughout the northland. The children of Mrs. Hanley were also respected—particularly the one the men called Patty. Lucretia Patricia was now 16 years of age—a tall, stately girl with the black hair and eyes of her Romany mother and the excellent complexion of her English father. Life in the tavern had sharpened her wits and her conversation. It was said in the neighborhood that Patty Hanley could have any young man she desired. A few of the old cronies whispered that she was waiting for a man who looked like her father.

Mr. Washington was only a few weeks in office when the man appeared. He was a handsome young wheelwright from Delaware, and when he asked for a bed his voice was soft as honey. His voice also trembled, for he had taken a fever during his travels.

Mrs. Hanley eyed him sharply and led him to a bed in the family's section of the inn. When the young man fainted, the gypsy ran a practiced hand over his money bag. It was full—here was a young man who deserved good care.

"There's a sick one in James' bed," Mrs. Hanley told Patty. "You're to watch him."

Lucretia Patricia heaped robes on the young stranger and placed hot stones at his side to sweat him. When he was able to open his eyes, she fed him venison broth and steaming rum.

"You have a name?" she said when the young man could speak.

"Alonzo Cannon, a Delaware man," the stranger whispered.

Lucretia Patricia Hanley, daughter of a murderer and child of a gypsy, became Mrs. Alonzo Cannon 10 days after Alonzo was able to walk by himself. And right after the wedding they left for southwestern Delaware. There, at a point on the Nanticoke River, Alonzo Cannon established a wheelwright's shop and a small pole ferry.

Patty Cannon was pleased with her new home during the first few years in Delaware. The Cannons prospered, and Patty bore her husband a daughter who was named Jenny. Three years passed pleasantly, with Patty occupied in the duties of motherhood.

Then the first trouble began. Patty began to take in over-night guests—travelers who crossed the Nanticoke on the ferry. The life in her mother's inn had accustomed her to the companionship of large groups, and she felt happiest when her table was crowded and the rooms of her house fully occupied. Alonzo Cannon was not greatly pleased, however, to find his home turned into a wayside hostel; his displeasure increased when it became evident that Patty welcomed disreputable wayfarers as readily as she did decent folk.

The change in the relations between Patty and her husband was a gradual one. Not until the end of the first three years was there an outright quarrel between the two. It came on a warm summer night, shortly after the Cannons had retired to their bedroom.

"I've had a fill of this inn-keeping," Alonzo said

sharply. "I don't want my wife to be a friend of strangers. We'll have an end to it."

Patty examined her husband's face coldly. "I'll choose my friends," she said, " and those who wish to stay here may do so."

The argument raged for an hour. At last Patty swept out of the bedroom, to spend the night in the room occupied by her young daughter.

Toward morning, Alonzo was awakened by a curious sound. He listened drowsily, cursed, and went back to sleep. In the moment before sleep returned, he thought he heard the click of a falling latch.

At breakfast, he tried to repair the damage of the night's argument. Patty, he observed, was as gay as usual; her tempers, reflecting her gypsy heritage, could turn from fury to good humor in a matter of moments.

"Last night," said Alonzo, "I was awakened by the call of an owl. A strange call, indeed."

"I heard it," Patty replied. "Strange it was, but an owl has the gift of mummery, I have heard . . ." And Patty became silent.

The next day Alonzo Cannon fell ill. He was seized by violent cramps; his face turned the color of flour and he suffered intensely from nausea. Patty called a doctor who bled the patient, in the manner of the times, but the bleeding did nothing to improve Alonzo's condition. He died in agony.

With the help of neighbors, Patty arranged for the burial of her husband. Then Lucretia Patricia Hanley Cannon found herself a widow in a strange country, encumbered by a child and without means of support.

"I can run an inn," Patty told the neighbors, "but it won't be here, in a house filled with memories."

For two weeks Patty traveled the roads of southwestern Delaware, in search of an advantageous location.

At last she found what she wanted—a solid, two-story building that stood in Maryland at a crossroads near the Delaware line. To make the arrangement perfect, a farmhouse could be purchased on the Delaware side of the line, a short distance from the inn. Patty, a woman whose childhood had been spent in a border town, knew there were certain advantages in living on a border, with a business in one area of civil jurisdiction and a residence in another.

The tavern and farmhouse were purchased, and Patty established a comfortable living. True, the neighbors complained that her inn was frequented by rough, strange men who plied curious trades on the Nanticoke River, but Patty could point out that an inn was a public place, open to all.

Remembering the bitter winters in St. Johns, Patty wrote to her sister Betty, inviting the girl to join her in Delaware. Betty could care for the farmhouse and daughter Jen while Patty ran the tavern. She also took, as bound boy, a seven-year-old lad named Cyrus James. When Cyrus was old enough, he would be useful in overseeing the slaves Patty had purchased.

When Betty arrived from the north, she found that her sister Patty was a prosperous woman. Child-bearing and the sorrow of her husband's death had left no mark on Patty's face; her hair was as black as ever, and the young men of the neighborhood were as attentive as they had been in St. Johns. It seemed to Betty that her sister had everything a woman could desire.

Pleased though she was with her sister's prosperity, Betty was not happy about the patrons of the tavern. As the daughter of an inn keeper, Betty was accustomed to rough men; but the men who frequented Patty's tavern were rough beyond any in Betty's experience. Perry Hutton was one such man—a tough, sour-faced youngster who seemed to occupy a high place in Patty's favor. Joe and

Ebenezer Johnson were two other constant patrons whose behavior troubled Betty.

"Why don't you discourage those men?" Betty asked her sister.

And Patty, smiling gently, replied, "They're my friends. In a little while, I'm going to have Joe Johnson manage the tavern."

"I shall not be friendly with them," said Betty.

Patty looked at her sister with a curious iciness that startled the girl. "You," Patty said, "are the daughter of a murderer and a gypsy. Be damned to your notions."

That night, the two sisters slept together in the farmhouse. Shortly after midnight, Betty was awakened by a strange sound.

While she trembled beneath the bed quilts, her sister rose and dressed. Betty heard the door of the farmhouse slam. Presently hoof beats echoed from the direction of the stable, then died slowly in the distance.

At breakfast, Patty joked with the servants and caressed her child, Jenny.

"You did not come back to bed last night, "Betty said at last.

"No. I slept on the couch downstairs."

"Did you ride somewhere? I heard a horse."

"You imagined it."

But Betty had not imagined the sound of pounding hoofs. Later in the morning she found mud on her sister's riding boots. At noon she noticed the farm slaves in an excited huddle.

"What's the trouble with you?" she demanded.

"Nothing, Miss Betty. Only they's a dead man on the Lawrel [sic] Pike."

Two slave dealers, it seemed, had been intercepted by robbers as they rode toward Lawrel. Only one had been murdered; the other, although seriously wounded, had managed to escape. According to his story, he and his companion had been attacked by four riders between Cannon's tavern and Lawrel.

Betty was not a fool. She began to understand the implications of the owl's cry and her sister's midnight ride, and her suspicions terrified her. At the same time, she loved her sister. And flight was impossible—she had no money. It was best, she decided, to forget the previous night and devote herself to little Jen.

Almost eight years passed before Betty found the courage to eavesdrop on one of her sister's midnight conferences. On a burning July night in the early 1800's she wakened at the owl's call and crept to the window. Her sister, she saw, was talking excitedly with Joe Johnson.

"Perry Hutton, it was," Johnson was saying. "The fool, the fool!"

"He killed the driver?" Patty's voice carried clearly in the night air. "I told him to be careful."

"No matter, He's gone. They'll hang him for certain."

"And what if he talks?"

"The ship is ready."

"What happened to the mail?"

"The sheriff got it when he took Perry."

The following morning Patty drew Betty into the farmyard.

Patty, now in her early thirties, had acquired a fierce, autocratic air with the passage of the years. It had become her habit to wear men's clothing and to carry a heavily weighted riding crop. She was carrying it now, and she slapped it furiously against her boots.

"I suppose you listened last night," she snapped.

"Yes," Betty whispered.

"If you blabber, my dear sister, I shall kill you. Now listen to me . . ."

The story Patty Cannon told her sister was terrifying. She was the leader of a gang of highwaymen. Joe and

Ebenezer Johnson were members of the group, along with a man named Butler, John Griffin, Ted Bowen and Perry Hutton.

Recently she had purchased a large sloop. If Hutton died without talking, she intended to put the sloop to use in a new business.

"I shall steal free Negroes from the north," she told her sister, "and sell them to the slavers!"

"Where will you keep them?"

"Here. Up in the attic."

"But how about Jen?" Betty cried.

"Jen," said Patty, "is old enough to marry. Joe Johnson wants her. They'll be married in a month."

Perry Hutton died without talking, however, and Patty, aided by the Johnsons, build a prison in the attic of her farmhouse. The room, solidly boarded, almost airless and only 12 feet square, was directly above Betty's room; in coming weeks Betty would hear the moaning of her sisters' captives.

Daughter Jen was married to Joe Johnson, just as Patty desired. The pair made their home in the tavern; and Johnson, aided by his brother, took charge of the kidnapping. Betty Hanley, tortured by the sounds in the attic of the farmhouse, received Patty's permission to live at the tavern with Jen.

Patty moved between the tavern and the farm, according to the requirements of the moment. When Johnson was in the north, she managed the tavern. When the farmhouse dungeon was filled, she stayed at the farm to guard the prisoners.

Despite her success in the kidnapping business, Patty still enjoyed the violence of an occasional midnight ride, a holdup and, in some instances, a brutal killing.

One fall evening a prosperous slave dealer named Bell rode into the tavern yard. "I'll have dinner," Bell ordered, "and I may stay overnight. I'm carrying money, and I don't like to be on the roads at night."

"You're a wise man," Patty agreed softly. "Have some ale in the common while I arrange your dinner."

Late that night Cyrus James saw a curious sight—one that he would remember for the rest of his life. Rising before dawn to attend to the farm chores, he saw the silhouettes of three figures against the faint light of the eastern sky. They were carrying a large object—a chest of some sort—toward an isolated corner of the farm.

Betty Hanley also had a curious experience on the day following Bell's disappearance. She smelled the odor of burning cloth. She hurried downstairs to find her sister poking something into the fireplace.

"I thought I noticed a stench of burning wool," Betty explained.

Patty looked at her coldly. "I'm burning an old skirt," she said.

As Patty Cannon entered the middle years of her life, she became heavy and as powerful as a man. She still affected men's breeches and jackets and when the mood struck her she would challenge the local tipplers to wrestling matches. They quickly learned not to accept—she could easily throw a man the length of the tavern. The neighboring farmers caller her Terrible Patty Cannon, and feared her as they feared the devil.

Only toward Jen and Betty was Patty gentle, and most of this gentleness was reserved for Jen. When Jen gave birth to a child, a small black-haired girl who was named Patricia after her grandmother, Patty's joy was intense.

On a morning in April of 1829, a tenant farmer who worked a portion of Patty's land felt his plough strike an obstruction. Examination disclosed the object as being a large wooden chest. A few blows of an ax split the cover and showed the chest contained a human skeleton. The farmer carried his news to Constable Thomas H. Hicks.

. . . when the mood struck her she would challenge the local tipplers to wrestling matches . . . she could easily throw a man the length of the tavern

Hicks talked to the slaves on Patty's farm; he also talked to Cyrus James, now a grown man and overseer of the farm help. "I seen them plant that box," James told Hicks, "and I know what's in it. The bones are the remains of a man named Bell. He never left the inn with his horse, and I seen Patty bury the box."

On the testimony of Cyrus James, Patty was indicted for murder. James also implicated the Johnsons and several other members of the gang.

Further questioning revealed that Cyrus James had been forced to participate in some of the robberies. Hicks arrested him, and then gathered a posse of six neighbors. The problem was to lure Patty Cannon from her tavern, on Maryland soil, to the Delaware side of the border where he could arrest her.

"Run tell her a slaver wants to see her," Hicks ordered one of the posse.

The ruse worked. Patty galloped up to the farmhouse, swung from the saddle with the vigor of a young man, and stalked into the farm kitchen to find herself facing Hicks' pistol.

"Well, young man," she said to Hicks as she stared imperiously at the faces of the posse. "I'm glad you thought me worthy of a half-dozen jailers."

The posse took Patty to Magistrate John Gibbons in Seaford, Delaware. On the testimony of Cyrus James, she was indicted for murder. James also implicated the Johnsons.

Taken to Georgetown, she was placed in prison to await trial late in May. Very much to her own surprise, she decided to confess her crimes. According to her account, Lucretia Patricia Hanley Cannon had poisoned her husband, killed 11 men with her own hands and assisted in the slaying of a dozen more. There was no doubt about it; a number of skeletons were unearthed at indicated points.

And on the night of May 11, 1829, young Patricia Johnson awakened to a strange sound. She had heard it before—a curious throbbing call that came from the woods near the tavern.

"An owl," Aunt Betty had told her. But the child knew it was not an owl. No owl made a sound like that. And no owl could make Patricia's grandmother rise from bed at midnight and ride into the darkness on her fine black horse.

Presently Patricia heard Aunt Betty go downstairs. The latch of the tavern door clicked; Aunt Betty was talking to someone. The odor of lilacs rose from the tavern garden. Suddenly a terrible cry filled the house.

"What is it?" Jen cried. "Aunt Betty!"

Betty had collapsed at the foot of the stairs. She turned her lined, tired face toward the daughter and granddaughter of Lucretia Patricia Cannon.

"She is dead," she said. "She took poison and destroyed herself."

And truly, Patty Cannon was dead, although there is some disagreement as to whether she died before or after her trial. With her death, the power of her gang was broken. The accounts vary; some indicate that two members of the group were executed while a number of others were imprisoned. The records, obscure because of their great age, are understandable vague. A pamphlet, published in 1841, implies that the Johnson brothers were punished, but the nature of the punishment is not revealed. In any case, the reader may be certain that Patty Cannon was the wickedest woman ever to walk on American soil. Her black record has never been matched.

A Federalsburg-Vienna Connection

In 1969 Ellenor Merriken published a charming little chronicle about Federalsburg, Maryland, and vicinity. *Herring Hill* contains some interesting and humorous oral tradition about Patty Cannon which I have not seen published elsewhere. From *Herring Hill:*

> Patty Cannon was a resident of Federalsburg in her younger days, and was practicing her lawless and wayward ways as proprietor of a tavern situated close to the present bridge crossing the river on Central Avenue, and on the east side of the river. Patty was born in Romania,

of gypsy heritage. She came to Canada with her mother and step-father Hanley, who as the name implies, was of British ancestry. In Canada, their activities were such that they were ordered to leave the country. From there they moved to New York State in the early eighteen hundreds where Jesse Cannon, who was thought to be interested in the slave trade, met her and brought her back to the Eastern Shore.

So much has already been written about her escapades. Whether true or not, here are a couple of stories that are supposed to be authentic. According to John Coulbourne's granddad, Michael Coulbourne, she stole one of Rufus Nichols' slaves. Rufus felt certain that she was guilty, and walking into the tavern shouted in a loud voice, "Patty! What did you do with my slave?" Patty swore she didn't know anything about his slave's whereabouts. Just then a voice was heard from the dungeon, "Here I is Boss!" and Patty was forced to release her prisoner.

That was the beginning of a rough time for Patty. When it got too hot for her here, she moved to Vienna and built the Patty Cannon brick house on the Indian Town Road; then moved from there to Johnson's Cross Road, now Reliance.

Another time that she was outsmarted was when Warren Kinder lost his two little Negro children, Plymouth and Martha Russum. He was very fond of these little kids. They used to come to the house every evening for some special treat after working in the field all day. One night they didn't show up and Mr. Kinder went to investigate. He noticed wheel tracks and hoof marks in the sand where the children had been working in the field and suspected right away that Patty had something to do with it. He went to see the Sheriff, and together they called on Patty at Johnson's Tavern. She pleaded innocent as usual and swore that she hadn't been off the place that day. Just then Mr. Kinder happened to notice a tiny black finger sticking out of a keyhole in a nearby closet, wiggling back and forth so as to draw his attention, and Patty was once more deprived of her prey.

The aforementioned version of Patty Cannon's' origin has been handed down through generations of the Whit White family, whose ancestors knew Patty. Mr. George Butler is a descendant of this family and believes the information to be authentic.

What is now considered the Patty Cannon House at Reliance, Delaware is not the original Patty Cannon Tavern. It belonged to her son-in-law Joe Johnson and was known at the time as Johnson's Tavern. Patty's own house stood a short distance from the corner on Stein Highway, as you turn toward Seaford from Federalsburg, almost directly in front of the present road to Galestown. It was situated right on the line between Delaware and Maryland; one half of the house in Maryland, the other in Delaware. According to legend, this was a great convenience for her since she was constantly pursued by law from both states for kidnapping and selling slaves. She could thus escape from one state to another when threatened, by moving from one end of the house to the other, where she was immune to arrest for the time being. Law officers were not allowed to cross state lines to arrest a person.

Patty Cannon's Home stood vacant for a great many years after her death, and was finally acquired by Mr. William Handy, who owns the farm where it stood. He moved it to the back of his buildings and used it for a tool shed until it was beyond repair.

The photograph of an abandoned and aging brick structure appears with the Patty Cannon stories in *Herring Hill* and is identified as the house that Patty occupied after leaving her tavern in Federalsburg and prior to moving to Johnson's Crossroads. This structure, which has stood without residents for

many years, is commonly know as the Webb House and is believed to have been built about 1800.

A couple whom I knew intimately before their death resided
in the Webb House for a short while in the 1920's and we often
discussed the imposing old structure. I am certain that if they
had been aware of any connection to Patty Cannon they would
have mentioned it to me. Neither has a search through numerous
volumes of Dorchester County history, architecture, and land
records uncovered any mention of a Patty Cannon connection.
Historians say it is not reasonable to believe that she was ever a
resident there.

The Webb house on Indian Town Road north of Vienna

But a few people have vague recollections that keep the idea
alive. Thomas Marine, who was born about a mile from the

house, told me: "I don't know how true it is, but I've heard that Patty Cannon built that house." The last time it was occupied, Marine believes, was in the 1920's.

Federalsburg may very well be concealing additional little-known Patty Cannon tradition. June Truitt told me that her father, who was involved in archaeological investigations around the area, always insisted that what we know as Johnson's Tavern, alias "The Patty Cannon House" in Reliance, was not the true location of the tavern. He is supposed to have identified the correct site, but June does not know the details of his investigation.

Mrs. Truitt also recalls another story passed down by town elders: "A man from Federalsburg was going to Seaford one day with some meat to sell to a butcher. On his way he stopped at the tavern in Reliance, and Patty said to him, 'On your way back, stop again.' I guess she thought he'd have some money with him then. Coming back, he went all the way around on another route; he was so scared of her."

Federalsburg, which developed at the navigable head of Marshyhope Creek, once known as the Northwest Branch of the Nanticoke River, was also home to Robert Messenger, author of *Patty Cannon Administers Justice*, and in *Herring Hill* I learned that Messenger and his brother, Burdette, are credited with building the first shell road in the village.

While I have seen no documents to substantiate any of the claims, other residents of this bustling Caroline County town insist that Patty was a frequent visitor. The crossroads which mark the heart of Reliance lie only four miles to the southeast.

Patty Cannon's Two Houses

In Dorchester County, Maryland, in the northwest quadrant of the offset crossroads that mark the village of Reliance, literally a stone's throw west of the Delaware line, stands a frame house that looks very much like hundreds of other turn-of-the-century dwellings throughout Maryland and Delaware.

Just outside the fence, however, a few yards from where Maryland Route 392 becomes Delaware Route 20, a State Roads Commission Historical Marker bears this inscription:

PATTY CANNON'S HOUSE

AT JOHNSON'S CROSSROADS WHERE
THE NOTED KIDNAPPING GROUP HAD
HEADQUARTERS AS DESCRIBED IN
GEORGE ALFRED TOWNSEND'S NOVEL
"THE ENTAILED HAT." THE HOUSE
BORDERS ON CAROLINE AND DOR-
CHESTER COUNTIES AND THE STATE
OF DELAWARE.

On September 7, 1934, the following article appeared in *Daily-Every Evening*, Wilmington, Delaware:

Wanted A Mythmaker

The neatly trimmed and newly painted house at John-son's Corners, near Seaford, known in history as the home of Patty Cannon, needs someone who can weave about it strange and weird legends. Tourists have taken to visiting this crime "shrine" and they want stories of horror that will chill their spines and congeal the blood. But congenial Mr. and Mrs. A. Hill Smith are not particularly given to the fabrication of such stories, whereupon the tourists leave, disappointed and crestfallen.

Back in the 1820's, as it often has been written, Patty Cannon used this house, then a tavern, as headquarters in her Negro kidnapping trade. She was the Lucretia Borgia of the Peninsula and her tavern was a carnal house of torture. Novelists, pseudo-historians and free lance writers have not helped to minimize these literary allusions one whit.

So well did these writers do their work that today tourists, visiting the Cannon house, will have naught but chambers of horror, blood stained floors and dark dungeons. But there are no dungeons. There are no slinking ghosts, and the Smiths are kindly, truthful folk, who see no particular point in transforming their placid home into a dime museum.

Under the diligence of Mrs. Smith's impeccable housekeeping, every last vestige of Patty Cannon's crimes have been swept away. The only relic in the home that might be construed as gruesome is a dagger found in the flue of the living room fireplace. Its history is unknown, but as a concession, perhaps, to the visitors, the owners have decided not to clean the rust from the blade.

"Visitors to my home would believe anything I told them," Mrs. Smith (who has since passed away) was quoted as saying. "If I poured a bottle of red ink on the parlor floor, they'd be thrilled to think it was blood. And even a couple of rusty chain links would satisfy their yen for mementos. They all want to see the attic, but when I tell them they would have to climb up through a trap door, they back out and give up the idea."

From the porch the visitor may admire the majestic silver maples, their broad spreading branches framing a vista of beautiful charm and tranquillity. The countryside is peaceful. There is not a suspicion of Patty Cannon or her infamous gang. But all of this is not what the public wants. Maybe, if the demand becomes more insistent, a professional legend maker might be imported to transform house and atmosphere into a place that would outdo even Patty Cannon.

Twenty one years later, on April 3, 1955, in a *Baltimore Sun* article, James Bready informed us that little had changed for Mr. Smith:

Motorists will stop, knock and ask to see the attic dungeon. But Mr. Smith informs his visitors that "nothing is now the same—no secret stairway, no leg irons, no balls, hobbles, gripes or clevises" as Townsend listed them. The present attic even has windows; though there is still no cellar.

A. Hill Smith poses next to the State Roads Commission Historical Marker on Maryland Route 392.

In 1965 it was Ted Giles' turn to visit the house and write his impressions; A. Hill Smith remained in residence:

The house, a two-story and attic structure in good condittoing, is occupied as a residence by A. Hill Smith, who has lived there since 1895. This house bears little resemblance to the original tavern. If the picture used in *The Entailed Hat* is authentic, then an extensive remodeling and modernizing job has been done. That there have been considerable changes is confirmed by the Smith family, who state that none of the elements that made it a place of terror in the early 1800's remain. Some of the beams and walls which formed the original may have been retained in the reconstruction, but the barroom, the dining room, the fearful "Keep" in the attic with its heavy oak paneling and iron rings and chains have since vanished. Today it is a cheerful and pleasant home, appreciated by the own-ers, their friends and relatives.

It is believed that Joe Johnson built the original house in the early 1820's. The records at the Court House in Cambridge, Dorchester County, state that James Will-son on January 14, 1822,[1] transferred the property to Joseph Johnson of Sussex County, Delaware. The line of subsequent ownership is not completely known, but later it belonged to Sally Moore, then to a man named Wilson, then to one whose name was Phillips. It was Phillips who did the major remodeling.

Matthew Smith, grandfather of A. Hill Smith, bought it in 1894. Thence it went to his daughter-in-law, Char-lotta F. Smith, and was subsequently inherited by her son, A. Hill Smith. The latter conducted a grocery store across the main road for fifty years, retiring from this work and closing the store in 1960. He and his daughter continue to live in the house.

But all those years of general peace and tranquillity which the Smith family enjoyed in the remodeled tavern ended a-bruptly in 1977 when it was purchased by James Good, an in-terior decorator who became an entrepreneur of things that go bump in the night—the mythmaker sought by the *Daily-Every Evening* in 1934 had finally been found. For Good's story let's turn to a contemporary article by Bill Radcliffe in *The Daily Banner*, Cambridge, Maryland, August 13, 1979:

Wanted: Exorcist For Patty Cannon

Ever since a rainy day in June of 1977, James Good has lived with a constant, gnawing feeling that someone is watching him. Even in the tranquil moments, the

---

[1] The record I reported in "The Sparse Paper Trail" says the purchase date was July 14, 1821, but it may not have been recorded until January.

thirty-two-year-old Denton native claims, the feeling persists. It only departs when he leaves his home at the corner of Maryland 577 and Delaware 20.

For the past two years, Good and his two sons, Jim, 12, and Chris, 8, have lived in the legendary Patty Cannon house, a sprawling green farm house on the Maryland-Delaware border.

. . . Good and his sons are convinced that their home is haunted by the spirits of the people murdered by Patty and her gang. Their suspicions have been confirmed by spiritualists from Milford, Delaware and Cambridge, [Maryland] according to Good. Last Tuesday, Good claims that a Milford spiritualist visited his home, "but she wouldn't come in. She walked into the yard, but that's as far as she'd go."

According to Good, the spiritualist claimed that she was powerless to rid the house of its many spirits. "The only thing we can do," he claims, "is to get an exorcist. I'm working on that right now."

Since purchasing the Cannon House in 1977, Good has spent close to $45,000 refurbishing the home's interior, which now serves as a showplace for his interior decorating business, Cannon Interiors. He runs numerous tours through the sprawling green house, showing his decorating abilities while entertaining his customers with tales of Patty Cannon. In the foyer of the house, $3 illustrated versions of *The Wretched Patty Cannon* are on sale, as are $6 plates depicting the Cannon House.

Although he admits that tales of evil spirits in the Cannon House might increase his business, Good fervently denies that his stories are contrived as an attraction for his interior trade. In fact, he believes that the tales may be more of a deterrent than a selling point.

"I wouldn't say anything if it wasn't true," Good said recently during a tour of the Cannon House. "My sons have both seen things, and if I was going to make this up,

I would have said I saw it myself. In a way," he continued, "it probably hurts my business. A lot of people don't understand about ghosts and spirits and they'll probably stay away."

According to Good, a premonition of his visions in the Cannon House arrived two weeks before the 1977 move when he saw "this terrible woman standing over my bed." Although the woman wasn't ugly, Good claims that the vibrations she put forth were demonic. "She may have been Patty Cannon."

As soon as he moved into the house, Good said he was aware of an evil presence. In his bedroom on the second floor, the Denton native was unable to sleep and was "haunted by terrible dreams." Shortly thereafter, he discovered that his bedroom was the alleged site of several of Patty Cannon's murders.

Less than two weeks after moving into the Cannon House, Good discovered a small opening to the attic above a second floor bedroom. When he hoisted his son through the opening, the boy scurried back claiming that he was scared by a picture of a "mean woman" that appeared to be staring at him from a chair. Good quickly enlarged the opening and crawled into the attic. There he found an old chair circled with black cloth, "but no picture."

Before moving to the first floor, Good had several other unsettling experiences in his second floor bedroom. On several occasions, he claims that his bed started shaking, or that something would slap him on the back before he fell asleep. One night, as he was reading the Bible, Good said something pounded on the wall of his bedroom. Then, he said, "I heard chains dragging across the attic floor and someone screaming."

Coming from what he claims was a "heavy black woman," Good said the scream was "Have mercy, have mercy."

Last summer, Good's sons were playing with a friend

in an upstairs bedroom, "when all of a sudden I heard this terrible scream." The boys claimed to have seen a large, black, hairy creature emerge from a closet and come toward them. The monster, they said, had bright red eyes. From that date forward, Good said his sons have not been allowed to enter the room, in which the closet door has been nailed shut.

Perhaps the most unusual story Good related about the Cannon House took place last fall, when he was planting chrysanthemums in front of the house near twilight. The light was growing dim, so he asked his son Jim to turn on an inside light. "All of a sudden the light started flickering," Good said. "It started slowly and picked up speed." Jim, who had recently learned Morse Code, read the flashing lights as "Help me; help me Patty Cannon." Good claims that no one was in the house and that the bulb was not loose.

Although the name was not recognizable to Good, he said that Cannon's main accomplice in her many crimes was a man named Joe Johnson, her reported son-in-law.

"I haven't heard that much in the past six months, but my kids saw the monster again on Monday night," Good said. "I can't afford to move out of here now, but what I'd really like is an apartment in Seaford so I could get out of here at night. I've been scared for the past two years."

When he first became interested in the Cannon House, Good said he was unaware of the gory history of the one-time tavern. "I didn't even know who Patty Cannon was," he said. "I just wanted my business out here."

Shortly after purchasing the house from Mary Handy, however, Good said he talked to the people who rented the Cannon house before he did, "and they told me they had heard things. They said that their little boy was in bed and saw something with a black face and red eyes looking in the window." The former renters also told Good that they had been jarred out of their sleep on several occasions by something shaking their bed.

Prior to moving into the Cannon House, Good claims to have had several experiences with ghosts and spirits, several of which took place at a farm house near Hobbs, Maryland. At the farmhouse, Good said, something would always wake him up at 3:45 a.m. every morning. On two occasions, he said he woke up and found a telephone next to his ear.

When he was a child, Good said he was standing in his front yard one evening when he saw a Model-T Ford gliding down the road towards him "at least two feet off the road." When the car pulled along side of him, Good said the passengers looked at him, stopped smiling, and moved on. "Then the car just flew over a fence and into the woods," he said. "I told my mother about it, and she said I was crazy, but I know that I saw it."

After several consultations with a psychic in Cambridge, Good said he has learned that he is clairvoyant. "She said I'm sensitive to spirits, and that's why I can sense them. The thing I have to do now is learn how to cope with it."

Despite his apparent fear of the Cannon house, Good said he plans on keeping his business in Reliance and turning one upstairs room into a museum. A mannequin of Patty Cannon has been placed in the home's attic.

"You know it's funny," he said. "You can live here for two years and it's still hard to believe it actually happened here. But you can't blame the house," he added. "She did it."

Good was later married, participated, he claimed, in writing a book about Patty Cannon, and turned the house into a paying museum. An article titled "Reliance Ghost House Pays Off" was written by Theresa Humphrey and appeared in *The Daily Banner* on September 29, 1980. Here are some excerpts:

... Good says the $1 charge to tour the home and learn its history helps pay for upkeep since he is now the owner. The fee, however, has led some in surrounding areas to believe that Good's tale may not be authentic.

Good, however, claims he is psychic enough, and his wife more so, to know that the house is haunted.

Married in August, Mrs. Good, 28, said when she first entered the house, she could feel the evilness in it. "Even now, I can still hear voices at night," she said. "When psychics are relaxed, they can pick up things from the past and that's what I've been hearing. They were conversations between a man and a woman. I've also heard a baby crying and I have heard chains rattling."

Mrs. Good has not been in the home as long as her husband who claims to have had much more bizarre experiences, similar to the Amityville Horror.

One of the upstairs bedrooms, where Patty Cannon is said to have committed most of her murders, is now called the "killing room." "I slept in there when I first moved here more than three years ago. I slept in there two or three nights by myself and I could feel the presence of someone in there," he said. "On the second day I woke up in the middle of the night and I could hear what sounded like a black woman screaming, 'Have mercy, have mercy.'"

Good said he had a spiritualist come to the house—a woman he would only identify as "Mary Smith." "She wouldn't come in here because of the evilness so we went to a neighbor's home and talked about the house," he said. "She said there was a treasure buried here (which he hasn't found) and that about 600 to 700 people were killed here.

... Good said he also had contacted a minister to "clear out the house," but the minister and his assistant, who were not identified, canceled at the last minute. "His assistant called me and said a spirit had appeared to him the night before and said, 'You're not coming in my house,'" Good recalled. " I suspect it was the ghost of Patty Cannon herself."

Good's sons, Chris, nine, and Jim, thirteen, are also psychic and have become accustomed to the strange goings on in the home, their father said. But Mrs. Good's daughter, nine-year-old Page, is still "a little scared," Good said. Page sleeps in the "killing room" and the boys sleep in the "torture room" where Patty Cannon tortured slaves," he said.

. . . Good said the book about Patty Cannon and the house is being written by Adi-Kent Thomas Jeffrey, who is also the author of *The Bermuda Triangle and Other Eerie Areas.* Good has been providing background material for the book and said he expects it will be published later in this year, although no firm commitment has been made by a publisher.[2]

On April 17, 1981, The Star Democrat in Easton, Maryland published an article written by Sam Smith and titled: "Home of 1800's Murderess Patty Cannon Is for Sale."

. . ."We are ready for a change," he [Good] said. "Both of us have experienced things here that the average person would not understand. My wife and I have psychic powers. One evening we were in the living room and my wife saw the Lavender Lady. She was allegedly stabbed to death by Patty Cannon. The Lavender Lady was supposed to have worn a lilac perfume at the time. Later we both smelled lilacs in the house," Good said.

. . . The Cannon house in Reliance is modernized today to the point that it scarcely resembles anything indigenous to 1800. The home is beautiful inside with several fireplaces and a modern kitchen. It's cozy and comfortable, hardly appearing to be the kind of place in which

---

[2] I can find no record of the book having been published.

scores of murders took place.

However, the attic in the home, described in historical writings as "the dungeon," is somewhat chilling. It is one of two rooms in the home that have not been touched by the craft of the interior decorator. A frail ladder with manacles and restraining devices surrounding it leads to the attic-dungeon. Once inside the attic, one is confronted by uncomfortable looking beds of straw. In one corner stand two black mannequins shackled to the rafters.

"I left the attic just like it was when Patty Cannon lived here," Good said. "On weekends I would open the home to tourists who were curious about the legend. They always wanted to see the attic. We had several mannequins chained to the walls and rafters," he said. "On a busy afternoon we could take in several hundred dollars from the tourists who paid a dollar admission. We also sold artifacts that we found during our digs on the property."

According to Good, in George Alfred Townsend's book, *The Entailed Hat*, it was written that Patty Cannon buried her gold pieces on the grounds around the inn. "My wife and I never used metal detectors to locate any of that treasure," Good said. "But we did do a lot of digging under the house in search for other kinds of artifacts. That treasure could easily be worth millions today," he said. "We did find other items such as glassware and even a club with blood stains on it."

A neighbor of Good's whom Sam Smith interviewed at the time he wrote the article is quoted as saying, "That place isn't any more haunted than my house."

Indeed, people who knew Good often smile when asked about his tales of ghosts and curious phenomena. One man told me, "It was all a hoax, you know. He wanted to bring people in to collect admission and sell them stuff. That attic was cleaned out and rebuilt years ago. All those chains and things—he's the one who put them there. There never has been one other person in all the years that place has stood there who said it was haunted."

Another resident of Sussex County shook her head and told me, "He was always trying to sell furniture that he said came out of the Patty Cannon House. Well, I guess it did; it went in the back door and came out the front."

Recently I acquired an unidentified newspaper clipping which I suspect dates to the Good era:

> It is said that the bricks which formed the chimneys to the house in which the infamous Patty Cannon lived and concocted so much deviltry, are now being sold to relic-hunters at the high price of twenty-five cents per brick. The house sometime ago was repaired and the old-fashioned chimneys with their mammoth fire-places were torn down and the bricks were used in other masonry. So only a very limited supply of the genuine Patty Cannon brick remains for relic-hunters. But a brick kiln is soon to be established here, and its owner and the owner of the old Patty Cannon property can make arrangements between themselves to furnish, for a quarter apiece, everybody in the land with a brick taken from the very centre of old Patty's big fire-place.

In 1982 Mr. and Mrs. John Messick bought the house.

"When we first came here," Mrs. Messick told me, "kids in the neighborhood didn't want to come over and play with our children. 'Oh, you live there,' they would say. 'Oh my gosh!'

"I wanted to have some curtains made for the living room once," she continued, "and I went to Seaford to find someone who could do the job. The lady that I talked to said she would make the curtains, but when she found out where I lived, she wouldn't come and hang them.

"However, we haven't had anything like that happen in years. Every once in a while something will be written about Patty and the house and two or three people will stop. If someone is interested in the history, I share what I know."

"From what you're saying," I observed, "Mr. Good must have taken all the ghosts with him."

"I suppose so," Mrs. Messick agreed. "We haven't seen anything like that."

Johnson's Tavern or "The Patty Cannon House"
as it appeared in 1997

The photograph of "Patty Cannon's house" which appears in Tidewater Publisher's illustrated edition of *The Entailed Hat* and in one of the reprints of the *Narrative and Confessions* has always puzzled me. While it bears a resemblance to the early drawings of Joe Johnson's Tavern, as well as to the modern structure on the site, there are also some significant differences. The caption under the picture reads: "Patty Cannon's own house stood a quarter of a mile beyond Johnson's Crossroads in the State of Delaware." Clearly enough, the inscription claims it to be the building in which Patty and her family lived until she purchased the tavern from Johnson in 1826.

"Patty Cannon's own house stood a quarter of a mile beyond Johnson's Crossroads in the State of Delaware."

Such an explanation might have satisfied me if I had not also been in possession of a photograph taken in 1928 and first distributed in the 1960's by Ted Giles. The architectural lines are so dissimilar in the two photographs as to preclude any possibility that they are of the same structure, however heavily the building may have been remodeled. The photograph published by Giles reveals a dilapidated T-shaped construction in front of which are posing a woman and three children: Mrs. William Irvin Handy, her sons, young Irvin and William E., and her daughter, Jane Ann. Giles claimed this to be the house in which Patty and Jesse had lived and where much of their mischief had occurred.

I showed the questionable picture to Mrs. Handy, now a spry octogenarian, who has lived on Patty's original Delaware homestead since the 1940's.

"That's the tavern," she said without hesitation. "That was the back of the tavern. It's the front as we look at the house now, but in Patty's day it was the back. The road didn't go to Federalsburg where it is now. It went on the other side of the tavern, and then it went over to the house up in the field, the one with all those trees on the lane, and from there to the next place down on the left. In those days the road went through the yards of the houses."

Returning to the picture of the tavern, which apparently was taken prior to the initial major reconstruction late in the nineteenth century, Mrs. Handy continued, "There was a porch on the other side in her day. Now they have a front porch on this side. They pulled some of the chimneys out when they remodeled."

It is also clear that the main unit is shorter in the old picture than it appears today, after at least two major renovations. Extending a building was not an uncommon practice; I own a nineteenth century Eastern Shore structure which was once extended by six feet to introduce a new stairway.

"Now this was Patty's home," Mrs. Handy continued, directing my attention to the photograph including her and the children. "It sat on the line, and the line ran through the house. My farm is on the line now, except that I own about four acres in Maryland. Patty's house was over toward the tavern. I don't know when it was moved up here. It was moved from the line up here and then shifted back into the barnyard. This [the present] house was built where it stood. It [Patty's residence] had three rooms downstairs and three rooms upstairs."

Looking at the photograph of the eighteenth century dwelling, Mrs. Handy explained that there was one upstairs room in the cross section with a window in the near end. The dormer contained a window for the second upstairs room and a third chamber had its casement in the end to the right.

Mrs. Handy and her children pose in front of Patty Cannon's house in 1928 before it was razed.

"For each room," Mrs. Handy explained, "you went up a pair of crooked stairs. When Patty got the dealers up in one of those rooms, she had them, because there was no connection between the rooms upstairs—there was no other way of getting out."

Except for a short period of time, the property has been in the Handy family for a number of generations. Isaac Handy, her husband's great uncle, lived in Patty's house until the present brick dwelling was completed around 1910.

An ancestor of Mrs. Handy's husband was named John Quincy Handy. His mother was an Adams, related to President John Quincy Adams. John Quincy Handy's daughter Anna was married twice and lived with her second husband, John Vincent, in the Cannon house.

Mr. Handy's grandfather also passed down the story that another member of the Handy family was the model for the liberty head which once graced our silver dollars.

"Grandfather Handy," Mrs. Handy maintains, "was plowing between here and the ditch one time and he plowed up a pot with some gold coins in it. He told us that. He didn't say what years they were. Back in those days I don't think they were concerned too much with what year they were, just the fact that they found some gold coins."

Were the coins once part of a Georgian slave trader's purse and interred by Patty for safe keeping in the same earth that claimed their former owner's body? Let your imagination journey where it will.

Mrs. Handy remembers R. W. Messenger, author of *Patty Cannon Administers Justice.* "I can *just* remember him. I went to school with his daughter until we were about in the fourth or fifth grade. He was a tall man—a big man. He lived in Federalsburg. When you go through—up to the top of the hill on the right, that big, tan, brick house—that was his home. He had a cannery there on the river, and he had financial problems and lost all he had. I don't know where he went from Federalsburg. I remember Mother and Father talking about him when he was writing the book. I can remember my father laughing because he was writing about Patty Cannon."

Our conversation moved from one reminiscence to another. About Jesse Cannon, Mrs. Handy recalled, "There are tales around here that Jesse picked Patty up in a tavern in Philadelphia—she came from Canada to Philadelphia—and brought her down here. She was one of those—what do you call those dancing girls?"

"Go-go?" I suggested with a smile.

And then Mrs. Handy really got my attention with a story I had never heard before. Referring to a comment by Ted Giles that there was a Joe Johnson buried on one of her farms, she said, "He didn't get that right. It's not Joe Johnson that was buried up there, it was Patty's husband—Jesse Cannon. The markers are down in the dirt now, all covered up. You know where the road goes to Oak Grove," she explained, "well, the next place on the right, where the great, long lane goes up to the house. Somewhere down in the ground there's a gravestone that says 'Jesse Cannon.' When we bought that place, the graveyard was just about all covered up, but Bill [Mr. Handy] said there was a stone there for Jesse Cannon, and his grandfather told him that was Patty Cannon's husband. You can't see it now; it's been plowed over for years."

Mrs. Handy did not know what dates, if any, were carved into the stone, but she suggested I talk with her son, Irvin, who lives on and tills the farm where the graveyard was located. "He was very young at the time," she said, "but he might remember something about it."

"Bill's aunt—his grandfather's daughter—" Mrs. Handy continued with two more unpublished recollections about Patty, "lived over here on the other side of the tavern. Her house is gone now. When grandfather Handy visited her, he used to walk over here to see us, and he would sit and tell us these tales. He said he remembered seeing Patty Cannon. He came from Cambridge up to Seaford one time, he said, and they stopped at the tavern. It was a long trip from Cambridge to Seaford in those days. He was about eight years old at the time and said he remembered seeing her. He said she was a stocky woman with a very pretty face. Over in the archives they say they've got 1829 as her death, but if he saw Patty Cannon, it wasn't in 1829, I'll tell you that. He was born around 1850.

"And I was doing some remodeling down there (the Handys once owned the tavern), and two school teachers stopped one day and came in. They used to go to Ocean City in the summertime for their vacation. They told me they met a cook in the place where they stayed who said she was raised by Patty Cannon. They were going down there, I would say, in the late 1920's and early '30's. Now if that cook was raised by Patty Cannon, Patty Cannon didn't die in 1829. So there's two references that came to me that I didn't ask for, and both claim the 1829 date isn't right."

I assured Mrs. Handy that there are newspaper reports, in

addition to other documents, which confirm Patty's death in 1829.

Before I left, Mrs. Handy shared three treasures with me: two timber-joining pegs which her husband saved when Patty's house was razed in 1949 and an old black-powder horn which he discovered in one of the walls.

Oak pegs and black-powder horn from Patty Cannon's house

"Can you imagine making enough of those things to put your house together," Mrs. Handy contemplated, dropping the solid oak pegs in my hand.

"When Bill found the powder horn between the outside and inside walls, he brought it up to the house. In those days we had a wood cook stove," Mrs. Handy remembered. "Bill shook it on top of the stove and it went *pfssst!* It still had some powder left in it."

Did the horn belong to Patty? Might she have poured the pistol charge which took the life of a slave trader from the very artifact I admiringly held in my hand? Again, who is to tell after all this time. It is certainly old enough—a short, cow's horn displaying a nicely carved dispenser end and an ancient wooden plug held in place by hand-wrought nails. As far as I have been able to determine, the horn and the pegs are the only documented period artifacts to have come from Patty's home.

When I called Irvin Handy and asked him about the lost graveyard, he thought for a long minute. "I remember there used to be a little patch of flowers out there in the field. We always drove around it. One year a fellow didn't know what was there and he mowed it off. And the next thing you know, another fellow who was working for us plowed it up. There was a gravestone out there, but I don't know what happened to it. I believe there was a Cannon on it, but I don't remember anything other than that.

"I've got a new piece of equipment," Handy continued, "which is called a ripper, and it goes about twenty inches in the ground. If the stone was there, it would probably have ripped it up last year. I've ripped the field twice since then."

Cannon's Ferry
and the Cannon Family

The Nanticoke River rises from several small branches in the heart of the Sussex County countryside northeast of Seaford, the site where navigation ends for vessels the size of schooners, tugs, and barges. It is a beautiful and often secluded waterway, with most of its thirty-six serpentine miles lying within the boundaries of Maryland. It is sometimes called that state's last wild river. Winding gently to the southwest, the ever-broadening flow arrives at Tangier Sound where it shares a mouth with the Wicomico and Monie Rivers and also Fishing Bay.

From Seaford—in Delaware—past Galestown and Sharptown—in Maryland—to now quiescent Vienna—once a port of entry—the shore is dominated by quiet farms, woodland, swampy cripples, and sloughs. After Vienna and the last of the farmland are left behind, the great Dorchester Marshes prevail to the western horizon. Along the eastern banks one encounters less expansive wetlands and the placid waterfront communities of Tyaskin, Bivalve, and Nanticoke.

The Nanticoke River below Woodland Ferry

A few miles above Sharptown, shortly after crossing into Delaware and past the mouth of Broad Creek, boaters need beware of a cable on which a motorized scow regularly chugs back and forth between the shores. Operated without charge by the

State of Delaware, the Woodland Ferry has a capacity of three passenger vehicles and boasts a service among the longest in the nation.

But the river crossing and the small collection of tidy homes and lawns at its western terminus have not always been designated by the tranquil geographical setting they inhabit; at one time the community and the enterprise were known as Cannon's Port and later as Cannon's Ferry.

The *Narrative and Confessions of Lucretia Cannon* has informed us that Jesse Cannon, upon his return from Canada with his new wife, was proprietor of Cannon's Ferry. The *Narrative*, however, is incorrect on this and other points.

Most historians believe that the ferry was founded by Jacob Cannon, a grandson of James Cannon of Nanticoke, while others credit James himself—or possibly Indians before him—for establishing the river crossing. At least one researcher, Richard Thek of Seaford, Delaware, contends that it may be the oldest continuously operating ferry in the United States. The earliest evidence I have seen as to the antiquity of the enterprise is a statement which comes from court records at "Snowhill Town," Worcester County, Maryland, and is dated November 4, 1766. The record states that 1500 pounds of tobacco were paid "To Jacob Cannon for keeping a Ferry over Nanticoke River the year past."

James Cannon, circa 1661 to 1711 or 1712, the progenitor of numerous Cannons in Maryland and Delaware, arrived in Dorchester in the Province of Maryland sometime before August 4, 1683, the date on which he signed John Taylor's will as a witness. From where he came is unknown, although "Ickford," the name he gave to his second grant of land, might be a clue. There is an Ickford Parish, partly in Ewelme Hundred, County Oxford, and chiefly in Ashendon Hundred, County Buckingham, England.

Robert E. Wilson, who published his genealogical research into the Cannon, Wingate, and Massey families in 1997, informs us that the Bible of William Turpin, husband to one of James Cannon's granddaughters, contains a reference which claims

Above: *an undated photograph of Woodland Ferry*

Below: *Woodland Ferry in 1997*

that the Cannon family originated in France. A large number of French Huguenots did emigrate to the Delmarva area and Cannons did intermarry with Huguenot families.

Wilson believes the Cannons may have settled in Virginia before moving across the bay to Dorchester County. Such a migration was not uncommon.

There is evidence without absolute proof, Wilson claims, that James had a brother named Thomas Canner/Cannon (the names Canner and Cannon are used interchangeably in some records) who settled on the Transquaking River in Dorchester County, and that their father's name was Edward. To lend credence to his theory that James and Thomas were siblings, Wilson points out that they each had children named Thomas, James, John, and William. But to complicate matters, another James Cannon (1675-1745), Wilson shows, lived in Western Dorchester County on Fox and Goose Creek.

On the north bank of the Nanticoke River, in what was then known as Nanticoke Forest, the James Cannon of interest to us received several grants from Lord Baltimore and made additional purchases: Cannon's Chance, Ickford, Noble Quarter, and Cannon's Increase are the names of some of these. Three-hundred-acre Cannon's Chance, the first grant, was surveyed for him on June 28, 1688, a year after the Nanticoke Indian Chief Ahopperoon renewed the peace made between his brother Unnacok Ca Simon and Lord Baltimore in 1678.

Down river from the mouth of Muddy Creek, James built his plantation home, a wharf, a tobacco curing house, and cleared land to plant the "divine herb," tobacco, which became his chief crop.

For river commerce James Cannon used a dugout canoe. Those forerunners of the Chesapeake Bay bugeye were often between forty and fifty feet in length and carried up to forty men. They were constructed by joining, side by side, from three to five logs. Traditionally propelled by paddles and poles, the white settlers soon added sail to make them even faster and more efficient. James owned two canoes which he lashed together to carry the heavy hogsheads of tobacco to a warehouse or to an outgoing ship.

On June 30, 1707, James Cannon was named attorney to Colonel Francis Jenkins, a prominent Somerset County official, and in 1709 was appointed Gentleman Justice of Dorchester, an important office in its day. James Cannon died several years later, bequeathing Cannon's Chance on the Nanticoke and his best suit of "cloaths" to his twenty-four-year-old eldest son, who was also named James. Other children sharing in the estate were Thomas, John, Matthew, Henry, Sarah Watson, Ann, Elizabeth, and William.

The second James married another Sarah, who bore him fourteen children to reach maturity, and added Goshen, Spring Hills, Friendship, and Cannon's Regulation, an increase of 577 acres to his three-hundred acre inheritance before dying in 1751.

A small addition to the Cannon land holdings in 1735 provides an interesting sidelight. In partnership with his brother John, James purchased thirty-five acres of the "Wooden Mines" in what is now Cypress Swamp, Sussex County, Delaware. Today the swamp lies just north of the Maryland line, but in 1735 it was part of Somerset and later Worcester County, Maryland. Only a few young cypress trees remain of the magnificent virgin forest which then carpeted thousands of acres. Cyprus logs—when the old trees fall—become gradually covered by detritus and take hundreds of years to rot. For nearly two centuries during our nation's early history, settlers "mined" this durable building material and used it to shingle their homes.

The second James Cannon prospered, growing grain, flax, fruit, vegetables, and tobacco. Horses, oxen, and Negro slaves provided the labor for his plantation. Cattle, sheep, hogs, and dunghill fowl furnished meat and material for clothing.

James left one hundred acres of Cannon's Regulation to his son Jacob, including fifty acres along the Nanticoke River which contained a wharf, a landing, and two houses. It was this Jacob, most claim, who was the first to operate a ferry at the present location.

Jacob married Elizabeth—Betty or Betsy in most references —who should not be confused with the character Betty Twiford (or Betty Cannon) in *The Entailed Hat.* Jacob and Elizabeth had three children who reached maturity: Isaac, Luraney, and Jacob, the latter unborn at the time of his father's death in 1780. Luraney, whose name is sometimes spelled Lurane or Lurany, was married to a Nicholson and later to a Boling.

It was during the first Jacob's tenure on the Nanticoke that the long boundary dispute between Maryland and Pennsylvania was finally resolved. In 1763, two eminent English mathematicians, Charles Mason and Jeremiah Dixon, were employed to survey the boundary. Their journal for December 17, 1765, includes this notation: "Twenty stones arrived at Wm. Twiford's on the River Nanticoke. . . ." The work was completed in 1768, and on January 11, 1769, England ratified the Mason Dixon Line as the boundary between the Provinces of Maryland and Pennsylvania.

The present border of Delaware was declared in 1775, and in 1776, at the time of the Declaration of Independence, Delaware not only proclaimed herself free from the British Empire but also established a state government separate from Pennsylvania. So Cannon's Ferry, begun on a land grant in Dorchester County, Maryland, came under the jurisdiction of Pennsylvania and then, only seven years later, became part of the State of Delaware.

Upon Jacob's death in 1780, Isaac was willed all his father's lands, housing, watercraft, and one mare. He was ten years of age. His brother, christened Jacob after his father, would be born later that year. Betty continued the business of the port and the ferry.

On February 2, 1793, as the result of an earlier petition, Betty and Isaac Cannon were granted by the Delaware Legislature the "sole and exclusive" privilege to operate a ferry across the Nanticoke River for fourteen years. Betty's petition, which she submitted on May 25, 1789, tells the story:

To The General Assembly Of The Delaware State

The petition of Betty Cannon, widow of Jacob Cannon, late of Sussex County dead. Humbly showeth—That the afs. [aforesaid] Jacob Cannon in his life time was at very considerable expense in having a cossway [sic] made over the marsh on the banks of the Nanticoke River to a ferry—lying on the road leading from the Broad Creek to the abovesd. ferry and since the death of the above named Jacob Cannon your Pettinor [sic] has at her request to the Court of Quarer [Quarter] Sessions of Sussex County procured a road laid out from Broad Creek to said ferry and has been at a considerable expense in clearing and making said road.

But a number of persons regrdless [sic] of the money expenses your Pettinor has been at in creating said ferry have by keeping boats at the same and ferrying travelers at lower rates than can be afforded by any person who has been at the expense of establishing the ferry, your Pettinor conceiving herself intiteled [sic] to an exclusive privilege of keeping a ferry on said road prays your honorable body to take her case into your serious consideration and grant her such relief as you in your wisdom shall think meet and your Pettinor as in duty bound will ever pray.

Ted Giles identified Isaac Cannon as Betty's brother-in-law, a rare error by Mr. Giles. Other writers have called Betty and Isaac husband and wife, a position which is also espoused by the Delaware historical marker in front of the Cannon Ferry House, which reads:

Isaac and Betty Cannon began operating a ferry here on Nanticoke River February 2, 1793. Their sons continued it, built stores and warehouses in the hamlet named for them.

The ferry became the property of Sussex County following the brother's deaths in 1843. First post office named "Woodland" was established in 1882 and the hamlet took the same name. The state acquired the county roads and ferry in 1935.

There are several things wrong with the historical marker and with the relationships described by Giles and others: The Cannons had operated a ferry at the Woodland location for many years prior to 1793, a fact shown clearly in Betty's petition as well as in numerous other records. Also, Isaac Cannon was neither Betty's brother-in-law nor her husband—he was, as we have seen, her son, who, with his brother Jacob, operated the ferry from the time Betty died in 1828 until they perished a month apart in 1843. They were by then wealthy shipping merchants and land magnates.

Isaac and Jacob Cannon must have been shrewd businessmen. In 1816 their Delmarva holdings included 5,473 acres of land, many houses, stores, warehouses, slaves, and a fleet of vessels which plied between Seaford and Baltimore. In Baltimore their properties came to include several brick dwellings and other buildings, a candle factory, a large ash house, two large brick warehouses, and all the ground and appurtenances between Concord Street and Fall's Avenue.

Cannon's Ferry was situated on what was then the principal highway transecting the lower Delmarva Peninsula, and the Cannons had been granted exclusive rights, in 1793, to conduct the crossing for fourteen years. This grant was renewed in spite of the fact that travelers were often obliged, as one complaint stated, "to wait . . . in the cold and rain and snow Hours before they can wake or Rouse with a loud strong voice or Conk Shell an Old Negro Slave upwards of sixty Years of age who has been the only Ferryman . . . to manage and Row a scow."

In later years the business of the Cannon brothers became even more extensive, George Valentine Massey II's history of the Cannon family informs us, "embracing a system of banking or money-loaning, which was characterized by its exacting methods. The partners were of opposite dispositions, yet the complement of each other in a business sense . . . ."

Their uncompromising methods apparently made enemies, perhaps resulting in Jacob's murder. Again from Massey:

> . . . when Jacob Cannon accused Owen O'Day, a former henchman of Patty Cannon, of stealing a bee gum (section of a hollow tree containing bees) from one of his farms, an argument ensued. O'Day shot Jacob Cannon on his ferry wharf, April 8 or 9, 1843, as he was returning from a visit to the Governor to whom he had appealed for protection from threatened assaults. Mr. Cannon died shortly thereafter on April 10. Young O'Day had the sympathy of most of the community and escaped. He was later apprehended at Chillecothe, Ohio, and orders were given for his extradition.

There is no mention of how Isaac died a month later.

Elizabeth Cannon, her two sons, Isaac and Jacob, her daughter Luraney, and Isaac's wife Mary are memorialized on the heavy, flat stones capping their brick vaults in the little graveyard between the ferry house and the church in Woodland. There is no evidence here of the elder Jacob's grave. Unless one applies a little arithmetic and ignores the historical marker only a few yards distant, it is easy to see how a casual observer might be confused about the relationships.

These are the epitaphs:

SACRED
to the memory of
ELIZABETH CANNON
Widow of Jacob Cannon
Who departed this life
August 5th. 1828
Aged 86 years
Also

to the memory of
MARY CANNON
The Beloved Wife of Isaac Cannon
Who departed this life
November 26th. 1831
Aged 58 years

IN MEMORY OF
ISAAC CANNON
who was born April 17th. 1770
and departed this life
May 6th. 1843
aged 73 Years and 19
Days

IN MEMORY OF
JACOB CANNON
who was born September 10th. 1780
and departed this life
April 10th. 1843
aged 62 Years and
7 months

In memory of
LURANEY BOLING
Born November 20th. 1778
Died August 17th. 1844

Isaac and Jacob died without issue, ending the family enterprise on the Nanticoke.

It was shortly after I completed my research and wrote this
chapter that I discovered Robert Wilson's study of the Cannons,
Wingates, and Masseys. In it Wilson claims that when Jacob
Cannon, the son of James II and the man most often credited
with founding Cannon's Ferry, died in 1780, he left behind his
pregnant wife, Betty, and *four* children: Ann, Isaac, Lillah, and

Sarah.[1] Isaac, Wilson continues, died in 1815, and his sons Isaac and Jacob took over the operation of the ferry and became wealthy but hated men. Nothing that I have seen from Massey's history of the Cannon family to the gravestones in the church yard at Woodland agrees with this claim by Wilson. He is incorrect, but I am not going to attempt to unravel it here.

A large mansion, Cannon Hall, still dominates the waterfront at Woodland Ferry today. Although Jacob Cannon built the house in 1820, it is said that his fiancee changed her mind about marrying him and he never lived there. Its fine wainscoting and dentiled mantels have long since been removed, "but the gaunt old house still stands," in Massey's words, "as if watching for Cannon ships."

In 1994 Cannon Hall was purchased by A. V. and Marilyn Griffies and their son Jeff. "We were looking for an old historical house to work on," Mrs. Griffies told me, "and we just love it."

I asked her about Laskowski's report of a murder and a bloodstain which remained on the floor in front of the kitchen fireplace. Mrs. Griffies had heard of neither, but offered me this story:

> I'd never seen ghosts and never thought about them one way or the other—whether they were real or not.
>
> It was about a year after we had moved here—at Christmas time. I was in the kitchen cooking and the TV was on. I was mixing something and I heard a noise in the attic above the kitchen. That's my son's office. I turned the TV off and it sounded like someone was walking around up there, but I knew my son and husband were both at work. At first I thought maybe Jeff had come home, but I looked out and his truck wasn't there.
>
> This house has noises all the time, especially in the wind, but it wasn't anything like that; it was somebody walking around. I didn't think about ghosts; I thought

---

[1] Jacob's will also included Luraney. Ann, Lillah and Sarah apparently died in childhood.

somebody was up there. I got so scared I called the police. I thought somebody would come down the stairs any minute. I stood by the kitchen door ready to run out.

The police came and there wasn't anything.

Then, a few weeks or a month later, I saw her in a room in the attic—it was just her head. She had medium-length blond hair, and she looked to me to be in her thirties, maybe late thirties. I can still see her now.

It was so clear and so fascinating; I just sat there and could not believe it. She was across the room and was floating towards me, and she kept getting closer and closer. I couldn't take my eyes off her. I wasn't scared. I knew what it was but it wasn't anything scary. It was totally fascinating.

Cannon Hall in 1997

We don't know who it is, but we think it might be Luraney's daughter. She lived here after her mother died.

We have felt her presence and my son has felt her
presence. Sometimes when you walk into a room, you can
feel she's there. She's been in my bedroom; she's been in
the bathroom upstairs; she's been in my son's bedroom.
It's hard to explain. When you walk into the room, you
just know somebody is there. It's been months since she's
been around. I can't wait till she comes again.

A short distance below Woodland Ferry, a small tributary
enters the Nanticoke from the northwest. The road to Galestown
crosses this branch on Maggie's Bridge. In the woods nearby, a
hidden, mostly desecrated graveyard holds generations of resting
Bloxoms. Maggie is said to be one of them.

"Sometime in the late Nineteenth Century" is the closest
anyone can now come to dating the tragedy of Maggie Bloxom.
There are few details known about the accident. Maggie was
thrown from her horse-drawn carriage and decapitated. The
girl's misfortune, an area resident insists, is a fact, but Maggie
Bloxom has also become a legend.

Some say that when the moon is full, Maggie can be seen
riding her horse, eternally in search of her head. "Stand on the
bridge," I was told, "and call her name out just right, and she will
come out of the woods." Others claim she carries her head in her
arms.

It seemed logical to me that a connection could be made between the story of Maggie's Bridge and the head described by Mrs.
Griffies, but her son Jeff says the family makes no tie between
the two events. "I know my mother uses the term 'head' when she
tells the story," Jeff explains, "but the vision was of a face rather
than a bodiless head." Are you wondering, as I am, about the
color of Maggie's hair?

Folklore everywhere is filled with stories of tunnels. On Delmarva, tradition includes tunnels to secrete the runaway slaves
at stations along the Underground Railroad and tunnels to hide

the kidnapped victims of Patty Cannon, who were moving, of course, in the opposite direction.

Cannon Hall also has its tunnel legend. Mrs. Griffies has been told there is a tunnel under the front hall. "When we rebuild the porch," she said, "perhaps we'll find out then."

Records attest that Isaac and Jacob Cannon owned and were leasing Patty Cannon's old farm to a tenant when the bodies were discovered there. Other testimony suggests that Patty, herself, rented from the brothers after Jesse's death and the disposal of his property by sheriff's sale. It seems obvious that there must have been at least some contact between Patty and Jesse and the brothers Isaac and Jacob, and that cargo from the Cannon-Johnson kidnapping operation must at times have passed through Cannon Port.

Some writers have intimated that Jacob and Betty had additional children and that Jesse was one of them. To some it seems altogether reasonable to believe that the family may have attempted to hide Jesse's relationship by disowning him, but all evidence is to the contrary.

The documentation provided by Massey indicates that Jesse was the great-great-grandson of James Cannon of Nanticoke, the lineal descent being through William Cannon (died 1764), Jesse Cannon (died 1790), and Levin Cannon (died circa 1794).

According to Massey, one of Jesse's sisters, Betsy, was married to Curtis Jacobs (1752-1831), a tax commissioner, justice of the peace, director of the Farmers Bank in Sussex, and also the appointed guardian of James Cannon IV's minor son upon the death of his father.

Milcah, also identified by Massey as Jesse's sister, is said to have married Jacob Wright in 1780. A son born to the couple in 1785 was named Jesse, Massey claims, in honor of Milcah's brother. Because a daughter delivered in 1791 was named Patty, it is believed that Jesse and Patty were probably married before August 13, 1791. Our knowledge of Milcah's marriage to Jacob and the resulting children comes from genealogical records of the Wright family.

Jesse, Massey reports, had at least one brother whose name was Edward.

Patty Cannon first emerges on a deed dated August 10, 1808, when Jesse and those claimed by Massey to be his siblings transferred their interest in Cannon's Conclusion, Luck by Chance, and Three Brothers, properties in the Northwest Fork Hundred in which they had inherited an interest.

In 1808, "Jesse Cannon of Levin" was commissioned a lieutenant in the Delaware militia and was promoted, in 1809, to the rank of Captain. Massey assumed this man to be Patty's husband and also that Edward Cannon, who served with him as an ensign, was his brother, but there are serious doubts that Captain Cannon was the same individual who was married to Patty.

Jerry Shields, who is presently engaged in an extensive investigation of the Cannon family relationships, traces the lineage a little differently. His version is James I of Nanticoke (died 1711); William I (died 1764); Jesse I (died 1790); and Jesse II, who was Patty's husband.

Concerning the 1808 land deed, Shields believes that among the persons named thereon, only Matthew and Milcah (Milly) was siblings to Jesse. He bases this confidence on two wills. The first is that of Jesse Cannon I which was made on October 12, 1790, and which names the following children: Hughett, Levin, Matthew, Jesse, and Milly. In the second will, Jesse I's brother William, who apparently had no children of his own, ordered his estate, in a May 1, 1795, testament, to be divided among his late brother Jesse's children: Levin, Matthew, Jesse, and Milly.

"It seems apparent from these two wills," says Shields, "that Jesse I was Jesse II's father, not his grandfather, and that Levin was Jesse II's brother, not his father." Edward and Betsy, Shields believes, were either cousins or nephew and niece to Patty's husband. He sees Milcah and Milly as being the same person.

It is probably fair to ask, if there were three consecutive generations named Jesse, why Patty's and Jesse's son was referred to as Jesse, Jr. and not Jesse III.

Again looking to Robert Wilson's study, he lists James I's

son William's children as Nicy (1715-1764), Curtis (1717-1785), Levin (1719-1789), William (1721-1795), Jesse (1723-1790), and Constantine (1725-1793). For Jesse's children Wilson shows Hughett (1748-1793), Levin (1750-1797), Milley (1752-1790, Matthew (1754-1790), and Jesse (1756-1790). Jesse, born in 1756, would appear to be about the right age to be our Jesse, but the 1790 date of death—if that were correct—would exclude him. Wilson, however, has *estimated* many dates of birth and incorrectly assigned the same year of death, 1790, to both parents and three of the children in this family.

This confusion is an excellent example of the difficulty faced by those who do genealogical research—especially in large families with frequently repeated given names. The indisputable evidence of Jesse Cannon's lineage may be out there somewhere, but it is yet to be discovered and published.

Putting aside the embarrassment of Patty, who married into the family—and to a lesser degree, Jesse—there have been many descendants of James Cannon of Nanticoke Forest who have distinguished themselves and the Cannon name as farmers, merchants, manufacturers, clergymen, professionals, academics, military men, legislators, and government executives. I have space here to mention only a few.

Each night when his daughter went into the tower of their home carrying a candle, Wilson Lee Cannon, Delaware shipbuilder and legislator, worried that Annie Jump Cannon (1863-1941) would set the house on fire. What she set on fire was the science of astronomy, classifying according to their spectra some 400,000 stellar bodies and discovering many new variable stars and five novae. Among her many distinctions was an honorary Doctor of Science degree from Oxford University, the first ever issued to a woman by that prestigious institution.

"My success, if you would call it that," she once said, "lies in the fact that I have kept at my work all these years. It is not genius . . . it is merely patience."

William Cannon (1809-1865) ran a general store, bought and shipped lumber and grain, operated grist and saw mills, owned a brickyard, organized a bank, and planted orchards. The latter venture would eventually lead to another important family enterprise. He published a newspaper, served as superintendent of schools, directed a railroad, and then, to conclude a phenomenally varied and distinguished career, he became Governor of Delaware, in which capacity he served during the Civil War, dying in office on March 1, 1865, of pneumonia.

William Cannon's term as Delaware's chief executive was marked by considerable friction and dissension, some of which William suffered at the hands of half brother James, who loudly proclaimed his intense feelings for the Southern cause. Tradition asserts that James' sympathy extended to blockade running, shuttling supplies for the Confederacy down the Nanticoke River. When finally forced to flee to Salisbury, Maryland, to avoid arrest, James is said to have been aided by his strongly pro-union brother, the governor.

One thing the siblings and their wives did have in common was a strong religious conviction and an antipathy for alcohol. James' son, James Cannon, Junior, therefore, grew up in an atmosphere of extreme piety. His mother later organized a local Women's Christian Temperance Union and zealously fought to abolish the twelve saloons then operating in Salisbury, but it was her son who finally accomplished that in 1902. James entered the Methodist ministry and went on to become one of the most formidable reformers this country has ever known.

"The furious zeal that he brought to his crusade for prohibition and the almost superhuman will that spurred him on were as characteristic of him as was his willingness to use questionable means if they promised to be effective," wrote Virginius Dabney in *Dry Messiah: The Life of Bishop Cannon.*

Bishop James Cannon has been called "the most powerful ecclesiastic ever heard of in America," and William Randolph Hearst, describing him as a bitter adversary in the fight for prohibition, claimed, "His was the best brain in America, no one excepted."

Bishop Cannon died September 6, 1947.

To market the surplus of peaches from their father William's orchards, Henry Pervis Cannon and Philip L. Cannon built a small canning plant along the Delaware Railroad tracks opposite the Bridgeville Station in 1881. Philip later withdrew when the future of the business looked doubtful, but Henry stuck it out and saw the operation grow from a 30 x 80 foot frame shed into a nationally prominent business, called by *Canning Age* one of the finest in America for its equipment, management, quality of product, and progressive methods. In 1911 Henry's business was incorporated as H. P. Cannon & Son.

Harry Laws Cannon took over active management of the plant in 1900, became vice president in 1924, and was named president in 1929, continuing also the Cannon tradition of public service and business leadership to his community and state.

At the time of Harry's death, on November 10, 1944, his son, Henry Pervis Cannon II, was serving as an officer in the United States Navy. After his discharge in 1945, Henry succeeded to the company presidency, enlarged and renovated the Bridgeville operation, and constructed a new plant at Dunn, North Carolina. Before his death in 1993, both properties were sold, ending a hundred years of canning history.

Patty Cannon's Island

Several islands lie close to the shore of the Nanticoke River between Woodland and Sharptown. We have heard a tale about one of these in *The Laskowski Papers*; another was spun by Townsend in *The Entailed Hat*. Ted Giles investigated two of them, and I shall allow him to tell that story. From *Patty Cannon—Woman of Mystery:*

Across the Nanticoke from Galestown, close to the east bank, are two islands. One extends fifty or sixty acres; the other about two acres. The story has come down from family to family for more than a hundred years that on these islands Patty Cannon and her gang chained their captives. Great trees, they assert, contained iron rings attached to staples driven into the trees, and held prisoners secure until time for shipment. The trees and rings were there seventy-five years ago; fathers and grandfathers saw them. But in the meantime the big timber has been taken out. Only a jungle of smaller trees and underbrush remains.

Job Russell of Galestown says that the larger island was called "Patty Cannon's Island." Today it is known as "Tick Island," perhaps to describe its major inhabitants. From the southern end it is separated from the mainland by a small, overgrown creek called Devil's Gut. Nearly three quarters of a mile north, Devil's Gut connects with Cod Creek, which is navigable for small boats most of the way and forms the balance of the island's eastern boundary. Of course the Nanticoke River is to the west. Cod Creek winds mysteriously through banks covered with pine, cypress, holly, laurel and other lovely trees.

"Tick" or Patty Cannon's Island" is in Maryland, and could have been a perfect hideout. Remote, not easily accessible, heavily overgrown, even today it is an eerie place. Small though it is, one could easily lose direction in the closely crowded bushes and trees. It's a perfect setting for diabolic deeds. Elijah Wheedleton of Galestown took the author to the island in his sleek, swift fishing boat. Wheedleton is a woodsman as well as experienced—life long—in the ways of the water. He broke twigs to lay on the ground so that we could cross the marshy land, and we reached the high grounds, that stretch like a ridge down the island's center, without sinking into the morass.

The island is what is known as a "cripple," which means a high and wooded place surrounded by marsh.[1] Job Russell says in some places it is called "spung." We searched the island, both on land and from the water. No

[1] Cripples are commonly considered to be swampy woodland bordering creeks and rivers.

tree is in sight that could have been a hundred and thirty years of age. Both Russell and Wheedleton knew from family stories passed from father to son that the big trees had once been there. But they vanished from the scene possibly fifty or sixty years previous.

The other island reputed to have been used by Patty Cannon is called Pickle Pear Island. It is in Delaware, north of Tick Island, and almost within sight of Woodland Ferry. Pickle Pear, being small and closer to settlements such as Laurel, Seaford and Sharptown[2] is more easy of access. A picnic grounds in 1963 was proof that it was known and used. The spectral tenancy of Patty Cannon's Island might well be imagined, but there was no such feeling about Pickle Pear. It is just a charming spot beside the Nanticoke. But Pickle Pear is also "cripple" or "spung," for it is high, well-drained land surrounded by marsh.

Joe Johnson, Patty Cannon's son-in-law, is reputed to have killed a man named King in a house in the area. And Job Russell's grandfather, who was also Job Russell, born in 1821 and who died in 1911 at the age of 90, would tell of seeing Patty Cannon. The grandfather's friend, George Lowell, raised by Tyrus Phillips and living on the road between what are now Reliance and Woodland, also talked of seeing Patty Cannon, who traveled back and forth on horseback. She was a person of interest, for rumors were rife.

According to Galestown residents, the work of the Patty Cannon gang was not confined to kidnapping and murdering, They levied toll on river traffic, and made prey of any boat, engaged in business, that passed up and down the Nanticoke.

Mike Wheedleton, Elija's grandson, visited Patty Cannon's

---

[2] Tick or Patty Cannon's Island is closer to Sharptown than is Pickle Pear.

Island in 1996 and told me there are again some large trees on the high ground—loblollies are relatively fast growing.

"On the Wicomico side," Wheedleton described the setting, "Cod Creek comes back, and Devil's Gut cuts through to the Nanticoke closer to Sharptown. There's a section of cripples and marsh, and the island is right smack in the middle of that."

Back in the nineteen-twenties, John Stevens, a local legend who lived behind the Galestown Cemetery on the Nanticoke River, is reputed to have been a bootlegger. Wheedleton tells this story about Stevens:

"John used to go to Baltimore. To get around the customs men—that's what he called the ones who checked for bootleg—he would take a couple of old cats with him in his boat. He would put those cats in a burlap sack. Of course the man would want to check the bag, and when John opened it, the cats would jump all over the man. Then he'd go back and fill his bag with whiskey. Later on he'd say to the customs man, 'Want to check my bag?' 'No,' the man would say, 'go on.'"

"It doesn't sound like it has a lick of truth to it," Wheedleton chuckled, "but it sure makes a great story."

Tradition is strong that John Stevens kept his stills on Patty Cannon's Island and that he told ghost stories about the place to discourage people from going there.

"Sure enough," said Wheedleton, "when I went back there, you can still find the old metal barrel rims."

Wheedleton told me he had been under the impression, since reading *The Entailed Hat*, that the wharf once owned by the Twifords was the property just inside the Maryland line on the northwest bank of the Nanticoke where his friend Thomas Marine once lived (more about Tom later).

But old rivermen, he said, see it differently. They identify sections of the Nanticoke by what they call fishing "retches."[3] The section on the Maryland-Delaware line where Marine lived

---

[3] I initially assumed that "retch" was a colloquial pronunciation for "reach," but the term is also commonly used on the Nanticoke River to describe the action of feeding a length of gill netting into the water from a skiff.

is known as Hawk's Nest Retch, and the long-abandoned wharf is called Truitt's. Further upriver, in Delaware, is Red House Retch. That, the fishermen claim, was the location of Twiford's Wharf. While oral tradition is not to be dismissed lightly, the watermen appear to be wrong in this instance. Twiford's Wharf and Truitt's Wharf are generally considered to be the same property, the farm once having been deeded to the Twifords and later to the Truitts.

None of the area residents I have spoken to are familiar with the Twiford name or know of any Twiford graves, but Wheedleton told me about a discovery he made in the spring of 1997:

"Down past Sharptown we were progging around in the marsh and we found a graveyard. It's around the first bend below Sharptown, on the fishing retch that's called Miracle Bend. There is an old wreck there, an old tug or steamboat that was called Josephine. On real low tide you can see the huge keel. Right past that there's a little piece of high ground which used to be fast land years ago. In the woods there's four or five graves, all Twifords."

"On the bank of the Nanticoke River below Sharptown," grave records for Wicomico County list the burials of John Twiford, his three wives: Elenor, Amanda, and Elizabeth, and Sina, daughter of John and Elizabeth. Dates range through the eighteen fifties and sixties.

Some believe that Sharptown was originally named Twiford, and George H. Corddry's *Wicomico County History* claims that Twiford's Wharf was established at the site of Sharptown about 1760. By 1800 the town had acquired its present name, most likely to honor Maryland Governor Horatio Sharpe. It became a vital ship-building center shortly afterward when Matthew Marine founded the Sharptown Marine Railway.

Tom Marine no longer lives on the farm at Truitt's Wharf but has moved only a few miles in the direction of Reliance where he lives with his wife, Elizabeth, and his son, Randy.

"When we moved on the farm," Marine told me, "they always called it the Patty Cannon Farm, and they called the old house— it's burned down now—the Patty Cannon House, but I can't say when she lived there.

"There was great big trees on the farm, and there was big rings on a wedge drove in there. And they said that's where Patty Cannon used to tie the slaves," Tom remembered. Randy Marine has saved one of the iron rings found on the property when his grandfather first moved there.

"And then, across that river is an island called Patty Cannon's Island. If you take a boat and go over there you'll see . . ." Marine paused in the middle of his sentence, then continued: "Well, I think all the trees broke off now. They cut 'em down. But years back there were chains in them trees. I saw the trees, yes sir! Some were on the farm and some were on the island. What they done with the rings—I guess people got them for souvenirs. They were a big ring with an iron wedge, you might say, and they drove that into a tree. There weren't no chains on the trees on the farm, but [if] you went across to the island, there were chains hangin' down. Of course they were all rusted.

"John Stevens took us to Patty Cannon's Island. He carried us over there to show us the rings and the chains on the trees. Years ago John kept stills over there. He told us the old barrel staves were rotten and gone but the iron rims were still there, and he walked right to 'em. It looked like they just slid off the barrels and stayed there."

I asked Marine to tell me more about John Stevens.

"John Stevens was a good old thing. He'd do anything in the world for you if he liked you. But if he didn't like you . . . just forget about it; he wouldn't do nothin'.

"When I was young, John used to say that Patty Cannon cut the slaves' heads off sometimes, and she'd save the blood and sell it to somebody that made something out of that blood. That's what he said. That's all I got to go by."

The Marines verified that Stevens was a great one to tell ghost stories.

"I would tell him," Elizabeth said: 'Mr. John, there are no ghosts.' And he would say, 'Yes there is!'"

And does Tom Marine believe in the supernatural?

"I've heard a lot of ghost stories, but I've never *seen* nothin' I couldn't make out."

Tom Marine's father also lived on the farm at Truitt's Wharf, and Willard Massey was resident prior to that. Tom remembers a tale Willard told his father when he first moved in: "Willard said Patty Cannon's ghost was there all the time but you would-n't hear her till after dark. At night she would come down the stairway to the bottom step. You go get her two cans of beer and give [them to] her, she'll go back upstairs and won't bother you."

Tom's father is alleged to have replied, "Well, I'll go get some beer and stick it up there and maybe she won't bother me."

Elizabeth Marine told me two stories which demonstrate just how much Patty Cannon was a part of local life and thought well into the Twentieth Century:

> When Randy and his sisters were growing up, their cousins would come over and stay, and there was a boy down to Galestown would come out and stay. The boys slept in one room and the girls in the other.
>
> The boys would go to bed earlier than the girls, and they'd get some string and tie it on the girl's quilts. The girls would go upstairs and get into bed, and here they'd come down the stairs just a-flyin': Pat-pat-pat! Pat-pat-pat!
>
> "What is the matter?"
>
> "There's somebody pullin' the covers off our bed. It's got to be Patty Cannon."
>
> Those boys would have to cover their head and laugh so the girls couldn't hear 'em.
>
> The girls said, "We can't sleep up there."
>
> I said, "Yes you can. Get yourself a pair of scissors, and before you get in the bed, look on the quilts. If you find a string, just snip it."
>
> This one night [there] wasn't none of 'em up there, and Randy went to bed hisself. After a while he hollered down the stairs: "Mom . . . Mooom . . . Moooooom!"

I said, "What is the matter with you?"

"Oh!" he said—it was close to Christmas—"I think Patty Cannon's wrappin' her Christmas packages."

I opened the stairs' door and listened. Weren't a thing in the world, I imagine, but rats. We had a mess of rats in the old house and they had gotten paper in between the ceiling part of the stairway and the floor that went upstairs.

I said, "Go to sleep, Randy. That ain't nothin' but rats cuttin' up some paper."

The lost Twiford graveyard was still on my mind, and I asked the Marines if they had ever seen any gravestones on the farm. They knew of a small graveyard, but the names are Haines and Wheatley.

A road used to go from the site of the old Truitt house down to the wharf, Elizabeth Marine told me. "In front there was a mess of stones. We got some out here in the front yard. You could take a tractor and a cart and drive out on the mud flats. Someone told me those stones was on the ships when they were comin' up the river. Then they would throw 'em out. They say a Mason-Dixon stone is down there underneath all that silt and stuff."

I thought back to Charles Mason's and Jeremiah Dixon's journal entry for December 17, 1765: "Twenty stones arrived at Wm. Twiford's on the Nanticoke River," and to *The Entailed Hat*:

"Now, I never been by this place before," Jimmy Phoebus muttered, "but, by smoke! yon house looks to me like Betty Twiford's wharf, an', to save my life, I can't help thinkin' yon white spots down this side of the river air Sharptown. If that's the case, which state am I in?"

He rose to his feet, bailed the scow, which was nearly full of water, and began to paddle along the shore, and, seeing something white, he landed and parted the bushes, and found it to be a stone of a bluish marble, bearing on one side the letter M, and on the other the letter P, and a royal crown was also carved upon it.

John Moll's conception of Patty Cannon's Island, from Patty Cannon—Woman of Mystery, by Ted Giles

Patty Cannon's Skull

It was a pleasant morning and finding the Dover Public Library from U. S. Route 13 was easier than I had expected; it sits near the center of old Dover amid brick buildings that have an air of history about them. Inside, two or three scattered patrons were quietly busy at their literary tasks. I introduced myself to the young man behind the desk and informed him that I had come to see "the skull."

"Oh sure," he said, and disappeared for a moment into an inner room, then reappeared with a red hatbox which he placed on the counter.

"Is there someone I can talk to about this?" I asked.

He pointed to where an elbow was protruding from behind a stack of books: "The director," he said, "Mr. Wetherall."

Director Wetherall and "Patty Cannon's Skull"

I picked up the container by its handle and walked toward the elbow, which I soon discovered was attached to a portly gentleman with a pleasant smile. I introduced myself again and explained why I had come.

"Has there ever been a forensic study done?" I asked the director.

"I don't believe so," Bob Wetherall responded. "I don't believe it's ever been run past the state pathologist or anything like that. It's obviously somebody's skull, and it very well may have come from the place where they said it did, but there is a lot of doubt. It's just word of mouth. Have you seen it?"

"No, I just picked her up before I joined you."

Wetherall ran the zipper around the container and flipped open the lid. Lifting out a small cardboard carton and laying it aside on the table, he smiled, "These are some extra little parts."

There, resting on a cushion of red velvet and displaying what could well be the ravages of more than a century and a half, sat "Patty Cannon's skull." The cranium was missing its mandible and there were no teeth that I could observe. A large portion of the bone between the nose and the left eye socket was missing. A hasty, mostly-uneducated appraisal of the sutures indicated to me that the owner was not a young person at the time of death.

"I came here in 1989," Wetherall explained. "Mrs. Batton, who was the director for many years, had written a piece about the library for the tercentennial reviews and I thought I would read that. When I saw this I said, 'We have Patty Cannon's skull?' They said, 'Sure,' and handed me the hatbox. It was supposed to be loaned to us by Alfred Joseph, who was Dover City Engineer at one time, but he is long since dead."

Wetherall removed a document which had been tucked in next to the skull, unfolded it, and handed it to me. Neatly typed on the letter-sized sheet was this title and explanation:

Patty Cannon's Skull

Just after the turn of the century James Marsh (my

uncle by marriage) was reading law in the office of Robert White of Georgetown, Delaware. Since during this apprenticeship period there was little income he took the position of deputy sheriff of Sussex County. While holding this job the bodies of Patty Cannon and one or two others who had been buried in the jail yard of the Sussex Jail were exhumed for reburial in potters field. The yard now is a parking lot and is south of the old jail which is now the Sussex County Board of Assessment Building.

In 1827 Patty had taken arsenic and died[1] while being held for trial for murder.

Somehow while moving these bodies Patty's skull came into the possession of James Marsh.

About 1907 James Marsh contracted acute tuberculosis and in an effort to save himself moved to Denver, Colorado. At this time he gave the skull to my father, Charles I. Joseph of Angola, Sussex County for keeping. From that time until the late thirties the skull hung on a nail in a rafter of my father's barn, by which time it had become quite a curiosity. To save it from damage or possible theft he put it in a box and stored it on the attic of his home. At his death in 1946 I took possession of the skull and in 1961 put it on loan to the Dover Library.

Alfred W. Joseph

Dover, Delaware
May 2, 1963

Like so many relics of its kind, Patty Cannon's skull may have cloned itself over the years: There is a footnote in *The Entailed Hat* which informs us that "The skull of Ebenezer Johnson can be seen at Fowler & Wells Museum, New York. . . . There, also, are the skulls of Patty and Betty Cannon."

The Ebenezer referred to is the senior Johnson whose death

---

[1] Patty died in 1829.

is chronicled in the novel, and Betty, in the same chapter, is identified as Patty's sister. One wonders if this is part of Townsend's tale or an attempt to supplement it with factual information. Jerry Shields believes that, particularly in his footnotes, the author was not romanticizing and that Townsend had probably been to the museum and had seen the skulls.

We also have the claim contained in the *Narrative and Confessions of Lucretia Cannon*, which informs us that Patty's skull was obtained by a "celebrated and highly respected phrenologist" for examination, and that, in 1841, it was in the possession of Mr. O. S. Fowler of Philadelphia.

The "science" of phrenology was the brainchild of a Viennese physician named Franz Joseph Gall, who, with a student, Johann Kaspar Spurzheim, in the early part of the nineteenth century, spread the idea across Europe and to America where it found its most devoted following.

Spurzheim died while touring the United States, and his banner was taken up by Orson Fowler, a ministry student who suddenly found his true calling. Fowler's enthusiasm infected his younger brother, Lorenzo, and together they toured the country, lecturing and analyzing the character and propensities of simple folk as well as the rich and famous by reading bumps and depressions on their skulls.

The brothers' New York office, known at one time as the Phrenological Cabinet, became a bizarre museum. After the 1836 death of Aaron Burr, for example, they had a cast of his head commissioned and declared—as a surprise to no one—that his organs of "Secretiveness" and "Destructiveness" were far larger than those of the average person. The collection grew to some four thousand studies of famous and infamous craniums and included about three hundred skulls. S. R. Wells became a partner.

References immediately available to me provided no additional information about the collection. Before I had an opportunity to expand my investigation, however, Jerry Shields told me that he had spoken to the New York Historical Society about

Fowler and Wells. The Society confirmed the depository's existence but has no record of its inventory or its eventual fate.

Is it possible that a Philadelphia phrenologist might have gained permission to removed the skull of a deceased criminal from the Sussex County jailyard? Of course it is. Fowler and Wells apparently made a practice of such collecting. Phrenology was all the rage, and what law or individual existed to protest?

Is it also possible that a deputy sheriff assigned the task of removing the remains of several former prisoners to potter's field could have "somehow" come into the possession of one of the skulls? Again, the answer is yes.

Beyond a determination of sex and age, I do not know what might be learned from the Dover Library skull, but modern forensic anthropologists are capable of some remarkable sleuthing today. I decided it would be interesting to have someone with the necessary knowledge take a look at the partially deteriorated cranium, but I have not been successful in raising any interest in such a project. There does not appear to be any apprehension that someone might debunk the skull; it is rather a matter of not taking it seriously to begin with. Most commonly I am told that the skull is too small to have belonged to such a large and powerful person as Patty Cannon, but *was* Patty Cannon a large and powerful person, or is it only her legend that has achieved that status?

Someday, I hope the artifact will be critically examined by an expert. Meanwhile, I think that the Fowler and Wells version stands a better chance of being authentic.

Another study should be conducted to answer the question of whether Fowler include an evaluation of Patty Cannon's skull in his writings? Phrenological journals from the period would seem to be the logical place to begin the search.

Aunt Patty

We have documentation to show that Patty and Jesse Cannon had two children who lived to maturity, Mary and Jesse, Jr., but little is known of them, and knowledge of their movements and life beyond the early 1820's is entirely speculation. Jesse, Jr., some believe, died in the Southwest in the 1840's. No one seems to know if Patty's children had offspring of their own.

The Cannons who descended from James of Nanticoke Forest were a fertile clan, and their lineage stretches far and wide across our nation. With attempts to pinpoint Patty's husband, Jesse, we have seen how difficult it can be to verify ancestry when a family is large, documents are scarce, and each generation contains multiple individuals with the same given name. Still, it is a thing that drives us: to know who are we, to identify the shadowy figures in our past.

Many search hopefully for ancestors who were famous. Some find them. And some retain and enlarge upon glimpses and suggestions, perhaps with tongue in cheek, perhaps because it can be fun.

I was leisurely browsing through Volume IV of Ed Okonowicz's "Spirits Between the Bays Series" one evening when I did a double take. There, on page 48 in the chapter "Patty Cannon: Kidnapper, Murderess, Ghost?" a man was referring to Patty Cannon as "great-great-great-aunt Patty." I knew immediately I had to talk to George Figgs.

I found four "George Figgs" listed in Maryland and Delaware, but not the one I wanted. The information, however, led me to his parents, and the following day I reached Figgs at his Pennsylvania home.

I opened the conversation by saying, "I understand you can tell me something about Patty Cannon."

"That's my great aunt," came Figgs quick reply.

"I've talked to a lot of people about Patty, but you're the first one to claim a relationship."

"Well," he chuckled, "I guess they wouldn't—bloody aunt Patty!"

Figgs is a fan of Edgar Allen Poe and proprietor of the Orpheum Cinema, a theater in Fells Point, Baltimore, which specializes in screening vintage movies. "Kiss Me Deadly" (1955) and "Breathless" (1959) were playing the day we spoke.

"I'm from Figgs Landing," George began to explain his claim. "It's on Chincoteague Bay right below Public Landing—around Watermelon Point, Girdletree, and Boxiron. Columbus Figgs had a trading post down there and he gave Figgs Landing its name."

When I pressed for an explanation of the relationship with Patty, George was unable to provide any detail: "You'll have to get to my Aunt Midge. She was a Figgs—she's my father's sister—and she married Johnny Parkinson from Deal Island. Johnny was a waterman, a skipjacker. He died a couple of years ago, but

Aunt Midge still lives on Deal.

"Back in the 70's, during the genealogical craze after *Roots*, Midge and her daughter Sandy did a lot of research and they found out that Patty Cannon was our relation. My father's side was originally from up around the Seaford-Reliance area in Delaware. That's Patty Cannon country. My great-grandmother would tell us stories about Patty Cannon. I guess she knew the relationship but she never told us. We made the connection later."

"What did your grandmother tell you?" I urged.

"Patty was so mean that she killed and ate one of her children in front of her mob to quell a mutiny. So the children that were left—Jesse and Mary—were surviving children. And her first husband—the one before Jesse—she was supposed to have hamstrung and killed him in front of her crew to quell another mutiny.

"The family said she was a big-boned woman with Indian or Gypsy blood. They thought she might have been part Nanticoke or Piscataway. They said she may even have been part black and that made her hateful about blacks.

"She ran slaves—had the reverse underground railroad. She would put them in the tavern, and if the abolitionists were coming down from Delaware and closing in on her, she would kill them and bury them out in the field behind the tavern. Of course that's how she got caught—you know that.

"Her ghost and the ghosts of her band are supposedly roaming the swamps around the Pocomoke [River]; up in Nassawango Creek; down by Shad Landing. She had camps out there where she had slave pens. If anybody told on her, they would die, and their children would die, and their animals would die. She was feared; that was how she ran her regime.

"If you went to her door—If you went to the inn and looked like you had any money, you would probably never be seen or heard from again.

"And another thing we were told was that she was so charismatic that she had everyone hypnotized. She was a mezmerizer and hypnotizer—the hoodo princess.

"My great-grandmother, Carrie Jones, would use Patty Cannon as the boogie man. She would scare you with, 'Patty Cannon is gonna get you if you don't behave.'"

I wondered if there was a Figgs' family version of her origin: "Did your grandmother believe the story about her coming from Canada, or was she a local?"

"We were led to believe that she was local."

George Figgs' parting words were, "It's hard to own up to being a blood relation to bloody Patty. That's some strong blood there." But it was clear that George was enjoying every moment of his disclosure.

I couldn't wait to talk to Aunt Midge and review her genealogical research. It took five telephone calls before I finally reached her.

"I'm afraid I really don't know anything," replied Mildred Parkinson to my questions. "The only thing I can tell you—and it's nothing I can verify—is that when we were children, my mother used to tell me that my grandfather was related to Patty Cannon. His name was William Huffington Cannon Jones. Mother said the Cannon part was because he was related to Patty Cannon. He was born somewhere around Reliance, Delaware. Other than that I really can't tell you anything. It was just a childhood thing."

"But you must have heard stories about Patty when you were growing up?"

"No, I don't think so."

"What about your daughter; has she done any genealogical research?"

"If she has, it's news to me. She's not very much into things like that."

Then, just before we said good-bye, Aunt Midge offered this parting remark, "Sometimes we remember things that don't really happen."

What Do We Really Know?

We end our examination of the life and the literature of Patty Cannon as we began it, with more questions than answers. Who was she? Lucretia Martha Patricia Patty Hanley (or Hanly) Cannon. To my knowledge the only given names which appear on documents are Martha and Patty, and Cannon is the single surname of record.

A footnote in *The Entailed Hat* informs us that neighbors claimed Patty came from "Delaware and Maryland stock, a Baker and a Moore." I must place my confidence in the footnote and on statements by Anthony Higgins, in 1930, and later by Val Massey and others, that Patty was—as much as some hate to admit it—almost certainly a home-grown product of Delmarva.

And where did Jesse Cannon meet his bride to be? While most

continue to repeat the claim made in the *Narrative and Confessions*—that Patty was living in Canada—I have seen no documentation to encourage such a belief. Think about the prospect for a moment. A wheelright from Lower Delaware (surely not a man of means) happens to be casually traveling through Canada with a large sum of money shortly after America has won its independence. There he meets the daughter of an English nobleman and his gypsy wife. He takes sick; she nurses him back to health; they fall in love and marry. To express the credence I place in such a scenario, I am inclined to borrow from the vernacular of a friend, who puts it this way, "Get real."

Other claims that the pair met in New York State, perhaps in a Buffalo tavern, or in Philadelphia, where Patty was a dancing girl, are equally without documentation.

Was Jesse Cannon a respectable, hard-working mechanic? Did he die shortly after his marriage to Patty, distraught over discovering her true, evil nature? Did Patty poison him? Looking back on the evidence we have seen, Jesse Cannon clearly looms as a member of the mob of cutthroats who kidnapped, robbed, and killed for a living. In 1821 he and his adult son, Jesse, Jr., along with his adult daughter, Mary, were indicted for kidnapping. Therefore, documents from Delaware courts clearly demonstrate that he lived into the 1820's. While we do not know exactly when he died, there is no logical reason to believe that Patty poisoned him.

At least one historian, apparently ignorant of the 1821 indictment, has attempted to use Dorchester County records to show that Jesse died before 1820. He points to seven transactions dated December 1 and December 8, 1819, in which "Jesse Cannon Junr." signed as witness before Justice Henry Smoot to the transfer of the following property from William Russell, of Dorchester County, to Joseph Johnson: "Negro Mary, aged 24 years; Negro girl Sall, aged 12 years; Negro man; Negro Stephan, aged 22 years; Negro woman Betts, aged 20 years; Negro Susan, aged 23 years; and Negro woman Edy, aged 28 years."

But what does this prove? When we search further in the Dorchester County records, we discover that on May 30, 1820, Arthur H. Williss of Dorchester County transferred three slaves to "Jesse Cannon" of Sussex County, Delaware. And on August 26, 1820, "Jesse Cannon" sold slaves to Samuel Laughlin of the Parish of St. Landry, Louisiana, those two transactions, sworn, in turn, before Justice William S. Harper and Justice Eccleston Brown.

Val Massey once flatly stated that Jesse died in 1822, but he presented no documentation in support of that pronouncement. It certainly would explain why Delaware's Attorney General failed to act on Jesse's indictment of 1821 and prosecute him along with Joe Johnson in 1822.

Continuing in the Dorchester journals, we are able to place a no-later-than date on Jesse's passing. On March 1, 1826, "Joseph Johnson and Ebenezer Johnson of Dorchester County [transferred] to Martha Cannon, widow of Jesse Cannon deceased, of Sussex County, Delaware: part of 'Willson's Plain Dealing' on the road from Willson's Cross Roads to Northwest Fork Bridge." The transaction was witnessed and acknowledged before Justices Wm. S. Harper and Ezekiel Wheatley.

This property included Joe Johnson's Tavern, and it is interesting to note that the area was still referred to, at least in this document, as Willson's Cross Roads, not Johnson's Cross Roads. For those who believe that Joe Johnson fled the state after his whipping, leaving Patty high and dry, this transfer is evidence to the contrary.

Then, to confuse the reader even further, a March 5, 1826, document: "Certificate of Negroes brought into this State by Emelia *Johnson*, [italics mine] lately of Sussex County, Delaware, who removed February 21, 1826, into the State of Maryland to live in Dorchester County," was witnessed by none other than "Jesse Cannon."

Recall that at this time Mayor Watson of Philadelphia and Attorney General Rogers were hot in pursuit of the Johnson brothers. It looks like the entire family may have been bailing out of Delaware.

Other questions remain unanswered also. What about Patty's arrest? It is certain the tavern did not become a battlefield as some contend, but did she surrender and willingly enter Delaware to be jailed and indicted for murder? And how did she die? Where is she buried? Where is her skull?

For me, the most important question is the degree of Patty Cannon's involvement in what certainly was one of the most desperate and despicable criminal gangs in our history. Was she the leader, or was she merely a woman who happened to be married to a criminal and was swept along with the tide of her circumstances?

We can credit the majority of her massive legend to the "penny dreadful" *Narrative and Confessions of Lucretia Cannon*, a clearly romanticized fiction, and to the accusations of Cyrus James. There were no other witnesses against her at her arrest, and she never had the opportunity to face her accuser in court.

George Valentine Massey II was interviewed by William Frank for an article which appeared in the Wilmington News on September 2, 1960, where Massey is quoted as saying about Patty Cannon, "The woman was a tramp and a very vicious kind of person, but not nearly as wicked as she's been made out to be. Evidence seems to indicate she had been led astray by the men whose company she kept. . . ."

In a reference to Cyrus James, the principal witness against Patty, Massey again is quoted, "I think he was brainwashed by the authorities. He was a rogue himself—and I have always felt that his testimony had little value. I'm sure he made up most of the yarns about Patty Cannon's cruelty."

Frank goes on to quote Massey as saying that ". . . the man who was hired by Quakers in the late 1820's to help prosecute Patty Cannon as a murderer and kidnapper of slaves, was prejudiced himself. He was the famous John M. Clayton. . . . Clayton had political ambitions and used questionable methods for political gain. [He] was somewhat lacking in tact and patience as well as in firmness and stability of character."

"And it turns out," Frank again quotes Massey, "that Joe

Johnson was the real leader of the kidnapping-highway robbery gang."

Massey replied to Frank's published interview in a letter to the editor: "While I have long enjoyed being an iconoclast, Bill Frank has built me into one of embarrassing proportions. When he asked me for material on Patty Cannon, whom I did not call a tramp, I unfortunately alluded to derogatory statements from the "Dictionary of American Biography," which I should have qualified more clearly for Mr. Frank. To me John M. Clayton is as much a hero as George Washington. . . ."

I do not wish to make an issue of the differences between Frank and Massey, but I shall quote directly from one of Massey's original typewritten pages in his Cannon family history. "The Quakers employed John Middleton Clayton to assist in his [Joe Johnson's] prosecution, a lawyer of unrivaled reputation in Delaware though known at times to use questionable methods for political gain. Mr. Clayton was somewhat lacking in tact and patience as well as in firmness and stability of character. . . ."

Often referring to Patty Cannon as an "extra ordinary woman," Massey minimized her involvement in crime. I quote from one of his newspaper articles, "The men did the kidnapping, while she [Patty] and her beautiful daughter Mary entertained the slave dealers."

Massey accepted Littleton Bowen's testimony that after the indictments and trial of 1822, Patty removed to Maryland and lived quietly, unmolested by the law, and welcomed into some of the best homes on the Eastern Shore.

Speaking of her death, Massey wrote, "[She had] no opportunity to refute the testimony of brainwashed Cyrus James—doubtless frightened into giving answers to please the jailers, and appease the hysterical mob."

Bill Frank, discussing in another article what he claims were Massey's attempts "to debunk the entrenched yarns about what a terrible, awful, godless, bloodthirsty, villainous female she was," laments the fact that Massey's account was never published in book form. Then he adds, "Even if it had been published, I doubt that it would have been accepted. People in Sussex rarely want their myths debunked or their villains exonerated."

When we examine the contemporary documents—the court records, newspaper articles, and letters—we discover that they seldom mention Patty. It is the writers—the newspapermen and novelists—and John Clayton who dwell on her as a fiend of unparalleled proportions.

While completing work on this collection, I was also engaged in taping oral histories from several elderly African American women. As the group ended a session one afternoon, I asked if they had ever heard of Patty Cannon.

"Yes," they all knew of her.

"What did you hear about her?" I asked.

After glances were exchanged, one of the group, a woman who has seen ninety-six winters, looked at me and said simply, "She was a conjure."

I love myths and traditions and legends, and I do not wish to —nor, probably, could I—diminish Patty Cannon's legend by even a hair's breadth. But when all the evidence has been sifted and examined, I must contend that the fiction is far stronger than the fact.

She Was Not Alone

Many residents of Delmarva believe that the Cannon-Johnson kidnapping operation existed as a venture unique to the Maryland-Delaware border country. Such a notion could not be farther from the truth as an investigation of contemporary newspapers will quickly demonstrate. The kidnapping of free blacks was widely practiced all along the border between North and South, even in free states, and often with tentacles reaching deeply into the North.

In the free state of Illinois, for example, blacks were apparently in constant danger from kidnappers, some of which had sophisticated criminal organizations and political connections.

Near Equality, Illinois, in the Old Slave House, as Hickory Hill Plantation came to be known, John Hart Crenshaw held kidnapped blacks against their will on the third floor. Sound familiar?

Indicted but never convicted of kidnapping, Crenshaw, who was called the Southern Illinois Salt King, was also a distiller, toll bridge operator, farmer, land speculator, saw mill owner, railroad builder, and a member in good standing of the Equality Methodist Church.

Tradition states that Crenshaw captured runaway slaves, a profitable sideline in the first half of the nineteenth century, especially so if their captor sold them back into slavery instead of turning them over to the sheriff as the law required.

A common method of kidnapping along the Ohio and Mississippi Rivers was to "employ" poor blacks on flat boats. At a prearranged point on the river, they would be seized and turned over to confederates who carried them south and sold them into slavery. Others were kidnapped and moved from house to house through a network often more organized than the legitimate Underground Railroad.

Crenshaw, who was listed as illiterate, had a large number of siblings and children and used them to his best advantage. Either he or a relative always seemed to be on the commission whenever it was time to sell saline lands to the public—remember his title, Southern Illinois Salt King. His son William was appointed Indian agent under President Pierce and was Stephen Douglas' campaign manager in the 1858 Senate campaign against Lincoln. A son-in-law ran the Democratic newspaper in Springfield. Another served as an officer in the Mexican War and as a general during the Civil War. Yet another was active in county politics and was elected circuit clerk. Brother-in-law Edmund Taylor held a commission in the Winnebago War of 1827 and was on Governor John Reynold's general staff during the Black Hawk War of 1832. In 1834 Taylor beat Abraham Lincoln in a race for the legislature. Later, he was a Springfield merchant and then receiver of public money in Chicago. He was a land speculator, sat on the boards of two railroads, and was a charter trustee of Rush Medical College.

Did I hear the name Abraham Lincoln? For years tradition claimed that Lincoln had visited with Crenshaw at Hickory Hill Plantation, a belief denied by Lincoln scholars. But recently a letter turned up, written by a woman who tells of having danced with Lincoln at the Crenshaw house when she was a teenager.

Crenshaw was only one of many Illinois kidnappers who preyed on free blacks. Others of prominence included Caleb Slankard and William H. Vaughn, a Bay City storekeeper who was a pirate on the Gulf Coast before opening his storeboat on the Ohio River. Newton E. Wright was known as a shrewd kidnapper who lived on Wolf Island in the Mississippi River.

And then there was James Ford, a kidnapper and river pirate known as Satan's ferryman, who was also, like Crenshaw, a salt operator in the Salines in the 1820's. In spite of Ford's many illegal activities, he served as delegate to Kentucky's first constitutional convention and was an officer in the militias and a justice of the peace in both Kentucky and Illinois. And—remember the story about Joe Johnson's later occupation—Ford also sat on the bench as a county judge in Kentucky.

Ford, according to old records, seemed always to be finding lost property and laying claim to it. Sometimes the things he found were whole flatboats complete with cargo, possessions, livestock—everything but the owners.

An organization of twenty to thirty gang members worked with him. He controlled his problems and stilled his dissenters by having them murdered and then by having the murderer eliminated. And did I mention that he was also sheriff?

Ford controlled the river from Shawneetown to Fort Massac and owned the land and highway on both approaches to his ferry. He murdered settlers and merchants by land and water and grew rich by "finding" their property. The law couldn't touch him because he was the law.

Finally, after he became so open and ruthless that the community could no longer tolerate his activities, an armed posse of vigilantes arrived one evening at supper. Ford was told to continue his meal but declined, tradition claims, by saying, "Tonight

I'm going to eat my supper in Hell."

There were seventeen lead balls in Ford's body when they nailed him into the wooden box which had accompanied the posse. While Ford was being lowered into his grave that night, the coffin slipped and plunged headfirst into the dark hole. Standing almost upright, his casket was sealed in by shovels without adjustment. I understand that in Illinois they still talk about the night that James Ford descended headfirst into Hell. That was in 1833.

The Legend Marches On

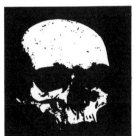

No one should be astonished that Patty's legend is alive and well after almost a hundred and seventy years nor that we continue to encounter legitimate new information along with much new misinformation.

On the internet I recently learned that "Patty Cannon and *her husband, Joe Johnson,* [italics mine] ran a slave sale trade," that they would "take the slaves in covered wagons to *Johnson's Ferry* [italics mine]," and that, when they were caught "in May, 1822," Joe Johnson was sentenced to thirty-nine lashes while Patty Cannon killed herself after being charged with murder.

The story is credited to someone who served as temporary "sitter" for the "Patty Cannon House" after James Good, the man who gave us all the ghost stories, left it in the custodianship of a bank.

In a 1997 *New Bay Times* article, Bob Hall enhanced the statistics of Patty's murderous inclinations as reported in the 1841 *Narrative and Confessions*. You will recall that she was credited by the author of that dubious biography with killing eleven persons by her own hand and assisting with the dispatch of more than a dozen others. In *New Bay Times* Hall claimed that, "Patty killed more than 20 men on her own and participated in at least 20 additional gang killings."

In his tale, "Patty Cannon, The Wicked Witch from the East—Eastern Shore, That is," Hall also makes this interesting observation, "With the help of her son-in-law, 'Killer' Joe Johnson, Patty . . . kidnapped free blacks, escaped slaves and persons who could be sold into slavery regardless of age, gender or ethnic origin. . . . Accordingly, the gang consisted of male and female, white, African American, Native American, and perhaps even Hispanic members." If we go along with that version, Patty might be historically prominent from yet another standpoint—She may have been America's first equal opportunity employer.

While the above-mentioned efforts seem satisfied with keeping the "facts" of Patty's history alive, novelists also continue to find in this infamous lady a source of inspiration. The latest effort in that genre is *The Devil's Crossroads* written by Kathryn Pippin and published by The Circle Press in 1996. In this two hundred and eighty page softcover, Pippin's villainess is "Lucretia Hanley," the offspring of a gypsy mother raped by a Chesapeake pirate. She is the proprietor of "The Sign of the Bacchus," a tavern at Johnson's Crossroads which serves as the center of operations for her gang of kidnappers and robbers. The name Patty Cannon is never used.

Lucretia becomes involved in a long-term affair with the Reverend Jeremiah Milton, a Methodist preacher who is both smitten and naive to the extreme. After eventually discovering the true nature of the love of his life, Jeremiah departs this world—we are led to assume—by his own hand.

The story of *The Devil's Crossroads* is told through the char-

acter of Henry Edwards, editor—when we are introduced to him—
of *The Clarion*, a newspaper in Georgetown, Delaware.

Edwards becomes involved with Lucretia and the red-headed
Johnson brothers while pursuing a story. In Pippin's tale there
are three Johnsons: Joe, Ebenezer, and Enoch. The editor is apprehended by them while attempting to assist the escape of a
comely slave woman named Hannah, toward whom he soon
begins to feel more than sympathy.

While Edwards is chained in her attic, Lucretia offers him a
deal. In exchange for his life, he agrees not to divulge the gang's
secrets and to leave Delaware. So much for all that integrity we
were beginning to believe he possessed.

Accepting a position in New York, our narrator enters into a
poor marriage, meets the likes of Daniel Webster and Andrew
Jackson, and is tormented periodically by his unrequited love
for the runaway slave whom the Johnsons shipped to Alabama.

When Lucretia is eventually arrested, Edwards returns to
Delaware to cover the trial. The Johnsons are holed up in "The
Sign of the Bacchus," surrounded by sheriff's deputies, but the
newsman, armed with his knowledge of the tavern, shows the
lawmen how they can break the standoff. There is a fire and
some loss of life, but the Johnsons are apprehended and brought
to trial.

Lucretia commits suicide. The Johnson brothers are found
guilty and hanged. Edwards falls in love with Claire Hayes, an
impertinent woman reporter who turns out to be the sister of his
college buddy. After working out the details of a divorce from his
institutionalized wife in New York, Edwards and Claire move to
Baltimore and are married. Edwards joins the staff of the *Baltimore Sun* while Claire becomes a novelist, writing under the
name Henry Hayes. Together they serve as station masters on the
Underground Railroad and live happily every after.

Oh yes—a slave whom Edwards rescues from the blazing attic
of Lucretia's tavern turns out to be Hanna's husband. Edwards
helps to reunite him with his wife and children and moves them
all to Canada. They also, we assume, live happily ever after.

All the light-hearted reading fun aside, as I conclude this effort to bring together the principal writings and oral tradition spawned by the life and legend of Patty Cannon, I want to direct your focus to a serious and scholarly work in progress. Several days after I had drafted the Foreword to this book, I learned that Jerry Shields has been engaged in an extensive exchange with correspondents in the Deep South, including, I understand, descendants of the Johnson family. A considerable amount of unpublished intelligence about this missing piece of the puzzle is slowly coming to light, and a new book will be written.

"When I wrote the 1990 pamphlet," Shields offered, "I was trying to analyze the previous material. I was relying primarily on secondary sources, but the new book will be mostly fresh research. While it is mainly about Patty and the Johnson gang, it is also going to be, I think, a study in the problems of digging up events and personalities of the past, particularly if, like Patty, they weren't politically, socially, or militarily prominent. Writing about those who operate in the public eye for much of their careers is challenging enough, but writing about people who were trying to keep their activities secret is much harder.

"The documentary record on Patty is pretty sparse, and how much of what has come down to us can be trusted? The written record can only tell us so much, then we have to rely on the word-of-mouth accounts which are difficult to prove but can't be entirely discounted either. Sometimes one must go on instinct.

"I am trying to get at the heart of the situation and answer questions no one else has answered to this point, or answered incorrectly. Thanks in large part to my Southern correspondents, I've found out more than I expected to in several areas, but there are still some questions hanging, including ones about her parentage and origins. Nobody, to my knowledge, has cracked that nut so far. If we dismiss the Canadian version in the 1841 *Narrative and Confessions*, as I tend to do, we're left just about nowhere."

The working title of Dr. Shields' new book is *The Search for Patty Cannon*. It promises to add much to our knowledge and understanding of the principals and their times, and I, for one, await its publication impatiently.

Postscript

"There was a song that the children used to sing," an elderly woman told me as she rocked on her Sussex County porch, "but I haven't heard it now for a long time:

"Old Patty Cannon
is dead and gone.
Can't you hear the devil
draggin' her along."

Patty Cannon Country Today

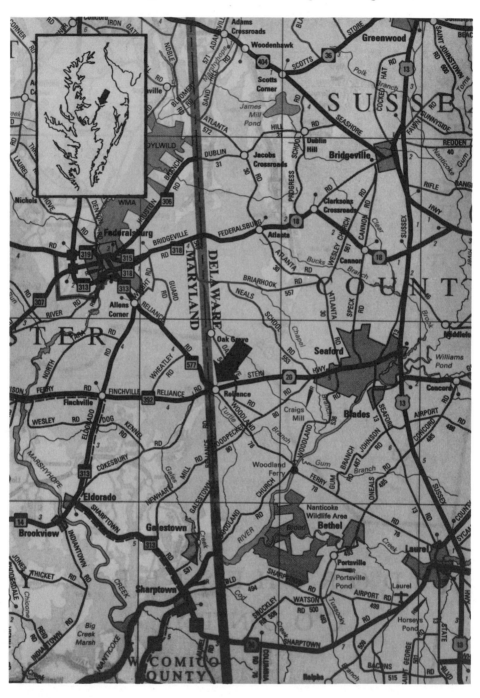